MIDNIGHT & SILVERED GLASS

EMILY MICHEL

Dragon Smith
PUBLISHING LLC

This is for the little girl who loved stories,
the teenager who lost her love of writing,
and the woman who found it again.

Author's Note

This book contains the following elements: profanity, open door sex scenes, alcohol use, difficult parent/adult-child relationship, past death of a parent, discussions of child endangerment, kidnapping, blade and hand-to-hand fighting, coerced marriage, storm at sea and discussions of drowning, brief depiction of a pregnancy (epilogue, not FMC).

I welcome comments on my website should you find something that should be included which was not mentioned above.

Heorthwerod and Witan are Anglo-Saxon words I picked up from the British History Podcast and follow the host's preferred spelling, which may differ from other historians. I use both concepts in ways that are true in some respects to the historical record, but as this is a made-up fantasy world, I took a lot of literary license.

Heorthwerod: hearth-wear-odd

For free short stories, bonus content, updates on current and future projects, and early looks at covers, excerpts, and review copies, sign up for my Magical Musings Newsletter at EmilyMichelAuthor.com/newsletter.

Chapter 1

*H*ad anyone told Betony that her fairy tale began at a ball, she would've laughed. Once upon a time, she loved balls. They were rare and precious events she was not allowed to attend until she was thirteen. She loved the gowns, the well-dressed men, the music, the dancing, and the food, but her years in Faerie had put a damper on her enjoyment. Now she had little patience for the small talk and the court politics.

Bet jumped as her door flew open and a chestnut-haired woman surrounded by outrageous layers of golden silk and tulle barged in. The woman slammed the door behind her and leaned against it, bringing a finger to her lips.

"I was never here," Rane mumbled through clenched teeth.

Bet smiled at her sister, twisted her fingers over her lips, and threw away the imaginary key. The pitter-patter of little feet and giggles seeped under the door as Jonquil toddled down the hall, followed by the heavier footfalls of his father.

"Get back here, you little imp." The thick wood muffled Nevar's voice, but the humor behind his words permeated the air as the women held their breaths.

When the last echoes faded, Rane pranced across the sitting room and dramatically collapsed onto a settee, releasing a great sigh.

"I love him dearly, but he had honey dripping off his hands. *Honey*. Why did no one warn me children were so…sticky?" Her hand fluttered about before it rested on her forehead in a theatrical gesture.

1

Bet chuckled and slipped into her bedchamber without answering. Every last person in her family had warned Rane, but as usual, her sister had ignored them all. Especially since nearly every story about sticky children had been about Rane herself. The Crown Princess of Lorea had been an...exuberant child. It was one of the things Bet loved best about her older sister.

To be fair, Rane was an exuberant adult, too. The current situation was not an outlier.

The swish of silk followed Bet, only to pause on the threshold.

"I forgot how they follow you," Rane said quietly.

Their mother's white dogs were curled on the rug at the foot, ears and paws twitching in their sleep. Two cats looked up from the bed. A half dozen mice sat upon the trunk shoved under the windows, and a blue and white bird perched on the far bedpost.

"Hush." Bet used her magic to soothe them all back to sleep. The bird puffed his feathers and let out a chiding whistle. Bet rolled her eyes but continued in a soft voice. "You're right, I'll need your help shortly."

The bird settled, and Bet turned to her sister. "Sorry, I know it takes some getting used to, even in Faerie."

Rane gestured dismissively. "I just forgot, and really, I missed it. Mother's dogs bother the shit out of Bash when you're not around."

Her sister was being kind. When Betony was growing up, her retinue of animals followed her everywhere in the castle, and the staff had always looked oddly at her parade. It was strange and had set her apart from the plain humans. The gift was not unheard of in Faerie, but it was rare enough *she* gave lessons to fairies. Rane's gaze raked Betony from head to toe, taking in her gown.

"Ooh, your dress is gorgeous. You did the embroidery yourself, didn't you?"

Bet lifted an arm and proudly examined her handiwork on the sleeves, feathers outlined in white thread on the cerulean gown. "Yes. Designed it and ordered the thread right after last year's Winter Solstice Ball."

Her sister's face went all innocent. "And I forget, what bird are you going as?"

Bet would wager every jewel in her chest that Rane hadn't forgotten at all, but she played along. After all, it had been a long time since she laughed with her sister.

"A Lorean blue *tit*." The same as the little bird perched on the bedpost.

Rane's signature snort started, changing quickly into an infectious laugh, one Bet could not resist. Soon, they were both red-faced with laughter, no better than twelve-year-olds.

"Stop…" Rane coughed. "We can't go to the ball like this!"

"Why not?" Bet dabbed a tear away with her handkerchief. She was not risking ruining the fine embroidery that took nearly a year to complete by wiping her face on her sleeves. "You're already married, and I'm not interested in a single man who will be there."

They would all be relatives or men she'd met a thousand times before. Men she'd rejected long ago by staying in Faerie so long. But Rane had asked her to return home. Their brother Ebon was off searching for the northern clan behind the raids on Faerie and Lorea with his new wife, the spymaster of Faerie. Mother had been most displeased at receiving only a brief note before they set sail.

Rane needed someone she could trust absolutely at court. Unlike many noble families, the Lorean royal children loved each other. Even more importantly, they *liked* each other.

"You never know. The ambassador from Fuartir and his entourage will be there. Could be an eligible bachelor among the northerners. And nearly every noble family is attending."

Bet stopped herself from grimacing. The northern barbarians, the fairies called them. Centuries of hot and cold wars, but in the last few years, relations between Lorea and Fuartir had thawed, bringing hope conditions may improve for everyone, Loreans, northerners, and fairies alike. The road would be long, and no serious progress could be made until the raiders were brought to heel, but the possibility of a lasting peace was more real than it had ever been.

But too many of the noble families of Lorea were barely better, greedy for power, prestige, or wealth. Her father worked hard to reward those who showed compassion, reason, and restraint. His reign had uplifted many commoners and narrowed the wealth gap. Unfortunately, she was already related to most of the families who showed the characteristics she most valued, but perhaps there was a diamond among the chaff who would be at the ball.

"Unlikely. I caught a glimpse of the ambassador yesterday. He's old. Not everyone is as lucky as you."

3

Rane grabbed a pillow from Betony's bed and threw it at her. Bet skillfully caught it and tossed it where it belonged.

"You're right. The goddess smiled down on me when King Armel chose Nevar to be his ambassador. You'll get lucky someday, little sister."

Maybe she would, but she wasn't worried about it. With the crown princess married and an heir produced, Bet felt no pressure to find a match yet. She was only twenty-five, and not only was the Lorean royal family long-lived, but she was also fae. Her fairy ancestry was apparent in her cranberry hair. And her magic. Mustn't forget that. No one would let her.

"Can you finish my laces?" she asked as she slid on her slippers. They sparkled with beads of silvered glass, shining jewels in the firelight.

Rane pulled until her laces were snug, but not tight, just how Bet liked them. She smoothed her skirt.

"Do you need help with your hair, too?" Rane tucked a lock behind Bet's ear.

"From you?" Bet snorted.

Rane scowled in jest, but her eyes twinkled. Moss-green, as were their father's. Hair like his, too, while Bet had the fairy-bright hair, and her eyes were a brilliant emerald. Ebon was a mix of their mother, with her darkling eyes, and their father, with the same dark chestnut hair as Rane. The only two features the three siblings shared were a heart-shaped face and golden beige skin. But at least Rane and Ebon blended in. Bet stood out like a rooster in a henhouse, though she was more chick size.

Bet whistled a three-note tune, and her feathered sidekick fluttered over. He took strands of her hair, twisting and weaving, while she shoved hairpins with cascading glass beads matching her shoes into the elaborate coiffure. Soon, the bird chirped his approval. The beads glimmered like stars in her hair.

"Ooh, me too!" Rane fought the squeal, and her voice came out all cracked.

With another whistle, the bird jumped to her sister and in a few moments, complicated braids spilled down Rane's back. While her sister was distracted, Bet slipped a small knife from under her pillow and into her pocket. It never hurt to be prepared, and the knife was easier to conceal than her staff.

The blue bird retreated to his perch on the bedpost, looking self-satisfied, the scamp. Just in time too, as someone pounded on the door.

"I know you're in there, Rane." Nevar's voice rumbled through the heavy wood. "You forgot your mask."

Her sister sighed and looped her arm around Bet's. "A crown princess's duty is never done. Still sure you don't want the job?"

Bet snagged her own mask, a bejeweled replica of a blue tit's head, complete with a tiny black beak, from the dressing table on their way out.

"I've never been so sure of anything in my life."

"Ah, well, can't blame me for trying."

Rane pulled open the door to a handsome man with reddish-brown skin dressed in green, his matching mask atop his tightly curled hair. He handed a gold mask to his wife and placed a tender kiss on her lips.

"You look beautiful, my love." His eyes shone in adoration.

Betony hoped she would find someone who looked at her with devotion, wonder, and passion all in a single glance.

"And Bet, you are a vision, truly," he continued, barely looking her way.

"Spoken like a dedicated diplomat," Bet said brightly. It was an old joke yet fitting. Nevar had been a diplomat, and still handled most of the matters needing a lighter touch than her sister's.

"Come, ladies, the ball awaits. And god forbid we have to stay past midnight." He offered his arm to Rane.

"I am not a fucking lady," Rane responded, but her voice lacked anger.

"No, you're a princess. And so am I." Bet tied on her mask. "What happens at midnight?"

"Parents pass out cold. Why do you think the king and queen always leave early? Rane assures me it's a Lorean phenomenon."

Laughter echoed in the hall as they walked to the ballroom. Rane was right. Who knew what this night would hold? Perhaps she'd find her prince after all. Stranger things had happened.

Chapter 2

*H*er bright hair sparkled with stars, and her laughter was a delicate melody that raised the hairs on the back of Dorin's neck. He waited for the princesses to disappear around the corner before he emerged from the shadows. He shook off the odd feeling, ducked down another hall, and trudged up some stairs, hurrying to the Fuartiran ambassador's quarters.

"You're late," Ambassador Vedel said, whipping around as Dorin slipped in. The gray-haired man wore a stern frown, and his impatience filled the air.

"Apologies, milord." Dorin hung the sequin-bedecked costume he'd been carrying on the side of the wardrobe. "I took a wrong turn and found myself in the royal corridor as the crown princess and her sister exited. I didn't want to draw any attention."

Only half a lie. He'd been exactly where he'd meant to be but hadn't expected company yet. The ambassador grunted and waved a hand before undoing the laces on his tunic.

"What do you think of our recent arrival?"

Princess Betony, he meant. The diminutive fae woman had only arrived a few days ago, and this had been his second glimpse of her. The first had been as she cantered into the stables with her fine white gelding and handed him the reins while she prepared to rub down the horse.

"I'm not sure," he answered honestly.

"Strange hair, that girl."

It was strange, yet whimsically beautiful. He wanted to run his fingers through it, see if it was as soft as the silk it reminded him of.

"I understand unusual hair is a mark of her fairy blood." Vedel should know this. He'd been the clan chief's second for decades, had helped Clan Fher rise to be the most powerful of the seven Fuartiran clans.

The ambassador shivered, and his lips thinned in disgust. He dropped the subject as he pulled on a new deep blue tunic. Dorin handed him a light blue velvet doublet covered in dark blue sequins that matched the tunic. Vedel glittered like a wave on a sunny day. Dorin buttoned the garment, brushed off a stray bit of fluff, and ran a comb through the ambassador's thinning hair. His blue eyes snapped with impatience.

"Very impressive, milord," Dorin said after a last look over to ensure everything appeared just right. He grabbed a wooden mask painted white and blue to mimic glacier ice. Large icicle projections stuck out from the top.

Vedel snatched the mask from Dorin's hands. "I will leave the ball as soon as the bells finish tolling midnight. I am unused to late nights, and I expect you to be here to help me undress. Do nothing foolish."

The ambassador strode from the room. Holding his tongue, Dorin bowed as Vedel left and pulled the door shut behind him.

The old man treated him as though Dorin wasn't a trusted manservant trained by the clan chief's own chamberlain, as though Dorin wasn't someone to fear. But correcting the ambassador was a terrible idea. Not only was he proud and a stickler for hierarchy, but he had no idea what Dorin actually was. Few did. The best way to get on Vedel's good side was to demonstrate his skills.

Dorin slipped through the door on the other wall and into his own small chamber, always at the ready to serve his lord. He stripped off a well-constructed but plain gray jerkin and woolen tunic, dropping them to the floor. He might miss all the hidden pockets in the jerkin, but he had a part to play tonight. Freshening up in the washbasin, Dorin enjoyed the piney scent of the soap, a small luxury he had brought from home that reminded him of the woods outside his village.

What had he thought of Betony? She'd noticed he was new and asked his name upon her arrival. When she realized he was with the ambassador's party, she'd apologized for mistaking him for a stable hand. Unusual treatment from someone so high in the hierarchy. How she'd laughed with her sister and her brother-in-law sent a stab of envy into his gut. He was lucky when his brothers ignored him and had spent most of his childhood praying to both Alet and Zovog they would forget he ever existed. Besides his mother, the only person in his family who didn't look at him as if he was something to be scraped off a boot was his sister. She was merely content to pretend he'd never been born.

Ablutions done, he pulled out his costume. Or perhaps disguise was the better term.

Dorin was medium. Medium height, medium build, medium brown hair, medium beige skin tone. Generically handsome enough to avoid being singled out for being ugly, not so handsome to garner undue attention. *Nothing* about him would draw undue attention, which was a key part of his pretense and allowed him to be unnoticeable.

Tonight, his job was to keep his eyes and ears open and report to Jani, who would pass along any news of interest to Chief Kalman. The chamberlain had known the ball would be an excellent opportunity to confirm gossip and get a feel for the pulse of the Lorean aristocracy. Many would be attending who rarely visited the castle of Avora, and what was said in whispers and innuendo was often far more valuable than what was said at the bargaining table. Information on whether the potential treaty with Fuartir was looked upon favorably, or with skepticism, or with hostility would be most useful. He had supplied Dorin with coin to buy an outfit worthy of a lord so he could sneak into the ball unbeknownst to the egotistical ambassador.

His disguise was the best he could afford. The breeches were an earthy green, well-made but with little decoration. The tunic matched, but the quilted silk doublet was gold with red, brown, and orange leaves embroidered on it, and his half-mask was a work of art. He had carved it himself from a single piece of maple he'd found outside the stable. The bottom section preserved the bark, but the top edge was covered in sculpted leaves and painted to match those embroidered on his doublet.

He tied it around his head and listened at the door. Silence. He cracked it open and glanced up and down the hall. No one. Perfect. Dorin stepped out, pulling on the hem of his doublet and adopting his persona for the night.

He straightened his back and lifted his chin as he moved into the center of the hall. He was no longer a trusted servant, but a young lord who belonged in these corridors in his own right.

"Good evening, milord," said a servant he passed as he strode to the ballroom.

The clerics of Zovog had trained him well.

He waited until the pages were busy helping other nobles before strolling into the crowded, brightly lit room as though he owned it. Tonight he wasn't Dorin, bastard son of Chief Kalman of the Fher Clan, tolerated only when useful. No, he passed himself off as Lord Drees from a small holding outside Teruelle.

Dorin grabbed a glass of red wine and mingled.

"A blessed solstice to you all," he said in an aristocratic Teruellan accent as he joined a small group of Loreans. Mid-level nobility judging by the costumes.

Already well in their cups, they returned his greeting enthusiastically. He was here to gather whatever gossip he could, gossip Vedel couldn't. The Loreans were too reticent around the ambassador and the other officials. Smart people, both the royals and their subjects. At best, the ambassador had only Fuartir's interests in mind. At worst, only his own. Another part of Dorin's job was to find out which.

They seemed to have no qualms about sharing with a young Teruellan lord. The women flirted casually, and the men clapped him on the back. But one person seemed to be on everyone's mind.

"I heard Princess Betony embroidered her own gown," a young lady said in an awestruck tone.

"Why did the crown princess call her sister back to court?" an older man asked an even older woman.

"I haven't seen Prince Ebon lately. Perhaps that's why," the woman replied.

In yet another conversation, a young lordling eyed the princess appreciatively from across the ballroom before saying, "I wonder when she'll start courting."

Dorin tucked away the bits and bobs of gossip, rumor, and tales. He would write a letter to the chamberlain before bed to be sent by pigeon if urgent, and by barge and ship if not. So far, it seemed ship would win out. Why the princess had returned and who she might court were of interest, but not critical.

Music filled the air, and couples whirled across the dance floor, led in large part by Crown Princess Ranunculus and her consort, Prince Nevar. Despite being the center of conversation tonight, Princess Betony was alone at the edge of the crowd, looking as if she'd prefer to disappear into the tapestries lining the walls.

Nonsense. No one so beautiful should sit out a ball. Not to mention, if there was anything to know about the royals, what better way to find out than flatter the lonely youngest daughter? Or so he tried to convince himself. It had nothing at all to do with his fascination with the fae princess. Nothing at all.

Dorin snagged two glasses of the bubbly wine the Loreans preferred and headed straight for her. She twisted a ring on her finger, but her alert eyes behind the blue, black, and white bird mask scanned the crowd.

"Who are you waiting for, my lady?" he asked, still in his posh accent.

She jumped and reached into a pocket cleverly concealed in the pleats of the dress. For an instant, Dorin was sure she had a weapon, but what could she possibly conceal in a pocket? Betony examined him and must have decided he posed no threat. The hand came out of the pocket, and she pasted on a fake smile.

"My goodness, you startled me, my lord…"

Her voice was sweet, too sweet, and belied by her eyes. They were sharp and considering, trying desperately to place him.

He gave her an enigmatic smile and held out one of the drinks he carried.

"Now, now. What fun is it to reveal my identity at a masquerade ball?"

She shifted away from the wall and took the offered drink.

"Fair enough, though you can probably guess who I am."

"True, but let's pretend I can't."

His words earned him a smile bright enough to take his breath away, if he was so inclined. Which he wasn't. He was not a flirty young lord, and he had a job to do.

"To pretense, then." He lifted his glass to hers.

A small chime rang out as the glasses touched.

"To pretense."

Betony sipped her drink, and Dorin couldn't tear his gaze from her pink lips touching the glass. Unthinking, he gulped a large swallow of the sweet, tangy concoction. The bubbles tickled his nose, and it took everything in his power to keep from sneezing the liquid all over the princess. Instead, he nearly choked.

"Are you quite all right, my lord?" The words seemed genuine, and she leaned in to pat his back gently in concern.

Dorin inhaled deeply, taking comfort in her warm touch. He placed his nearly full glass on a table. Whatever it was, the stuff was deadly to his sophisticated persona. Next time, he would forgo the bubbly and stick to a less festive drink. Water was never a bad choice.

"Yes, thank you. I do not think this is for me."

"Want to know a secret?" She placed her glass next to his.

He raised a brow, and she smiled.

"It's not my favorite, either. The bubbles tickle my nose. It makes me want to sneeze."

Dorin couldn't help it. He barked out a laugh. "Precisely my problem."

"Well then, my lord, we are of the same mind."

She hooked her arm through his and started walking to a table loaded with food and beverages at the far end of the ballroom.

"Where are you taking me? My mother warned me not to go off with strange women."

"Why did you approach me in the first place? I am clearly the strangest woman here."

"Oh, surely not."

He glanced around. Well, perhaps she was right. Everyone else had hair in natural colors: blond, brown, black, a few gray-headed elders. A flash of red here and there. But her hair was the color of the lingonberries that grew in the temple garden he had helped his mother tend as a child. He remembered gathering them so she could make jam. He pushed aside the painful memory.

"For the moment, I am. Here we are!" Betony plucked two small glasses filled with a golden liquid and handed one to him. "The ambassador from Fuartir was kind enough to provide mead for Solstice. I snuck a taste earlier, and it's positively delightful. Cheers!"

As he sipped the drink from his homeland, the strangest notion crossed his mind—how would her lips taste after drinking this? He almost choked again.

She grinned at him, as though sensing his thought. "Good?"

He nodded and drained the glass, as did she. He thunked the glass on the table and held out a hand with an elegant flourish worthy of the lord he was pretending to be. "Would you care to dance, my lady?"

The princess placed her glass next to his and took his hand. "Yes, I would."

Dorin led her out to the other dancers as the band struck up a lively country tune. He wrapped an arm around her waist and pulled her close. The heady scent of rosemary and something light and floral filled his senses, sending his heart racing.

"Do I need to lead, my lord?" Her nose twitched with humor as he paused, taking in the feel of her.

"No, I've got it. Just noting the tempo."

He stepped to the beat, whirling and twirling in time to the music as his mother taught him so many years ago. He was okay with a waltz, could never keep the formal dances straight, but this…this, he could handle.

He held Betony close, watching her breaths quicken, her cheeks flush. Her musical laughter blended beautifully with the instruments. Everything she did was beautiful and graceful.

This was…fun.

And it had been a dog's age since Dorin had fun.

Chapter 3

$\mathcal{S}$omething about the young lord's eyes entranced her. Otherwise, he was nearly forgettable. Mouse brown hair, a height that blended into the crowd, and a body neither broad nor thin. Had he not approached her, Betony never would have noticed him.

But he had, and his voice did strange things to her insides. The thrum of it set off a resonance, and her whole body vibrated every time he spoke. And those eyes—when the glimmer of the fairy lamps hit them, the gold flecks in the medium brown sparked with amusement and, perhaps, attraction. Goddess, she hoped it was attraction.

He led her across the floor in a wild dance, and she realized his body was not all it seemed. He was graceful and strong, leading her through spins and twirls, dips and jumps as though he'd been born to this. With her hand on his shoulder, and his on her waist, the power of his muscles was obvious. Why hadn't she noticed before? He was more muscular than at first glance.

Nevar had played this trick when he first arrived in Lorea. He'd been hiding his years of sword training from his stepmother. With good reason, it had turned out. The hag was still locked in prison for almost killing him.

So why was *this* man determined for people to underestimate him?

Betony had little chance to think on the question. The music swept her up in its exuberance, and the lord's movements grew more complicated. It was all she could do to keep pace. Laughter escaped her lips, blending with the music, and before long, she forgot all her questions.

She let go of any suspicions and enjoyed the moment. He knew who she was, but for tonight, on the longest night of the year, she would pretend she was just a woman dancing with just a man with no politics, no past, and no thoughts of tomorrow.

The music ended, and the dancers clapped, surrounding Betony and her partner, who had taken over the dance floor. She curtsied with a flourish, and her lord gave an overly dramatic bow. Whistles and cheers greeted their performance. He leaned in closer.

"Want to get out of here?" he whispered.

Oh yes, she certainly did. The flash of what she could do with this man with a smidge more privacy left her even more breathless than the dancing. She grabbed his hand and pulled him toward the open doors leading to the gardens. Though it was cold outside, the heat from all the bodies made the ballroom nearly intolerable without a few open windows and doors.

Protests arose, and invitations to dance another round followed them, but Bet paid them no mind.

"Sorry, it seems the lady has other ideas," her dance partner said, laughing.

She led him outside onto a wide balcony overlooking the gardens. On the right, stone steps led to where the winter roses bloomed in the garden, their purple-tinged petals standing out against the snow and their soft scent wafting through the snowflakes. The holly leaves glistened in the moonlight, and the air was crisp and clean.

With a long exhale, Bet released the tension of being surrounded by so many people. It was unusual for her to be the center of attention. Her parents had worked hard to keep the court's focus off her, and Bet had not objected, not after the ball shortly before she turned eighteen. It had been a disaster she had no wish to repeat ever.

"Thank you." She leaned against the iron railing. Her human blood protected her from the physical effects of iron on a fairy, though it did interfere with her magic to a large degree. "It was getting a little crowded."

He smirked, seeing through her lie immediately as he joined her at the railing. His hand inched closer to hers. "It was always crowded, my lady."

She held her breath, wanting his touch once more. Though they'd held each other close, this seemed more intimate. The doors to the ballroom remained open, yet no one else was out here, and the voices and music seemed a world away. Bet let out a sigh when he didn't move.

"I suppose you're right. Let's say it *felt* more crowded."

"I will grant you that. You do not enjoy the limelight, do you?"

"No, I do not. In Faerie, I blend in. Here, I stand out. I always have, but I convinced myself I could fade into the background when needed."

"You shouldn't have to fade into the background."

Finally, *finally*, he covered her hand with his. Tendrils of desire traveled up her arm, strong enough she almost pulled away, but the steady warmth that followed in their wake soothed the lingering regret over the past.

"It's safer," she murmured.

"Safer for whom?"

Bet glanced at him. Those golden-flecked eyes still glittered in the moonlight, as fiercely as they had inside.

"For everyone. Things don't go well when I'm the center of attention."

He was quiet a moment but held on to her. The strains of the next song floated through the doors.

"No one is paying any attention now." His voice once again set her heart strings vibrating. "Dance with me again."

He didn't tug on her, didn't grasp her waist, didn't do anything other than wait for her response. His patience made up her mind. Betony stepped into his embrace and grabbed his free hand, placing it on her waist. He drew her close, and they waltzed gently across the balcony, observed only by the stars, the moon, and the roses climbing the rails.

The last notes died out and polite applause drifted into the wintry night. He brought her fingers to his lips and kissed them.

"Thank you, my lady," he said before dropping her hand.

She dipped a slight curtsy but couldn't keep the smile from her lips. "Thank *you*, my lord."

"Aren't you cold?"

"No, not yet. Part of being fae."

"How does your family handle it?"

So in tune with his voice, she detected the small tremble telling her the answer mattered. Betony carefully considered her words.

"My family—my parents, my brother, my sister—have never made me feel anything other than love. Well, maybe caution. My parents made sure I had training for my gifts so I wouldn't hurt myself or others."

They'd been almost perfectly successful. She shook away the memory. It had been their desire to keep her close that had led to the incident at the ball seven years ago. No one's fault in particular, but the situation couldn't arise again. After all these years in Faerie, training with the best wielders of magic and the best warriors, it wouldn't.

"You are lucky. Not every family is as understanding."

His shoulders hunched, and the pain of rejection radiated from him. This time, she covered his hand with hers.

"I know. But everyone *deserves* that kind of understanding."

He smiled sadly. "Perhaps."

Shaking his head, as if ridding himself of whatever pain the past had caused, he plastered on a smile that was a bit too wide, and a bit too practiced.

"Look at me, two dances with a beautiful woman and I become as morose as a moose."

"Maybe a third dance will make your smile real." She was unable to stop herself from calling out the false one.

It worked. The smile softened and melted her heart.

"As you say, my lady."

He pulled her once more into his arms, and though there was no music, they danced to the patter of snowflakes on the stone and the voices murmuring inside. When the band struck up another tune, it shut out the rest of the world, leaving only a man and only a woman dancing in the snow, like the stories Rane used to read to her when they were young.

Her companion stiffened as the music ended. He raised her hand and kissed her fingers once more.

"You must forgive me. My time here draws to a close." He stepped aside.

"Will I see you again?" she asked, his warmth seeming much further away than the arm length currently between them.

"Oh, I'm sure," he said with a wicked grin. "But in case you don't recognize me, let me leave you something to remember me by."

He closed the distance between them, wrapping an arm around her waist and cupping her cheek. He lowered his mouth to hers and kissed her. For an instant, it was only a gentle brush of his warm lips, tasting of flowers and honey from the mead, but she stood on her tiptoes and pressed into him. With a groan, he deepened the kiss, his lips growing insistent. She opened to him, and his tongue traced her lower lip.

Betony shivered with the pleasure of it, but before she could return the favor, the bells tolled once, marking midnight on the solstice. More would ring soon, and the pealing of all the bells in Avora would fill the air. He pulled away. She blinked at him in confusion.

"I really must leave." His fingers trailed along her arms.

"But I don't want you to go."

He framed her face with his callused hands. "Close your eyes and keep them closed until the bells stop ringing. Imagine I'm here with you."

She looked deep into his eyes and saw a desire fervent enough to shock her.

"Do you trust me, Princess?"

It was madness, but she did. Betony closed her eyes, and her breath quickened. One peal, two…

His lips brushed hers again, then were gone, along with his strong, sure hands. Betony waited until the last note of the last bell faded until the sound was nothing more than a memory.

She opened her eyes and touched her lips, still warm from their kisses. He was gone. On the railing was his mask, the leaves almost lifelike. She picked it up and held it close. This was a night she would never forget.

Chapter 4

*W*hat in Zovog's name had he been thinking? Death themself would never understand the risk Dorin had taken tonight. Dancing with the princess. Flirting with her. Fucking kissing her. He'd gone mad, obviously. Might as well admit it.

He rushed through the corridors, only slowing when shadows or voices hinted at others about. The ambassador would be more than displeased if Dorin wasn't waiting for him when he returned from the ball. No one questioned his presence, and he arrived at Vedel's quarters as the last bell quieted.

Dorin slipped in, closing the door behind him, and darted across the room to his own chamber. He pulled off his fancy doublet as he went and shoved it into the still open trunk, not bothering to close the door between his room and the ambassador's. He stripped down to his drawers and quickly yanked on his trousers and tunic.

Just in time. Voices murmured in the hall outside and the door cracked open. Vedel stumbled in, barely supported by an equally drunk Lorant, the warrior from the chief's personal war band sent as the head of the diplomatic guard. The burly man glared around the room, but before he could call out, Dorin strode in and helped him settle the ambassador into an armchair near the hearth. Lorant collapsed into the other.

"Get me a whiskey," Vedel said. "And one for Lorant, too."

Dorin calmly strode to the sideboard and poured two snifters of whiskey from their homeland. The smokey scent of cherrywood filled the room.

This was a drink, none of the Lorean bubbly crap. Yet it called to mind the sweetness of the mead, which lingered on his tongue along with the taste of the princess. He wished he could join them in sharing a dram to fend off the remaining confusion.

He carefully placed the glasses on the small table between the two chairs, and Vedel waved him away. Dorin took his place next to the sideboard and did the thing he did best. He listened. The aristocracy often forgot servants were about. He'd learned plenty in the past by simply remaining quiet and pretending he didn't exist.

Vedel sipped his whiskey. "So, Lorant, did you have your chance to dance with the fae princess?"

Lorant barked out a laugh. "No. I kept trying to corner her, but she moved about the room like a lynx in the forest. Then she disappeared with that godsdamned southlander lord."

Dorin suppressed a tight smile. His disguise had worked, and he'd kept Princess Betony far from this brute.

"Likely for the best. As much as the chief wants to solidify an alliance with the Lorean court, could you imagine being tied to a woman such as her? Too dainty, and too magical."

Lorant raised his glass. "She'd likely freeze to death at the first sign of winter in Cseobar. And I wouldn't want children with hair that color."

It took every ounce of willpower to keep from introducing the ambassador and his guard to his fists. How dare Lorant assume he was good enough for her?

A few dances with her, and he was ready to…what? Reveal his true purpose and throw away years of work? No, he was being ridiculous. The safety and happiness of Princess Betony was firmly out of his control, as it should be.

"Still, a marriage is the easiest way to form an alliance," Vedel continued, ever the seasoned politician. "And the sooner the chief can do so, the sooner the Witan will proclaim him king. But I doubt one of his heorthwerod could catch the eye of the fae bitch."

Ah yes, his father's ulterior motive for dealing with the Loreans. Sure, more trade and fewer skirmishes between Lorea and Clan Fher would be mutually beneficial. But if he made a significant agreement with King Rowan, Kalmar would have a solid base from which to build the kingdom he wanted. Not content to be merely a clan chief, an equal on the governing council of the Witan, he wanted to rule all of Fuartir. And a treaty with Lorea would be an important step.

Dorin didn't care, not really. His mother and the other clerics had raised him to serve his chief, to serve his clan, and someday he would serve his country. As the unacknowledged, mostly unknown, bastard of the chief, the best he could hope for was to be the secret sword of Clan Fher. To raise his father's stature among the other clans of Fuartir and guarantee his clan's preeminent place on the Witan. As brutal and violent as Kalman could be, the other clan chiefs were far worse, and the best hope for the northern lands was to install his father as king. Or so he'd been told, and so he believed.

"Shame to end the raids. They've brought wealth and glory to our clan." Lorant held his glass to the fire and studied its amber depths. "I suppose there is still Faerie. Plenty of opportunity for gold and glory with the fairy bastards."

"Not for too much longer, though. Once we've made a treaty with Lorea, the Queens will see the benefits. Kalman wants to better the relations with Faerie as well once he's secured his own crown." Vedel polished off his whiskey and held out his glass for more. Dorin filled it. "And our stay here this winter is an excellent opportunity to build his case with the Loreans."

Keeping Faerie as an enemy would make it easier to gather the other clans around Chief Kalman of the Clan Fher. Dorin wasn't a politician; he was a servant, a gatherer of gossip and whispers, and a knife in the night. He served his lord and his chief, he did not question them. And right now, his chief wanted some sort of leverage to treat with King Rowan.

Why else would the king risk a hundred years of peace and prosperity with his closest neighbors, both diplomatically and personally? Chief Kalmar would have to offer something of extraordinary value for Rowan to even consider moving forward with any deal without the Queens of Faerie knowing.

He hated that they viewed the princess as merely a pawn in the game his father played. He hated that *he* was a pawn in the game his father played. But Betony was no one's pawn, and he'd do everything he could to keep the kind and beautiful woman out of the ambassador's plans. She deserved so much more.

Lorant thunked his empty glass on the table. "I must go before all the pretty maids have finished their duties and retire alone for the evening. It's a fucking shame if any of them go home to a cold, empty bed."

"Ha!" Vedel said. "If you find a spare, send her my way, won't you?"

With a leer, the guard strode out of the room, leaving Dorin to ready the ambassador for bed. He kneeled in front of Vedel and pulled off his boots, then helped him stand. Carefully, he untied the doublet and tugged it off. As the ambassador took off his trousers, Dorin unfolded his favorite nightshirt. The ambassador put it on and climbed into bed.

Dorin tidied the ambassador's clothes and set the whiskey glasses in the hall for the night servants to gather. Soft snores followed him to his small chamber. Sleep was still another hour away for him. First, he needed to finish his letter for the chamberlain.

He poured himself a dram from a small bottle he kept in his trunk. He savored every drop as he added the rumors, scandals, fears, and hopes he'd collected over the past week.

The Loreans still did not trust the northerners. They were concerned about the raids on the coast. Worried how it would interfere with shipping, grumbled about how to trade with the northerners without a guarantee of safety for the merchant ships.

Clan Fher was not currently raiding while trying to negotiate with the Loreans in good faith, but there were six other clans. No one could guarantee *they* wouldn't attack the merchant vessels. The Loreans were used to dealing with long-established kingdoms, not the loose affiliation of chiefdoms up north. The King of Teruelle and the Queens of Faerie could enforce their agreements with Lorea. His father could not. Not yet.

He poured out every last drop of gossip into his letter, some bits from lurking in the halls and talking with the other servants. The rest from the upper echelons of society at tonight's ball. Which lords and ladies were courting, which were fucking behind their spouses' backs, which had debts, which had fingers in the shipping industry, and who might have the king's ear.

Dorin tried to convince himself that was why he'd danced with Princess Betony. She'd be privy to information no other lord or lady knew, perhaps even appreciate his attention enough to let a secret slip. But he was lying to himself.

He spoke to her, danced with her, because he'd wanted to. Because he sensed some connection to the shy wallflower.

It was no wonder why the Loreans mistrusted the northerners. Here they were, here *he* was, sneaking into a celebration and reporting everything he could learn to his father's chamberlain. Dorin had never loved these little spy missions, but tonight was the first time he felt dirty because of it. Damn beautiful princesses with hair the color of berries and musical laughs. And damn the circumstances of his birth.

He finished his note to Jani, along with the last drop of his whiskey. He folded the paper and tucked it into the pocket of the jerkin he would wear the next day. Nothing urgent, so this could go by boat. He'd see if Conrad and the *Blenny* were at the docks. The old smuggler was always happy to earn a gold coin to discretely deliver a letter to the *Zovog's Revenge*, where the Fuartiran captain would forward it with the pigeons kept aboard.

Dorin blew out his candle—he was fascinated by the fairy-light lanterns, but Vedel refused to have them in his rooms—and crawled into his bed. Laughing green eyes and perfect pink lips haunted his thoughts, keeping him up until sleep finally claimed him in the darkness before dawn.

Chapter 5

*B*etony had played the dutiful daughter for three whole days before
the ball last night. Three days of utter boredom. After the magical
kiss from her mysterious lord, the castle stones weighed on her. She needed
an escape.

Bet slipped off to the stables after breakfast. She hadn't slept well. Every
time she closed her eyes, his voice echoed in her memory, thrumming
under her skin, and made sleep an impossible goal. She drifted off near
dawn, only to have a scandalous dream featuring her new obsession. She
hadn't even glimpsed his face—but those lips did wicked things to her
dream body, and she'd awakened gasping with pleasure.

His mask looked on from where she'd hung it next to her mirror. If he
ever came looking for it—unlikely, but possible—she would be the one to
present it to him, and she'd learn his true identity.

Too bothered to get any more sleep, she dressed. Betony brushed her
fingers over the mask as she left, and warmth spread through her as the
dream came to mind in vivid detail. She stumbled to the kitchens for a
quick breakfast, and then left the confining stones behind for the freedom
of the forest. Years spent in Faerie had her as much at home in the Argent
Forest as in Avora Castle. Maybe more so.

After last night, all but one stable attendant would be sleeping, but she
didn't need anyone's help to saddle her horse. She grabbed a saddle
blanket off the pile in the tack room, and with a small smile on her lips, she
saddled Hesli her white gelding. As she led him out of his stall, a stranger

entered the stable.

No, not quite a stranger—there was something familiar… Ah, yes, the ambassador's manservant. She'd mistaken him for a stable hand when she first arrived home.

He noticed her and froze, and a peculiar expression crossed his face.

"Good morning," she said smoothly, hoping to allay his…fear? No, he wasn't afraid. Hmm. "I'm sorry, I didn't catch your name when we last met."

He donned his typical passive formality, putting aside whatever he'd felt at the sight of her, and bowed.

"Dorin, Your Highness," he mumbled in a thick Fuartiran accent.

Before she could wave away the formality, Hal, the head groom, exited a stall further down. He rushed out when he saw Betony.

"Milady, what are you doing?"

"Going for a ride." Out of the corner of her eye, she saw Dorin tuck his hands into his coat pockets and slink out of the stables. Too timid to brave a royal, poor man. "You all worked late last night, and I don't want to bother anyone, so I saddled Hesli myself."

Hal *tsk*ed. "It's our job."

Betony bit back a sigh. Though she'd grown up with Lorean hierarchy, she preferred the way things worked in Faerie. Able-bodied adults took care of themselves and helped anyone who needed it—children, elders, those with disabilities. Even the Queens saddled their own horses. Once Rane assumed the throne, things were likely to change. Her sister generally dismissed pomp and circumstance. It had lessened over the years, she'd been told. But Hal, older than her father, was a stickler for tradition.

"And you do it well. But you know how it is in Faerie."

"Aye, and you're just back. I'll make sure the lads and lasses appreciate your consideration."

She knew she couldn't stop him, so she gave a regal nod and mounted Hesli. Looking at where the manservant had stood, she asked, "Does he come often?"

"Who?" Hal scanned the stable, looking for whoever she was talking about.

"Dorin?"

Hal still looked confused.

"The Fuartiran ambassador's manservant?" Betony elaborated.

"Oh, is that his name? His accent is so strong, I barely understand him. He comes to borrow a horse every now and then. Goes into town from what I heard."

"What for?"

"Can't say, milady. Guess you scared him off today." He lowered his voice. "Them northerners don't much care for magic."

"Thank you, Hal. If anyone asks, I'm riding in the Argent. I'll return by dinner."

He grunted in acknowledgment. She pointed Hesli toward the gate and tapped her heels to his side. The *clip-clop* of his shoed hooves echoed in the quiet courtyard. She passed the Fuartiran manservant outside the gate to town.

Don't much care for magic, huh? That was an understatement. From her previous conversations with Fuartirans, from everything she'd read in the libraries here in Avora and Neraida in Faerie, they sought to *control* magic. Only their priests were allowed to wield it unfettered.

Betony settled Hesli into a nice trot through the capital city as she shook off the gloom from those thoughts. It was too fine a day to worry about what happened across the Roheda Sea. Nary a cloud in the sky, and the sun was almost warm.

The day after winter solstice was a day off for most. Shops were shuttered and smoke poured from the homes' chimneys. The fragrant scent of bread, roasting fowl, and sweet potatoes filled the air, mingling with the cold snap of a winter morning. A light dusting of snow covered the rooftops and cobblestones.

They cleared the city gates and Bet urged her mount into a canter, steering him toward the Argent Forest. Outside the city, a little more snow had accumulated, and the sun glinted off its surface. The leaves were long gone from the branches of the birch trees, and between the snow and the white bark, they gleamed like silvered glass. The forest lived up to its name today.

Hesli wound through the trees, and Betony's shoulders relaxed, the tension draining from her the further they got from Avora. She loved her family dearly, but she needed some distance today. It was strange, knowing this was her home again.

She had missed out on the balls and other festivities her sister and brother had enjoyed when they were new adults. Away in Faerie, she didn't participate in the typical duties of the royal family. No charities to visit, no festivities to plan, no diplomatic missions to go on. No way to make human friends.

Now, Ebon and Sarsa were off adventuring and protecting both their realms. Rane and Nevar were busy with Jonquil, still so young, and their duties. Bet was essentially alone.

She would figure out her place at court. Perhaps she'd speak with Commander Miren to see about training the guard in Faerie fighting techniques. She could serve some shifts in the hospital. Both her fighting and healing skills were impeccable, and she could be a true asset for both the commander and the hospital's healers.

Betony entered the clearing. Anyone else would notice only an iced-over pond at the far end, and trees and dormant grass waving in the breeze. But her fae eyesight granted her the ability to see through the glamour to the dilapidated stone cottage with smoke wafting out of its chimney and a pile of firewood stacked neatly to one side.

Before she could dismount, the door to the cottage flew open and a tall woman with bright yellow hair and purple eyes rushed out, a feral smile on her coral lips.

"Hello, goddaughter," she said.

"Hello, godmother." Betony slid off Hesli, landing in the sparse snow. She pulled the saddlebags off the horse. "I didn't expect to see you here."

Hyssop waited for Bet to approach before enveloping her in an embrace and kissing both cheeks. Bet returned the gesture.

"I was not planning on being here, but the Sisters were kind enough to invite me for Winter Solstice. Your grandmother insisted I come as she wanted to spend the night reading. The wine flowed freely, and Curlew did not want me to return to Neraida until morning."

Fairies marked Winter Solstice more somberly than humans, celebrating quietly with friends and family. Besides the Lorean royals, Hyssop had few of either left after her nearly three hundred years. It was a kindness of the Sisters to invite her, though it seemed the usually quiet occasion became a bit rowdy.

"It's past morning." Betony walked into the cozy cottage, which was in much better repair inside than out.

Hyssop let out a quiet growl, tinged with humor as well as irritation. "Apparently, Wren thought it would be fun to hide everyone's shoes. Her sisters have found all but mine, but she will not come out to help look."

Bet bit her lip to prevent the giggle threatening to escape. "Ah, I see. Let me put the bags down and I'll talk to her."

"I will be grateful, goddaughter."

Hyssop sat in a rustic chair at the smooth table in the middle of the one-room cottage. Her godmother picked up the steaming cup of tea she had abandoned to greet her. Betony hung the saddlebags over another chairs. A gray cat sat on yet another, and she stroked his head in greeting.

"Hello, Zol. Couldn't keep them out of trouble?"

He meowed gruffly, then licked a paw and used it to clean behind his ears, as if embarrassed by the youngest pixie's behavior.

Bet climbed the ladder to the loft, where six pixies cowered.

They were in their small forms, about the size of the birds each was named after. Four sat on their tiny beds, knees to their chests, heads down. Bet couldn't tell if they were laughing or crying. One lay on her belly on the floor, chin resting on folded arms as she peered under a bed. Peeking out from under the last bed were two tiny feet shod in golden slippers.

May Veitha, God of the Hunt, grant me patience.

"Greetings, Sisters," Bet said quietly to avoid startling them.

Pipit looked up from her bed, and a squeak came out from the last.

Curlew, the pixie lying on the floor, turned toward Bet, lips pressed together and shook her head. "I can't get her to come out."

"Wren," Bet said. "You need to come out."

"No! She'll kill me."

Below them, Hyssop snorted.

"You're not helping, godmother," Bet ground out.

"I've been trying all morning," Curlew said.

"Why don't you all take a break? Go patrol, or gather, or hunt, or…something. I've got Wren."

With a last look under the bed, Curlew flew from the loft and out the open door. Her sisters followed, leaving Hyssop at the kitchen table and Bet perched awkwardly on the ladder. The cat trotted after the pixies. There were seven sisters, but Lark, the eldest, now served as Jonquil's godmother. Curlew had assumed the leadership role for the time being.

"Godmother," Bet said, "would you mind taking Hesli to the pond for a drink while I talk to Wren?"

"Is this your boon?" A wicked twinkle shone in Hyssop's lavender eyes.

Her godmother's boons were to thank for both Nevar and Sarsa but shouldn't be wasted on small requests. Perhaps, someday, Hyssop's boon might bring Bet her true love, but for the moment there was little reason for the youngest of the Lorean royal children to hurry into marriage.

"No magic required. Only a little privacy. When I ask for my boon, I will do so in no uncertain terms."

Her godmother chuckled softly as she put her mug down, then pushed back from the table and slipped outside without a word of protest. Bet sighed in relief.

"Are they gone?" Wren asked in a tiny voice.

"Yes. Are you going to tell me how Hyssop's shoes ended up on your feet?"

The pixie crawled out and sat on her bed, her orange wings trembling. "She fell asleep and they were so pretty. I didn't think there would be any harm in trying them on."

She tried to pull off the shoes, tugging at the sparkly leather, but they held fast.

Though Wren was about Betony's age, she'd been bound to an evil hobgoblin as a child, along with her sisters. Since they'd been freed, the older pixies had indulged Wren's childish fancies. Mostly, they were harmless, but sometimes trouble followed. And it was Wren's luck her godmother chose enchanted slippers for Winter Solstice.

"You know what you have to do."

"I don't want to," Wren sniffed. "She gets scary when she's mad."

"You made a mistake. It's time to confess and apologize."

The pixie was a fierce warrior, taking on all manner of trouble in the Argent Forest. Hobgoblins, ghouls, dire wolves, ogres, trolls, armed men, and fairies who were bent on harm, the same as her sisters. But when her antics landed her in hot water, she was no better than a ten-year-old caught stealing pastries.

"Fine, but if she turns me into a toad, you owe me a prince. Or princess, I'm not picky."

Bet tried not to laugh as Wren flew the arm's length separating them, her dragonfly wings shimmering as they beat faster than the eye could see and landed on her shoulder. She ducked under the cranberry-colored tresses, her tiny fingers digging into the sensitive skin of Betony's neck.

Slowly descending the ladder, Bet made shushing noises to the nearly inaudible sobs coming from the pixie. Hyssop was indeed frightening. No one wished to get on her bad side. But she tended to be more bark than bite with those she cared about. Besides Rane and Bet, she was the only person to treat the pixies as family. Her godmother would scare the tits off Wren, but no harm would come to her. And perhaps the pixie would learn a little restraint.

Betony walked into the cold, her breath puffing in front of her face. She pulled up her hood and found Hyssop and Hesli at the pond for a drink, but there was no sign of the other pixies. Chickens.

Bet approached, making as much noise as possible in the quiet clearing. It didn't pay to surprise a powerful fairy warrior like her godmother.

"Wren has something to tell you, godmother."

Hyssop turned, one yellow eyebrow sharply arched, her lips pressed together. But humor glimmered in her eyes, and little wrinkles across her forehead gave away her amusement to any who paid attention.

"Oh?"

Wren peeked out from Bet's hair. "I'm sorry, Lady Hyssop. I took your shoes. I just wanted to try them on, but…"

She stuck out a foot and tried to remove the shoe. Nothing happened.

"Allow me." Hyssop reached out a finger.

Wren squeaked and trembled but kept her foot still. Hyssop touched the shoe and spoke a word in the ancient fairy tongue. A golden glow lit her finger and the shoe. It grew until it slid off Wren's foot and kept growing until it was large enough for Hyssop to slide her foot in.

"Now the other, you naughty pixie."

Wren pulled tightly on Bet's hair but stuck out her other foot. In a moment, the golden shoes were back on their owner's feet, and Hyssop glared at the tiny pixie. Wren let go of Betony and flew out a few feet. She glowed with her own magic, a shimmery rainbow bubble, as she grew to her full size. She was still smaller than Bet, who was petite by human standards.

She bowed low. "My apologies, Lady Hyssop. I did not mean to inconvenience you, and it won't happen again. Is there anything I can do to make this up to you?"

Hyssop tapped a finger to her lips. "Pack your things. I could use someone with your…talents…at Errozar."

Wren gulped. "Err-Errozar?"

"Yes. While Sarsa is away, the Queens have requested I step in and run the guards and monitor the spy networks. Your assistance will be a fine way to offset today's inconvenience. Only a few weeks. Winter is the quiet season in the Argent, if I recall correctly. Few travelers and many beasties in hibernation."

Wren bowed again. "You do indeed, my lady. I'll pack and join you momentarily."

Hyssop gestured grandly. "Spend some time with your sisters, but I expect you overmorrow."

A grin bloomed on Wren's face. "You are as kind as you are forgiving."

She returned to her small form and, with a whir of wings, flew off into the cottage.

"Errozar?" Bet said once the hum of her wings vanished.

Zol appeared from the other side of the woodpile and rubbed against Bet's ankles. She picked up the grimalkin and cuddled him like an infant. His purrs reverberated in her chest.

Hyssop scratched under the cat's chin. "Why do you think I enchanted my sparkliest shoes and wore them to a Winter Solstice celebration in the middle of the woods? I couldn't come begging a favor."

Unreasonable fairies with their ridiculous honor. Can't owe anyone anything without expecting payback of some sort. It was the one aspect of fairy culture Bet still had trouble grasping, even after living with them for seven years.

"You are one conniving fairy, godmother." Bet chuckled and shook her head.

"Well, thank you, child." Hyssop positively beamed. "I should return to Errozar. Find me there if the need arises."

And with a crack of thunder, her godmother vanished. Zol darted out of Bet's arms and ran into the cottage.

"Show off," she muttered, following.

One by one, the pixies returned as Betony pulled out the bread, cheese, and dried fruit. A flagon of ale joined the food on the table, as well as leftover spice cake from last night. She enjoyed her lunch with the pixies and reassured Wren that Errozar was not nearly as haunted as rumor made it out to be. A quick glance out the window as she packed the flagon told her it was time to be on her way.

No need to tempt fate by being out in the Argent Forest at night. She mounted Hesli and rode home.

Chapter 6

etony had stolen Dorin's breath away when he saw her standing in the stable. As he had mumbled his name, he prayed to Alet to turn her attention elsewhere, avoid recognizing his voice. It seemed to work.

Dorin stared as she rode by him, fixing her in his memory. Last night was one he never wanted to forget. A night when he'd been as much himself as possible. A night when he danced with a beautiful woman who hadn't judged him for anything—not his parentage, not his lack of wealth, not his abilities. A night when he kissed a princess, and she'd kissed him back with all the passion he could have hoped for.

The city was quiet. He preferred it like this. Cseobar, the port town he called home, was a fraction of the size, and he felt overwhelmed sometimes when visiting large cities. But today, few people were on the streets, and he could allow his gaze to linger on the buildings, small and large, and the lovely goddess groves interspersed at regular intervals throughout the city. The trees reached their bare branches toward the feeble winter sun, though each had at least one evergreen. Those stood out like a bluebird on a gray day. Like a fae princess at a royal ball.

Dorin found Conrad sleeping off the night of carousing on the deck of his barge, leaning over a pile of ropes and snoring softly. His nearly bald pate gleamed in the winter sun. Dorin walked over the gangplank but stopped before crossing onto the deck. It was impolite at best to board a vessel without the captain's permission, even a captain such as Conrad.

"Ho, the *Blenny*!" Dorin called out.

Conrad snorted as he jerked upright, lost his footing, and grunted as his ass hit the deck of the barge.

"Who the fuck—" His scowl quickly found Dorin and his mouth snapped shut.

"Hello, Conrad." His country Fuartiran accent was spot on, with enough smoothness to sell his role as manservant to an ambassador. "I have a letter that needs to be delivered."

"It's the day after Solstice, Dorin. A holiday. No working, only sleeping, eating, drinking, and fucking."

Dorin pulled out a gold coin. It gleamed in the weak midday light.

"I'll make it worth your while."

Conrad lumbered over and snatched the coin from Dorin.

"Fine," he grumbled. "Come aboard."

Dorin stepped onto the deck and pulled out the folded and sealed note.

"I need this delivered to Captain Mertok on the *Zovog's Revenge*."

Conrad took the note, too, but more gently this time. He tucked it into his pocket with a sneer.

"Going down to Nimel tomorrow, anyways. I woulda done this for a silver."

Dorin shrugged. It was Jani's money, which meant it was the chief's. It was no skin off his nose.

"My thanks just the same. Safe journey."

Muttering about cursed northerners, Conrad stomped to the small cabin and slammed the door. Dorin whistled all the way back to the castle.

Over the next few days, Dorin seemed to run into Princess Betony constantly. He spotted her in the halls, in the courtyard, in the stables, even in the streets of Avora. He would duck out of sight before she noticed him in return, but not before allowing himself to savor the sight of her.

After hearing Conrad had returned from Nimel, he went to the docks to buy a bottle of whiskey from the sometime smuggler and gathered all the gossip worth knowing from the port city. There was little. Lorea seemed to have gone into hibernation since the ball. Few people came, few people left. Deep winter on the Roheda Sea was dangerous, and travel ceased shortly after solstice.

There was little activity in the castle or the city. Betony made occasional forays farther out, sometimes accompanied by her sister or brother-in-law and always by a guard. Dorin ingratiated himself with the stable hands, bringing small treats in return for borrowing mounts. None seemed to know where she went or who she met. They were a close-lipped bunch when it came to the royal family, and as Betony had been absent for much of the last seven years, they didn't even try to speculate.

Returning late, he found her sneaking into the stables. He tiptoed behind her and watched as she sang softly to the horses, going from stall to stall, stroking the noses poking over the doors. The cats came out for some scratches, even the old orange tom with one ear no one could get close to. He flopped over and allowed Betony to rub his belly. Mice peeked out from under the straw, and the hounds in the kennels next to the stables quieted. The animals seemed to sway to her tune.

That should be impossible, yet no matter how hard he rubbed his eyes, there they were. Her voice trailed off, and he tried to slip out before she spotted him.

"It's Dorin, right?" she asked gently.

Too late.

"Yes, milady," he mumbled.

The cleric who trained him once said his voice was his most distinguishing characteristic. The temple had sent him to study with an acting troupe. They had taught him to disguise his too memorable voice in many ways. Higher, lower, how to roughen it, different accents, from educated Lorean to the poorest Fuartiran farmer. He went with the last here.

"You can stay, if you want. I don't mind. I was just visiting my friends."

His gaze darted from her to the exit. Dorin knew exactly what he should do. Go back to his room and rest. Draw no further attention to himself. But the loneliness in her voice called to the loneliness in his heart. If the princess called the barn animals her friends, then who else did she have in her life? Besides, much like the animals, her voice lured him, lulled him, and her kindness was more than he could resist.

"Thank you," he murmured, and settled on a hay bale inside the door.

She picked up where she left off, each cat taking a turn at her feet, each horse getting a few moments of her attention. He found himself drifting on the melody, reminded of nothing less than his own mother's voice. They were completely different, but the feeling... His mother had been the one person to love him as a child, and her songs, though sung slightly off key, surrounded him with her love.

Princess Betony sang like the birds in the trees, her voice rising and falling in some natural rhythm he couldn't put a name to. Her song filled the room with love and kindness, as his mother's had. The animals sensed it, and so did he. As long as Betony was here, he was safe. Dorin hadn't felt safe in…forever. More than half his lifetime ago.

Her voice faded, and he lingered in the space between wakefulness and sleep. A soft blanket covered him, and he kept his eyes shut tight, pretending to sleep. Her footfalls barely made any noise as she left, and the stable door closed with a soft click.

He was in danger of falling for the woman. By Zovog's scythe, he was fucked if anyone ever found out. And may the god of death help him, he almost didn't care.

Dorin cracked open his eyes. No one. He stood and folded the blanket, leaving it on top of the bale. The other animals had all dispersed, leaving the orange tom to lick his balls in the middle of the stable. The horses whickered softly as they settled in for the night.

He returned to his room, ghosting past the ambassador. As he listened to the snores and farts of His Lordship, Dorin wondered what he'd done to deserve Zovog's attention. Falling for a Lorean princess was a death wish if he'd ever heard of one. If King Rowan didn't kill him for reaching far above his station, his father would out of spite.

Crawling onto his surprisingly comfortable cot, he waited for sleep to find him. And waited.

He turned over on his side, resigned to another sleepless night. The princess's song still lingered in his mind. It had been a long, long time since anyone had sung him to sleep, not since his mother died in a raid from a rival clan when he was eight years old. The memories came flooding back.

He'd been asleep in their tiny cottage outside the chief's manor. As word of the raid spread through the village, all the children were ushered into the compound. His mother took her place with the other clerics of Zovog to help the warriors defend the defenseless. The high priest brought him the bad news at dawn the next day after finishing his rounds through the grievously wounded and offering the release of death. Fewer died that day thanks to Piroska.

That evening, Dorin had stood in front of his father and his father's wife as they heatedly discussed his fate. Lady Rahel wanted nothing to do with him, of course. He was a reminder her marriage to Chief Kalman was a political one, and she could never compete with a dead lover. She won in the end, and his father, never a warm, loving man, gave him to the clerics of Zovog to train. For ten years, he learned the skills of death, until his father called him to serve his clan in the only way he could.

He pushed aside the old hurt and focused instead on Betony. She was everything his family was not, patient and kind. He finally drifted off, her lullaby weaving through his dreams.

The next day, Vedel sent Dorin to fetch something for his upset stomach. He held his tongue, but the urge to tell the ambassador that perhaps he should try a little more moderation with the rich Lorean foods was strong. Unsure where to go for such a remedy, he began at the most obvious place, the kitchen.

"There's mint in the garden, lad," the cook said after listening carefully. "Start there, and if His Lordship needs somethin' else, come on back and I'll give you directions to the closest apothecary. Or ask Princess Betony. She's a healer, a skilled one at that."

Mint in the garden? The frigid season would soon set in, the crisp cold of solstice giving over to the bitterness of full winter. Though mild compared to Fuartir, the winters here could still become long and dreary, with enough snow to keep most indoors. The mint should have withered at the first hard freeze weeks ago.

He walked through the door the cook pointed out. There was no evidence of snow, yet the courtyard he'd walked through to get here had a few piles in the corners. In fact, the garden bloomed as if it was in the full warmth of a summer day. The temperature was mild—not summer hot, but certainly not cold enough to be winter.

The gardener chuckled at the shock on his face. "First time in a fairy-blessed garden, lad?"

Fairy-blessed. Of course. The hairs on the back of his neck rose. In Fuartir, magic was reserved for clerics. His mother had been a powerful magician, though she never used it at home. No, as a gift from Zovog, it was only to be used in their service, to worship or to defend. He'd seen her wield the power of fire and lightning at ceremonies.

Fairy magic, and thus the magic of the fae-born humans, was suspect. It was used as the fairy best saw fit, not in service to the gods. Dorin's training and duties had carried him into Faerie, Lorea, and Teruelle over the past twenty years. He was more comfortable with magic than most

Fuartirans. Yet seeing such a blatant use of it still sent a lance of trepidation down his spine.

"The snow will still fall, it just melts quickly," the gardener said. "What are you looking for?"

"Mint."

The man pointed at a pottery container where the mint grew as thick as grass before he returned to layering manure and straw around the plants. It smelled to high heaven, but the earthy odor spoke of renewal in the months to come. The basic principles of agriculture were part of his education as a supposed chamberlain-in-training. A fitting cover for his true purpose.

Laughter drifted out of the kitchen, laughter he recognized. Dorin froze in the middle of picking a few sprigs of mint. A moment later, Betony chased the young Prince Jonquil into the garden. The toddler squealed with joy as his aunt followed him around the table, keeping within easy distance to grab him in case he found himself in trouble, but far enough away so the tyke believed he was escaping her grasp. Her nose twitched as she tried and failed to keep a solemn expression.

The smile that blossomed made his heart race. Her eyes gleamed brightly in the mid-morning light, as bright as the finest emeralds the raiders had ever brought to Fuartir. But mostly, it was the joy and love she fed into the space, a blanket of comfort missing from his life.

The gardener nudged him, and a wry grin split his weathered face. "It don't hurt to look. She's lovely both inside and out. But that's all it can be. She ain't for the likes of you."

The heat rose up Dorin's neck and colored his cheeks as he turned back to the pot of mint. He'd been trained better than to be caught staring. Or to fucking blush.

"I know," he mumbled in his soft, unassuming country farmer voice. "She's awfully pretty."

And he left it at that. The squeals turned to giggles as Betony caught her nephew and swung him in her arms. She bounced him on her hip and carried him over to where the gardener worked.

"Can you say good morning?" she asked the wriggling boy.

The dark-haired child turned his face into her shoulder, suddenly shy.

"Jonquil, it's polite to say hello."

"Hewo," the child whispered.

"Hello, young prince. Good morning, Princess," the gardener replied in a robust voice.

"Good morning, milord, milady," Dorin murmured.

"Thank you." Betony ruffled the prince's hair. "Good morning to you both. Make sure you talk to Cook when you are done. I'll have her save a sweet bun for each of you."

The gardener bowed, and Dorin took his cue and performed a hesitant bow.

"Very kind," the gardener said as Betony waved and carried the child back into the kitchen. "See, lovely lass."

The gardener wasn't wrong, but he might have had some choice words for Dorin had he known the direction of the younger man's thoughts. Lovely was only the half of it. His hands still remembered the feel of her and his lips the taste.

Dorin returned to the ambassador's quarters and brewed a pot of mint tea. Vedel chased him out shortly, saying he stunk of manure. He went to the servants' bath and scrubbed the stench away with the rosemary soap the castle was known for. It reminded him of Betony, though she had a sweet floral scent as well. He splashed cold water over his head. His thoughts needed to stay as far from the princess as possible. Nothing but trouble and heartache lay in that direction.

But as hard as he tried, he could not get her off his mind.

Chapter 7

*C*abin fever set in.

After years in Faerie, even a few days of restriction were enough to set her teeth on edge. Bet had forgotten how little freedom of movement she was granted in Avora. Every time she left the castle, she was supposed to have an escort. Her little trip the other day had sent Miren and Jadran into conniptions. Now she understood why Rane had snuck out of the castle so often when she was younger.

After promising to not go riding solo again, they let her out of the Council Chamber with only stern looks. What could they do if she disobeyed? Not only was she a royal, but she was an adult. They'd tried confining Rane to the castle, but she had managed to sneak out anyway, and thus this little package of delight sucking his thumb as he ran his fingers through her hair.

Perhaps one day in the not too distant future, she would have a child of her own to snuggle. For the time being, she was content with her nephew.

She carried him to the nursery where Lark waited, foot tapping in impatience. The pixie took the sleepy child from her and tucked him into his crib. She tiptoed out and closed the door quietly behind her.

"I said to have him back directly after breakfast," Lark grumbled. "If he doesn't get a morning nap in, he will overtire before dinner. And you do not want to witness such an event."

Bet smiled sweetly. "We played in the kitchen gardens for a few minutes. No harm done."

Lark lifted a brow, then returned the smile. "I suppose not. I am used to my schedule, but now you've returned, I will have to…rearrange."

"Thank you, Lark. You are a marvelous godmother."

The pixie's shoulders pulled back and her cheeks pinked. "I take my duty seriously, and I am happy to help Rane. She's been a true friend."

"As have you. We are lucky to have you."

Lark was an exemplary godmother, more involved than Hyssop in the day-to-day care of her charge. Though Hyssop had always been exactly where she was needed when she was needed. The fierce fairy had an impeccable sense of timing.

The pixie, on the other hand, was protective of her young charge, only allowing Jonquil out of her sight when in the company of the few she trusted. Bet hoped as the boy grew, Lark would loosen up a bit. Making friends as the heir to the throne was hard enough without a fearsome warrior watching your every move.

"I am off to visit my sisters for a few days," Lark said with a lingering glance at Jonny's room.

"Jonquil and Rane will miss you, but he'll be fine. Enjoy your time away and tell them hello from me. Oh, and Wren is at Errozar."

Lark opened her mouth, but only shook her head. "I'm sure I'll hear the whole story, and then some, from Curlew. I am glad you are back, Betony. Rane has missed you."

"I have missed her." Truth, but being home still felt…foreign.

With a last bow, Lark shrank and zipped down the hall.

Well, now what? A maid was stationed outside the room to fetch Rane if Jonny woke before his normal time. There was little to do around the castle in the winter, and for once, her current embroidery project wasn't calling her to finish it.

Her thoughts flew to the other day. The hospital always needed helping hands, and she should put hers to good use. Surely a guard could be spared to walk her to the bottom of the hill. It would only be a few moments.

Betony hurried to her room and changed into a plain brown split skirt and jerkin over a green tunic. She braided her hair and tied a matching green kerchief over it, both to make her hair color less obvious and to protect it from whatever she might encounter at the hospital. She hooked her expandable staff on her belt and tucked the hawkbill knife into a pocket of her long wool coat.

The small fairy-wrought blade had been a gift to her grandmother from King Rowan when he married Beatrice, and Gran believed it was finally the moment to pass it along. She'd given it to Betony as a birthday present a month before she left Neraida. Though Betony preferred her staff for fighting, the small blue blade gave her a backup and was useful in so many ways to a healer. And this knife was a perfect fit for her delicate hands.

She strode confidently to the castle gatehouse, but her pace slowed when she noticed only a single guard on duty. This was not looking promising.

Nevertheless, she persisted. Perhaps his partner had merely taken a short break.

Plastering a friendly smile on her lips, Betony greeted the guard. "Good morning. I was hoping for an escort to the hospital."

The returning smile died before it fully came to life at her words.

"I'm so sorry, Your Highness. We can't spare anyone at the moment. Perhaps this afternoon. Definitely tomorrow."

"Oh. I understand." She tried to keep a brave face, but her disappointment must have shown through.

"I am truly sorry. I promise things will be different tomorrow."

"Perhaps I may be of service," said a soft, masculine voice in a thick accent.

Betony turned to her right. The ambassador's manservant, Dorin, stood a few paces off, awkwardly studying his feet. He seemed to appear at the oddest times. She had noticed him lurking in the halls and avoiding her in the courtyards. She had chalked it up to shyness, but he didn't seem so shy at the moment.

"I couldn't impose," she said, but was grateful for his kindness.

"I am going to market. It is not an imposition."

"Your Highness, Captain Jadran would have my ba—my head if I let you go off with a Fuartiran."

The guard had a point. Just because Dorin was shy and seemed perfectly harmless didn't mean he was. Dorin straightened, and his posture, the way he carried himself, seemed familiar for a moment. He met her gaze for the first time, but looked away so quickly she had no idea what color his eyes were. Facing the guard, he placed his left hand over his heart and bowed sharply.

"I swear I will see Princess Betony safely to the hospital or may Zovog's thunder take me and Alet's rainbows never light my way to the halls of heaven."

Her eyes widened. A strong vow, possibly the strongest among the Fuartirans. Her memory of common Fuartiran oaths was a little fuzzy. His tone caught the guard's attention, who eyed him more carefully now.

"Watch as Dorin walks me down the hill," Betony said when the silence stretched and the guard seemed torn. He really was sorry he couldn't let her go, but Jadran was a force to be reckoned with. "Send a guard shortly before dinner to bring me back. Who is going to attack me between here and the hospital?"

The guard blinked.

"Please," she said.

"Alright, milady." He narrowed his eyes and addressed Dorin. "But if anything happens to the princess, you will answer to me, to the commander, to the king, and worst of all, to the queen. I wouldn't want to be in your shoes should that happen."

"I understand. Princess Betony will be safe with me," Dorin said.

The guard nodded, and Dorin gestured broadly at the gate. Betony walked out the gate, with the manservant two paces behind on her left.

"You can walk next to me, Dorin."

"Thank you, Your Highness, but I cannot."

He was back to almost mumbling. Time to try some old-fashioned Betony charm. It rarely failed her. Maybe it was due to her diminutive stature, maybe it was some part of her fae magic, or maybe her intentions showed through, but few ever denied her requests.

"What takes you into town today?" When in doubt, ask them questions.

"The ambassador is feeling better and wants a delicacy your cook does not have. I'm going to market to find it."

"Ah. A noble quest, especially on a fine day like today."

It was a fine day, with the sun shining in a bright blue sky and the temperature above freezing. She glanced over her shoulder and caught the fading grin. Again, something about him seemed so familiar. Perhaps he reminded her of someone in Neraida.

"What is it you're looking for? I might be able to shorten your search."

She couldn't make out his mumbled response.

"I'm sorry?"

"Dried mouseberry."

Mouseberry? Oh, mouseberry. Bet giggled and looked over her

shoulder again. Dorin's cheeks were bright red, and he still refused to meet her gaze. Mouseberry was one of the few aphrodisiacs that actually seemed to work, but it was Fuartiran and hard to come by in Lorea.

"Your best bet is the apothecary near the western city gate. If they don't carry mouseberry, ask them for pumpkin seeds or palmetto. Not as effective, but more common here."

He mumbled his thanks, and Bet had to bite her cheek to keep from laughing more. It wasn't the poor man's fault, and who would expect to discuss aphrodisiacs with a royal?

Soon enough, the hospital loomed before them. She turned to thank him for escorting her safely and release him from his vow when a black cat streaked out of a nearby alley, yowling. It ran right to her, meowing in panic. Bet reached down and the cat rubbed against her fingers. It stared at her and meowed again, frantic. The message came to her in jumbled images, harsh sounds, and the sharp tang of fresh blood. A familiar face— a sweet young man who often acted as a messenger for the hospital. Veitha's hounds!

"What is wrong, Your Highness?" Dorin asked, his voice clearer than it had been since his vow.

"This cat's person needs help."

There was only one thing she could do. Betony hiked up her skirt and took off running, directly toward the trouble.

Chapter 8

*D*orin's oath demanded he follow, gods damn it.

Not that he'd minded making the oath, but somehow he knew he'd regret it.

Betony was fast, and he worked hard to keep up with her. She dashed across the street and darted into the alley the cat had come from, and Dorin was right on her heels. She unhooked the thin cylinder, about as long as her forearm, from her belt and twisted her wrist.

The ends of the cylinder shot out, the blue metal glistening in the sun. The staff was a bit shorter than the princess, and she wielded it like an adept fighter. Dorin drew the utilitarian dagger from its sheath at his belt and kept to the shadows.

At the far end of the alley, two burly men, muscled like dockworkers, held a thin young man between them while a third worked him over as efficiently as any bloodthirsty warrior. If their victim was half one of their weight soaking wet, Dorin would eat his shoe. He felt for the skinny runt. He'd been the skinny runt, once upon a time.

From the day he moved from the temple of Zovog into the chief's manor at eighteen to be trained by Jani, his older half brothers had tormented him every chance they got, regularly challenging him in the training arena and giving him a thorough drubbing. In the early months, they would sometimes catch him unawares outside the arena, too. Four and five years older, they were perpetually bigger and stronger.

Dorin couldn't fight back, not without revealing his training. Disguise, poison, and stealth were a midnight man's specialty, and only his defensive skills kept the beatings from leaving him with more than bumps, bruises, and sprains. Jani took notice, and a word with Kalman stopped the abuse. The clan couldn't afford to lose such a valuable weapon as Dorin.

"Stop!" Betony called out, slowly twirling her staff in a hypnotizing rhythm.

One of the men holding the youth leered at her, and Dorin didn't like it at all. He gripped his dagger and prepared to step into the light, to teach this asshole some respect.

"You gonna stop me, little fae?" He laughed malignantly and spat at her feet before releasing his hold on his victim.

Princess Betony stilled her staff, stilled her body, in a way Dorin knew meant danger. It was the stillness of a warrior before battle, the stillness of an assassin before a kill. The stillness of the center of a storm.

"Yes."

So quick it was a blur, she brought her staff down on the goon's foot, and Dorin could hear the bones break from where he stood. The man howled in pain, but not for long. In her next move, she shoved one end into his belly and pushed all his breath out. Another hit under his jaw— his eyes rolled up in his head and he collapsed at her feet.

Fuck, she was good. Better than any aristocratic lady he'd ever met. She might even impress the clerics of Zovog. The hitter looked at his fallen companion, then looked at her. He ran like a hare from a pack of hunting dogs. Right past Dorin in the shadows. Dorin stuck out his foot, and the man tripped.

"He's mine," Dorin growled.

Betony locked eyes with him and nodded before turning to the remaining goon. The hulking man seemed to be reevaluating whatever choices he'd made in his life that brought him face-to-face with a tiny fae woman who was going to beat the shit out of him.

The man at Dorin's feet tried to scramble up, but Dorin placed his booted foot in the middle of his back and pressed him to the ground. Dorin, too, was stronger than he looked.

"Stay down." He kneeled next to the asshole and held his dagger to the man's throat. "Unless you want this to end bloody."

The man shook his head vigorously.

"Noted." Dorin spun the blade and crashed the pommel on the goon's skull. The man's body went lax, and Dorin stood to watch the princess make mincemeat out of the last man standing.

The remaining ruffian dropped his victim, who curled into a ball on his side, moaning. The burly man pulled a knife, and it trembled slightly in his grasp as Betony stalked toward him with her staff held ready.

"Drop the knife, and no one else need be hurt." Her posture belied her sweet words. Someone was going to get hurt.

"What's he to you?" the man asked. "He's just some scrawny weasel who thinks he's too good to pay—"

He cut himself off, as if realizing he'd said too much.

"Pay what?" Betony said in a cold, dangerous voice. "For protection?"

The man didn't answer, his first wise move. He glanced toward the end of the alley, and Dorin flashed his blade. Before the prick could make a run for it, Betony brought her staff up right between his legs. His face reddened, and a pained wheeze spilled out of his lips as he dropped his blade. She stepped closer.

"He's under my protection, you utter shitstain of a human being."

And with an effortless flick of her wrist, her staff connected with his head, and he went down like the rest of his crew.

Betony didn't wait to see if he rose. She rushed to the young man's side. Blood leaked from his mouth, both his eyes were red and starting to swell, and pitiful groans escaped his mouth between pained gasps of air.

She kneeled next to him and dropped her staff before placing a gentle hand on his forehead.

"What can I do?" Dorin asked.

"Go see if the city guards are coming yet. If not, whistle three times, high then low."

Dorin took off for the end of the alley. As he did, she murmured, "It will be alright."

He stuck out his head and glimpsed a pair of guards at the far end of the street. He whistled as the princess instructed and waved his arms. They saw him and broke into a loping run. Dorin rushed to Betony and the injured young man. Golden tendrils of her magic surrounded her patient, and his moans had stopped.

The first man to go down was stirring when the guards appeared.

"What's going on?" the guard demanded.

"These three men were beating this one," Betony replied calmly, still focused on her patient. The golden glow faded.

"You expect me to believe the two of you did this?" The guard swept an arm toward the three groaning goons.

She looked up, and all the color drained from the guard's face.

"Your—Your Highness. Apologies. Yes, of course." He stuck his fingers in his mouth and emitted a loud, high whistle. His partner joined him and they discussed what to do next.

"Dorin, could you please help me get this young man to the hospital? I've done what I could for him right now, but he needs more healing." She helped the youth to sit.

Dorin bowed. "Of course, Princess."

He tucked his dagger into a sheath and moved in front of the young man, facing away from him and kneeling.

"Wrap your arms over my shoulders. I'm going to stand up and carry you to the hospital. Your Highness, please ensure he is stable and doesn't fall."

The youth did as he said, and Betony stared for an instant, wide eyed, before following them toward the end of the alley.

"Your Highness, we need statements," the guard pleaded desperately.

"I'm sure you'll find me when the time arises," she called over her shoulder, her nose twitching with amusement.

"Yes, yes, of course."

The two guards turned to the wretches, binding their wrists as they slowly regained consciousness.

Their strange party hurried to the hospital. Betony opened the door, and the smell of herbs and vinegar greeted Dorin as he walked in. Immediately, he was surrounded by helping hands that removed the young man from his shoulders.

"Betony, what happened?" asked an older woman wearing clean but worn clothes.

"He was beaten. I was able to do some minor healing before we brought him to you, enough to stop the bleeding and ease the pain, but he needs more."

"Yes, of course. Thank you. Please sit and help yourself to refreshments when you've caught your breath."

As soon as they carried the injured man away, Betony swayed on her feet, brushing against Dorin's side. Before he could think twice, he wrapped a supporting arm around the princess and guided her to the benches behind them. He eased them down and let go as soon as they were sitting, heart leaping at the intimate contact, despite how short it was. His body might react to it, but even with the more relaxed hierarchy in Lorea, touching a royal could lead to serious consequences.

"I am sorry, Your Highness," he said. His training had kept his heavy country accent even through the fight. Dorin clutched his hands in front of him.

"No, thank you." She covered his hands with one of her own. Her grip was surprisingly firm, given their softness and delicacy. He should stop being surprised after what he'd witnessed. The princess was obviously a warrior and a healer, as well as a royal. "I used too much energy healing that poor young man. You acquitted yourself well."

"Glad to be of service, milady."

"You don't have to keep calling me milady or Your Highness, Dorin. Betony is fine."

He merely shook his head, and she sighed in resignation. Dorin wished he could call her by her name, but he feared the feel of it on his tongue would be his undoing. Before either of them could say anything else, a girl brought out a tray of refreshments. Betony took the tray, and the girl bobbed a quick curtsy before rushing off. Two cups of tea, a roll each, a chunk of cheese, and some dried fruit.

Dorin scooted over and the princess placed the tray between them. He missed her presence next to him. It had felt both comfortable and exhilarating. Confusing. Some distance was for the best.

He drank the tea to be polite but left the food for her. She needed it, he did not. Once he was certain she wouldn't faint and needed him no longer, Dorin stood.

"Your Highness, I believe my oath fulfilled. You are safe at the hospital, and the ambassador waits for me."

She looked at him, and he quickly dropped his gaze to the floor. Dorin couldn't risk her recognizing him. The night at the ball had been perfect, a memory he would treasure. But the look of disgust she would wear when she finally realized she'd kissed a manservant, a Fuartiran, that night, he couldn't stomach the thought. Best she never found out, and she might recognize his eyes. The same as the rest of him, they weren't particularly memorable, but no need to chance it.

"Surely, there must be something I can do to thank you for your assistance. A drink at the Fiddle and Drum? Not tonight, but tomorrow?" There was a note of desperation, of loneliness in her words.

Again, his mouth got ahead of his senses. "I would like that, milady."

What the fuck? No, he would not like that. He needed to intercept these thoughts before they made it out into the world. An outing with the princess was one more chance for her to identify him as her dance partner at the ball. One more chance for the ambassador, or even worse Lorant, to discover his unseemly fascination with the fae princess. One more chance to bask in her beauty and kindness.

Fuck.

The smile she graced him with would live in his heart forever. Perhaps the risk was worth it to put such a smile on her face.

"Wonderful!"

He affected a shy smile, keeping his cover intact. "I will meet you at the gate, then?"

She bit her lip and wouldn't meet his gaze. Wicked thoughts went straight to his gut, and he subtly adjusted himself before she looked up again.

"No, meet me at the tavern at sunset. I'll have a guard escort me."

The princess was lying, but he didn't know why. And frankly, he didn't much care. They kept her too close for her own good. He saw what it was doing to her, dimming her beautiful light. If he could help in this small way, he would.

"Of course, Princess."

She took his hand and squeezed, her brilliant smile returning. "Again, my thanks for your help today. Should the ambassador question your whereabouts, please have him call on me so I may inform him of my deepest gratitude for your service."

He bowed deeply and, before he could do anything else rash, turned on his heel and strode away. He followed the crowd toward the city gate and found the apothecary the princess had mentioned earlier. Another piece of luck held. They'd recently received a shipment of mouseberry. It appeared Conrad the smuggler had been busy.

Dorin hurried back through the city and to the castle, trading a nod with the guard, the same one who had signed off on his journey with the princess. The ambassador was not in his chambers, probably in meetings with the Loreans, their whole reason for being here. Negotiations and cultural exchange all winter. A veritable holiday compared with the harsh northern weather.

He opened the wardrobe and pulled out the medicine chest the ambassador insisted they bring from home. Dorin had tried to explain that Lorean medicine was generally more advanced than Fuartiran. But Vedel was old and set in his ways. The herbal concoctions of the clerics of Alet were sufficient for him.

Dorin tucked the paper-wrapped package of dried berries in a drawer, and a glint of bright iron caught his eye. A black leather bracelet studded with polished rivets lay in the drawer. What was this doing here?

He picked it up and tucked it into a hidden pocket of his jerkin alongside some of the other tools of his trade. Since he was in charge of the ambassador's medicine chest, it was unlikely to be missed. Why would the ambassador bring a magic-suppressing zelizka to Lorea, a kingdom that welcomed and encouraged magic? No innocent answers came to him. In fact, all the answers that came to mind sent shivers down his spine. Perhaps his own training as an agent of death brought to mind only the nefarious reasons. For now, he would keep the bracelet safe to avoid a rash act from becoming a diplomatic incident.

Chapter 9

"I heard you had an exciting day yesterday."

Rane plopped on the turfed bench flanking the table in the kitchen garden. Bash, her fairy hound, settled at her feet and blinked her bright blue eyes lazily. The rich, bitter scent of coffee steamed from the mug Rane held. Bet wrinkled her nose. Her sister had taken to the drink favored by her husband, but it had never grown on her.

"I can't believe you drink that stuff."

"Oh, what fools do for love!" Rane slurped loudly, grinning. "So, do I get the details?"

Betony sipped her tea and considered what she should tell Rane. If anyone would understand feeling cooped up in the castle and the joy of an escape, even if only for a few hours, it was her older sister. From all accounts, she'd been attempting it since before Betony was born. But the past few years had changed Rane. Not tamed her, exactly, but she'd grown into her responsibilities as heir to the throne, wife, and mother.

"Not much to tell. Went to the hospital, rescued one of the hospital's messengers from some bullies, came home."

Rane waved her words away. "I already heard all about *that*. The man, Bet."

"Well, he was young and too skinny, and—"

"Ugh, you're impossible." Her sister smiled and nudged her shoulder with her own.

Betony returned the grin. She knew exactly what Rane had been getting at, but she found herself reluctant to discuss Dorin. He'd haunted her thoughts all day and her dreams last night. He'd handled himself well in the fight, though Fuartirans highly valued combat skills, so most could brawl competently. But as she drifted into sleep, he first competed with the mysterious lord from the ball, then replaced him. His firm but gentle hands roving her body. His soft lips following in their wake. The voice from the night of the ball transformed into Dorin's country accent, vibrating strings that curled deep into her core.

"Ambassador Vedel's manservant was kind enough to escort me to the hospital, helped me with the villains, and carried their victim to the hospital." She went with the bare facts, hoping Rane would let the matter drop. It was unlikely, but she had to try.

"And does the ambassador's manservant have a name?"

And her attempt to appease her sister failed.

"Dorin." It was almost a whisper. Why had she invited him to the Fiddle and Drum? Sure, she owed him for having her back yesterday, and a fairy hated to owe anyone anything. But she wasn't a fairy, and he was merely fulfilling his oath.

And yet...

He wasn't handsome the way Nevar was. He wasn't tall, or brawny, or eloquent, nothing she'd been attracted to before, though he was handy with the blade he'd pulled. Dorin was ordinary, plain, simple. Something about those qualities was appealing, perhaps because with him she could pretend to be ordinary, plain, and simple, when she was anything but. She was a fae princess, destined for a life less ordinary.

"There is nothing wrong with you spending time with him, you know." Rane said, pulling her out of her thoughts, "if you enjoy his company."

Bet's cheeks heated. While their real-life interactions thus far had been a few chance encounters in the castle and yesterday's escapade, her dreams revealed a depth to her attraction she refused to share with Rane. Her sister would tease her mercilessly. Betony was starting to have some sympathy for Ebon over how she had provoked him when he first courted Sarsa.

"I know. He keeps putting up a wall between us."

"Well, Fuartir isn't Faerie or Lorea. From what Nevar tells me, their society is more stratified. Give him some time."

Was a day enough? He'd agreed to meet her, though he'd seemed surprised at the words tumbling from his lips. So had she, if she were honest.

"So, if I were to, say, sneak out to meet him without an escort, I could count on you to provide a little cover. Especially since I kept my mouth shut when you did the same with your husband way back when."

Rane rolled her eyes and the corners of her lips turned up. "Absolutely, dear sister. I am a paragon of discretion. Dally with the ambassador's manservant to your heart's content. I'll make sure Father and Mother give you some space. At least, for as long as I can."

Relief flooded her. "Thank you."

"Are you sure you're the same prim and proper girl we sent to Faerie seven years ago?"

"Sometimes. And sometimes I think I'm becoming something else."

"Good. I love both versions of you, but I like this one more."

"Me, too."

And the two sisters broke into giggles.

"Rane!" a man's deep voice called from above.

Nevar's head stuck out a window, and the high-pitched wails of a distraught toddler filled the air.

"I can't find Jonny's stuffed dragon."

"Did you check the toy chest?" Rane put aside the mug and stood.

"Yes, and under the bed, and in the wardrobe, and in every damn vase in the hall. We need Bash."

The hound lifted her head and whined. Rane scratched behind her ears and rose.

"We'll be right there." She planted a kiss on Bet's hair. "Sorry, duty calls. Just slip a note under my door and I'll make sure everyone thinks you're in the library or sick or out for a walk in the garden. Come on, Bash!"

She rushed off, the dog running ahead, before Betony could thank her again. Nevar closed the window, shutting off the frantic cries of his son. Poor little prince. With Lark taking a break, Nevar and Rane were scrambling a little with the day-to-day care. They'd adjust, and Lark would return soon. Jonquil had the entire palace wrapped around his chubby little finger.

Rane mentioned the library. That would be the perfect place to spend the day distracting herself from the upcoming meeting at the Fiddle and

Drum. She was no Ebon, whiling away as many hours as possible surrounded by books, but she enjoyed a satisfying story and welcomed a little research on occasion. Especially when it had an immediate application. Surely, the library would have some books on Fuartir.

The depths of winter nipped at her nose, and there were no more parties or official functions scheduled until the spring thaw. Diplomatic missions often went into hibernation like the bears in the Argent Forest. The Fuartiran ambassador had decided to stay through the winter, and communications between his homeland and Avora would be unavoidably slow given the state of the rivers, the roads, and the sea.

But even the library was no respite today. It was too quiet without her brother in residence. Ebon loved books, and if he wasn't asleep, training, or eating, the library was the most likely place to find him. At least until Sarsa came into his life.

Betony loved Sarsa almost as much as she did Rane, and mostly because she brought out the best in Ebon. He had become more adventurous and less serious since meeting the powerful shapeshifting fairy who had saved the Faerie Court. Since then, they'd begun rebuilding the elite Errozar guard and had gone on several missions for the good of both Lorea and Faerie. They had left for their next adventure, heading north, before she'd arrived for the ball. Idoya knew what they were up to, but they would keep each other safe, and whatever information they gathered would be valuable. The Queens' spymaster and the Protector of Faerie, almost like the tales she loved when she was little.

Still, the silence screamed in Ebon's absence.

She flipped through a few books, but none caught her attention. She found an old, dusty volume on Fuartir and took it to her room. Bet spent the rest of the afternoon trying to read it, but it was drier than the deserts of Teruelle. She closed the book and put it aside.

A few facts stuck in her head. Fuartir was less a kingdom than a loose confederation of seven chiefdoms. Many clan chiefs of the past had tried to consolidate power and proclaim themselves king. None had succeeded.

But those facts helped her put the rumors she'd heard since returning to Avora into perspective. It seemed Chief Kalman of Clan Fher was closer than any in recent decades. He'd managed to win the position as Speaker for the Witan, the council of chiefs that governed the interactions between the chiefdoms and with other realms. Kalman had been using this to further the interests of Fuartir and his own ambitions.

Vedel was Kalman's man. The guards with him were Kalman's men, known as the heorthwerod, his war band. The ship that had sailed them to Lorea's port city of Nimel was Kalman's. Should they come to a reasonable agreement to contain the raids on the Lorean coast and further trade, Kalman would be in an excellent position to become a king.

Perhaps Dorin would be willing to answer a few subtle questions tonight. It might help her to understand everything if she talked to an actual Fuartiran.

Betony paced for a few moments, her gaze going to a pendant hanging on the wall next to the bedroom door. The small stone with a fairy rune carved into it had been a gift from Hyssop when she turned thirteen. Her godmother may not have tucked her in for naps, or known where to find her favorite soft toy, but she did arrange the most useful gifts. Not to mention the boons she had granted to Rane and Ebon, bringing her a new brother and a new sister in the process.

The charm made her invisible. Maybe not exactly invisible. It drew shadows to her, reflected and refracted the air around her, and muffled her footsteps. The charm had helped save all of Faerie when she'd loaned it to Ebon a year and a half ago. Rane had often "borrowed" it for her escapades when they were younger, but now that her responsibilities included a child, she rarely took unnecessary risks. But Betony, always the reliable child, the one who never snuck out of the castle, the one who never wanted to be a bother to her parents or the staff, had changed.

Her freedom in Faerie was a privilege she wasn't granted in Avora. The place that should have felt like home but no longer did. She itched to be out and about, walking among people as an ordinary citizen. It was how Faerie treated its nobility.

Veitha help me, I'm so tired of it.

Betony glanced out the window. The sun hovered low on the horizon, casting a golden glow on the snow. Finally! Flurries tumbled through her stomach at the thought of meeting Dorin far from the stifling formality of court.

After jotting a quick note to Rane, she dropped the fine woolen gown, exchanging it for breeches, a warm tunic, a woolen jerkin, and a coat. She slid her small fairy-wrought blade into a pocket and hooked her expandable staff on her belt. Tucking her telltale hair under a warm cap, she snagged the pendant and looped it around her neck, murmuring a single word to blend into the shadows. She cracked her door and slipped into the hall.

Though Rane needed her in Avora and her parents wanted her home for a bit, Betony still needed to be who she had become in Faerie. And that Betony didn't stay indoors. That Betony didn't keep to herself. That Betony didn't shy away from the ordinary citizens.

She slipped the note under Rane's door and found the old hidden corridor, pressing on the stone marked with the royal crest. Fairy lights lit up as she stepped into the dusty passageway, guiding her to the exit. She emerged in a quiet alley, murmuring the magic word and sending the shadows back where they belonged. The wall slid shut behind her. She hurried to the bustling street and blended into the crowd. Time for some ale and one of the Fiddle's meat pies. Maybe some harmless flirting.

And maybe something more.

Chapter 10

*A*s the sun set, Dorin washed quickly. The ambassador should be at dinner for a while, certainly long enough for him to sneak off to meet with Betony. The madness of this decision was obvious, yet Dorin couldn't seem to help himself. And the thought of going back on his agreement to meet her was beyond the pale.

Though he wished he could change into clothes more appropriate for meeting a princess, he would draw far less scrutiny dressed as he was, so he wore a creamy tunic with a bit of black embroidery on the cuffs and neckline, black trousers, and his usual gray jerkin—the one with all the hidden pockets. A well-dressed manservant.

He drew on a cloak and slipped through the ambassador's chambers and down the hall. But turning a corner, he ran into Lorant.

The guard greeted him with his customary sneer. Other than being born, Dorin had done nothing to earn the captain's contempt, but Lorant was his half brothers' friend. They'd trained together, and the grown man in front of him was as much of a bully as his brothers. As a trained warrior, Lorant couldn't fight Dorin without cause.

Dorin worked hard to give his brothers' friends no excuse to fight him. Rodric and Illes had never informed their friends of his identity, too ashamed to have a bastard-born brother working as a manservant. As far as the others were concerned, he was some orphan given a chance to better himself. Only the chief, his chamberlain, and the clerics who had trained him knew exactly what Dorin was, part of what made him effective in his more clandestine work. A midnight man was a story told to scare children. A story to keep unrest at bay. A story that was all too true.

Sometimes Dorin was certain Lorant could sense a small measure of his true nature. The lords and the heorthwerod were well-versed in swords, battle-axes, and shields, noble and honest ways of killing people. Those trained by the Zovog temple trafficked in poisons, rumors, and daggers to the back, methods the more honorable warriors feared. Dead was dead, and poison was often less messy than a battle-ax.

"Where are *you* going?" Lorant demanded.

"The ambassador is at dinner, and I have some personal errands to run. I'll return soon."

"Personal errands? You have no personal life, Dorin. I've never even seen you at a whorehouse. Can't find any woman willing to fuck an orphan? Are you still an untouched greenhorn?"

Dorin balled his fists at his sides. Lorant relied upon his contempt for a man who seemed to have chosen a more peaceful path. He saw Dorin as weak and without honor. He wanted—no, needed—Dorin to throw the first punch, so he could put him in his proper place with fists and blades. Dorin liked being underestimated and didn't want to show how skilled he was in all manner of combat. He would if he had to, but this wasn't a hill he would die on at the moment.

"Enough, Lorant," the ambassador said from a little further away.

"Milord." Dorin bowed. Shit, there went his night. There went his chance with Betony. A princess wasn't likely to forgive a lowly manservant who failed to show. *Like you had a chance, anyway.* "You're back early."

"Apparently, the kitchen staff have the night off for some celebration or another, so we are on our own for dinner. There was an assortment of meats, cheeses, and breads for any who wished to partake. I find myself wanting a hot meal. There's a tavern I've heard mentioned many times and wish to try. Let us change and you can escort us tonight."

Dorin couldn't say no. It would be an insult of the first order to refuse an invitation to dine with the ambassador. Maybe he could explain to Betony—

No, it was better this way. She was a princess, a fae, and he was the bastard son of a northern chieftain, a manservant, a spy, and sometime assassin. He would leave at the end of winter, never to see her again. Time to put aside the reckless hope anything at all could ever happen between them. The kiss they shared at the Winter Solstice Ball would be the one precious memory from this part of his life.

"Of course. I suggest changing into something less…extravagant before leaving." Dorin eyed the velvet doublet, the soft cap, and the gold-buckled shoes. "To avoid drawing undue attention."

"Ah, excellent advice. Jani trained you well."

The ambassador pushed past both Lorant and Dorin. The sneer returned to Lorant's mouth as they followed him to his chambers. Dorin fought the urge to punch it off his smug face. If only they knew how well-trained he was.

A short while later, the ambassador was kitted out in his simplest doublet, trousers, and boots. He mimicked the look of an ordinary citizen, only the thread of gold embroidery on the neck of his doublet giving him away. It couldn't be helped.

They requested mounts from the stable and rode down the hill into town.

"What was the name of the tavern, Ambassador?" Lorant asked as they passed the hospital at the bottom.

"The Fiddle and Drum," Vedel said.

Dorin's stomach clenched, and despite the frosty night air, sweat beaded on his brow. The god of death was having fun with him tonight.

"What the fuck is a fiddle?" Lorant glared at Dorin as if he would have the answer. He did, but he wouldn't tell Lorant unless someone's life depended on it.

"It's a musical instrument," Vedel replied. "Lovely tone. Wish we had them in Fuartir."

No, it would be fine. Betony would see him walking in with the ambassador and leave. She'd either assume he couldn't avoid bringing them, or he'd brought them on purpose. Perhaps it would be better if she believed the latter—end this farce before it could truly start. The strings on his heart twanged painfully at the thought.

They rode through the streets of Avora, passing open shops selling a variety of goods. Fairy lights shone brightly as people stopped in on their way home from work. What he wouldn't give for the safety of the fairy lights. Each year, dozens of homes had to be rebuilt in Fuartir because fire broke out, often due to unattended candles.

The men went around to the back of the building to secure their horses, then strode into the lively tavern. They found a table big enough for three. The musicians were tuning their instruments, the faint rumble of the drum creeping across the room, the squeal of the strings on the fiddle sending shivers up Dorin's spine.

"Sorry, folks," the fiddler said with a smile. "Won't be a moment. Violet here don't like the cold."

"He named his instrument? How quaint." Lorant's cold tone gave lie to his words.

Dorin ignored him and signaled to a server. The buxom lass sashayed through the growing crowd. She smiled and batted her lashes at Lorant.

"What can I get you gents?"

"What do you recommend?" Dorin asked in return.

"Can't go wrong with the Fiddle's meat pies."

"Very well, three ales and three meat pies, if you please."

"Sure thing!"

The ambassador paid the woman, and Lorant ogled her round backside as she left.

"What do they serve for dessert?" The peckerhead adjusted himself under the table. Lorant's lust-filled, vile gaze turned to a condescending glare when he looked at Dorin. "Meat pies and ale. You know how to show your betters a good time."

Dorin gritted his teeth. Lorant desperately wanted to provoke him. The best he could do would be to deny the asshole the satisfaction. But Dorin wondered exactly why Lorant wanted a reaction. It could just be his sparkling personality, or it could mean something more was going on. He'd have to keep his eye on the guard.

The musicians started a lively song, and many of the patrons clapped along. Dorin tapped his toes and noticed the ambassador did, too. Lorant merely glowered at everyone, obviously having the worst time of his life, listening to fantastic music in a roomful of happy people. Served the asshole right.

Dorin searched the crowd for any sign of the princess. A whisper of lingonberry hair, a tinkling laugh, her sweet scent of rosemary and spring flowers. Nothing. With any luck, she'd forgotten all about her invitation. With slightly less luck, she'd taken a look at his companions and run right back to the castle.

The server returned after a couple of songs, carrying the ale and pies.

She set them in front of each man, and Dorin's mouth watered as the rich scent of beef and gravy wafted up. He took a bite and swallowed in bliss. It tasted better than it smelled. Even Lorant's scowl disappeared after his first bite.

"Excellent suggestion, Dorin," Vedel said after gobbling half his pie and slurping a generous portion of his ale.

"If you'll recall, sir, it was the barmaid."

"Doesn't matter, dogsbody." Lorant spewed crumbs as he talked with his mouth full.

"There's no need for name calling, Lorant," Vedel said placatingly. The sly twist to his lips indicated he was merely humoring Dorin.

Fuck them both. He plastered on a fake smile and pretended he was in on the joke. It wasn't the first time he'd been patronized, and it wouldn't be the last. A bastard son with a dead mother was an easy target, and bullies like Lorant loved an easy target. But one day, Zovog willing, Dorin would show him the truth. Between Chamberlain Jani and the clerics of Zovog, Dorin was the most deadly "dogsbody" in Fuartir.

"So, Dorin, what gossip is making the rounds at the castle now that solstice has come and gone?" the ambassador continued after washing down another bite of meat pie with some damned fine ale.

"This is a bad season for gossip, milord," Dorin said.

"Useless," Lorant muttered into his cup.

Dorin pretended he hadn't heard. "Winter back home is an excellent time to gather and gossip, but the Loreans live further apart, especially the powerful lords and ladies. After the winter solstice, there is unlikely to be any large gathering until spring."

"And how is this *information* supposed to help?" Lorant's voice dripped with acid.

"It means there won't be any large changes to policy for the next few months," Dorin said.

Lorant had never been very bright, so the implications would be lost to him, but the ambassador was a conniving, greedy lord with a keen need to further his career, and the implications were apparent to him.

"Ah, we have the opportunity to persuade King Rowan of our good intentions, our fine moral character, and lay out all the benefits to Lorea of forming an alliance with Clan Fher with no competition from rival clans, and without the interference of Faerie or Teruelle."

"Exactly, milord."

Lorant glared at him. Dorin didn't care. Lorant could hate him, could try to undermine him, but in the end, Dorin would run circles around the brute's intellect.

"Anything else?" Vedel asked.

"The fairy godmother has departed for a few days. I don't think it's important but I'll keep an ear out. Rumor has it Princess Betony is not supposed to leave the castle unaccompanied. And there is hope in the staff that the crown princess will soon see to having another heir."

Lorant snorted.

"Is there something bothering you, captain?" The ambassador glowered at the head of his guard.

"Why are any of these rumors important?" Lorant said in a tone that expected agreement.

Dorin may not like Vedel, but the man was a talented diplomat with over a decade of experience in negotiating with the other clans and the other realms.

"I don't know," Vedel said, "not yet, but the smallest bit of information may give us an advantage in negotiations. If the fairy often travels, that can tell us when the young prince might be vulnerable. If the princess isn't supposed to leave the castle alone, we must ask ourselves why. Is there a specific threat or general anxiety? The answer might inform certain decisions. And any monarch worth their salt wants more than one heir. Succession gets interesting if the next in line dies young. Or goes missing."

Dorin had wanted to show up Lorant, prove he was smarter and more valuable than a simple guard. But the ambassador's words stuck a blade of ice in his gut. *The young prince might be vulnerable. Or goes missing.* Dorin might be a deadly assassin, but kidnapping or harming a child was an atrocity to both Zovog and Alet. Enough youngsters died from illness and unintended injury. Zovog might be the god of death, but they were not without compassion, and Alet would not grant easy admittance to heaven for a child-killer. Chief Kalman was ruthless, as was his ambassador, but would they really use a toddler against Lorea?

Castigated, Lorant finished his ale and thunked the cup on the table with a wry chuckle. "Apologies, ambassador. You are far more ruthless than I gave you credit for."

Dorin hoped not, but that was all it was. Hope. Under the right circumstances, his father would use whatever tools were at his disposal to secure his chiefdom and bring all the clans under his banner. There was nothing Ambassador Vedel would appreciate more than to be the man who helped make it happen. He could go from a simple lord to a jarl under a King Kalman.

"Shall I get another round of ale?" he asked instead of slipping a dagger into Lorant's ribs or an emetic in the ambassador's drink.

"Yes, thank you," Vedel said carefully, as if he knew exactly where Dorin's thoughts had wandered.

Dorin stood and froze. A heart-shaped face with emerald eyes waited directly behind Vedel, surrounded by shadows. All the color had leeched from her and a strand of her magenta hair escaped her cap. A stone around her neck glowed purple. She extracted her staff from her belt and glared at Vedel and Lorant.

Fuck, she'd heard their conversation and had picked out the same subtle threats Dorin had. Betony's narrow gaze locked on his, and betrayal warred with anger.

"Wait!" Dorin shouted.

Her eyes widened before she took off out the front door, shoving a few patrons out of her way. They turned to glare at each other, ignoring the young woman running away. That was a strange reaction, unless…

The shadows. The glowing charm. She had some sort of magic making her hard to see. Magic he could see through, thanks to the blessing from the clerics of Zovog at the end of his training.

Lorant stood and grabbed his shirt. "You don't speak to the ambassador that way, bastard."

Dorin drew his thin dagger with the hand hidden from view of the crowd, whose attention returned to the stage after the disturbance caused by the princess. He poked it into Lorant's belly and almost smiled as the color drained from the guard's face. Lorant hissed in a breath and let go of Dorin's shirt.

"Take it easy," Vedel said.

Dorin pushed Lorant away. "You fucking fools. Guess who overheard our conversation? Just take a fucking guess."

"You can't talk—" Lorant began.

Dorin shoved him into his chair and held his blade to his neck. "Tell me once more what I can and can't do, *Lorant*, and I'll dance in your blood like a true son of Zovog."

"What is this all about?" Vedel demanded.

"The answer is Princess Betony," he spat.

At least Vedel had the grace to look abashed.

Lorant sneered and folded his arms across his chest. "You're seeing things."

"I don't think he is." Vedel's gaze appraised Dorin with a keen eye.

"You are correct, Ambassador. As far as the princess knows, you're planning on taking her beloved nephew for some nefarious scheme. The first thing she'll do is warn the guards. The second thing she'll do is tell her father, or worse, her sister. If even half the rumors about Crown Princess Ranunculus are true, she will hunt you down and pull your fucking brains out your fucking nose."

He shoved Lorant again, and the chair tipped, tumbling him to the floor. Once again, attention turned toward them.

"Escort Vedel to the horses and wait for me there."

Lorant scrambled to his feet, grasping his own dagger. A part of Dorin wanted him to draw the blade, any excuse to teach this asshole a lesson. But fate intervened.

"Do as he says, Lorant. Let's go, we're drawing attention." Vedel pulled out a couple of gold coins, a reasonable recompense for the trouble they'd caused. "Apologies. You know how young men get over a woman when too much drink is involved."

The crowd's gazed returned to the musicians, and Dorin ran into the night. There was no sign of the princess. He hadn't expected her to linger, but sometimes Zovog's grace played in his favor. Not tonight.

There was only one thing to do. He had to catch up to her before she told anyone what she'd overheard. He could explain this away, all of it, if she'd give him a chance. Just a couple of drunken northerners spouting off.

Curses came from people at the intersection to his right. Dorin ran towards the disturbance, faster than he'd ever run before.

Chapter 11

Betony rushed into the street, bouncing off pedestrians, a streetlamp, and darting in front of horses. Curses followed in her invisible wake.

The evening had started pleasantly. She'd walked into the Fiddle and claimed a seat at the bar. The barmaid had greeted her warmly and served her a cider while she waited for Dorin. The butterflies in her stomach fluttered delightfully. She tapped her fingers and bobbed her head to the music, caught up in the heady sensation of freedom and anticipation. It might be only for one night, but it would do.

Then Dorin entered as the band began their second set, flanked by two others dressed in plain but exceptionally well-made clothes. Betony blinked as she recognized the Fuartiran ambassador. His well-dressed companion had a familiar face, but she couldn't place it.

She'd left a coin for her drink and activated her invisibility charm before they could spot her.

Why had Dorin brought Vedel and the other man? The ambassador didn't seem the sort to frequent a tavern like this. The Fiddle and Drum was a homey respite for the royal children, with a prosperous enough clientele to avoid the most unpleasant altercations but enough ordinary citizens so they could delude themselves into thinking they blended in. It usually worked.

Perhaps he'd thought better of meeting her alone. Perhaps he'd merely run into them on the way here. The Fiddle and Drum was a popular tavern, well-known among the castle staff. And perhaps schemes were afoot. She would never know unless she did something to find out.

Betony slid off the stool and took cautious steps to avoid the bustling crowd as she snuck behind the ambassador. She leaned against the wall, the voices of the Fuartirans barely audible from her position a few arm lengths away.

"Succession gets interesting if the next in line dies young. Or goes missing," the ambassador said coldly.

Betony imagined the smirk on his face, and her knuckles grew white on her staff. One more word, just one more, and she'd take him out as a threat. And maybe he'd even remember enough to tell any and all comers to stay away from Jonquil. Lark was fierce and deadly. Rane would do anything for the people she loved. So would Bet, and they were only the first line of defense. Commander Miren and Captain Jadran, though no spring chickens, were accomplished warriors. Even Cook would brain the man with a pot.

Vedel sipped his ale, his air of boredom almost as irritating as his companion's hostility. But what did Dorin think? She shouldn't care. He was nothing to her. She'd merely been infatuated with a man who helped her, who had seemed kind. Not with a man who wouldn't stand up for a child.

He looked up and caught her angry gaze, and his eyes went wide.

Dorin could see her. How? It didn't matter, not now. She needed to warn…someone. Jadran. Yes, Jadran would know what to do.

She had run out, never looking back.

It was after dark. Jadran would be at home in his lovely cottage outside the city walls with his beautiful wife and two teenaged children, closer than any mad dash to the castle. He would sort this out.

Her stomach turned as a hoof nearly connected with her jaw. She rushed closer to the buildings and clutched the corner of the shop next to the tavern, nearly losing the cider she'd consumed. A coldly speculative discussion about kidnapping, maybe killing, a toddler. *May Veitha light their hair with a flaming arrow and Idoya refuse them the peace of the earth.* She'd even invoke Nevar's God and the hell he sent such wretches to.

Betony rounded a corner and halted in front of a line of horses secured to the hitchrail behind the tavern. No, this wasn't the right direction. Her fear and his betrayal had turned her around.

Something scratched at her senses. The soft scuff of a boot on the cobblestones behind her had her whipping around. Dorin stood there, eyes narrowed. Betony flicked her wrist, and the fairy-wrought iron staff extended with a soft metallic scrape until it was nearly as tall as her.

"Why? Why would you threaten a toddler?" Some of the power of her words was lost in the sob trying to force its way out. She swallowed it.

He held up his hands in surrender, but she stayed vigilant.

"I threatened no one." His voice was different, clearer, more understandable, more resonant. It pricked her memory, but she had no time for such folly.

She twisted her staff until the end pointed at his throat. He didn't flinch. Interesting.

"You said nothing. You sat there and said *nothing* when they threatened the life of my nephew. The future King of Lorea. Don't deny it."

"Why don't you deactivate the lovely charm and we can discuss this?"

"No." He could apparently see through it anyway, and at least once she beat him, she could slink off with no one else the wiser.

Dorin sighed and held his hands palm up.

"Aye, I did nothing when they threatened the young prince. What am I, a lowly manservant, supposed to say to the Ambassador of Fuartir? I know my place, milady."

"And I know mine."

She lunged, and he jerked aside, grabbing her staff. He wrested it this way and that, and she held on tight, trying to use his momentum against him. He let go and backed off. She spun the staff, creating a whistle as the metal cut through the air.

Betony snapped out again, but he seemed to sense what she was going to do before she did it. He turned so his side was facing her and took the blow on his forearm. It failed to stop him. He grasped her staff again with his other hand, and she twisted away, hoping he wouldn't let go. But he did, and she stumbled a couple of steps, losing the opportunity to use the force of her twist to throw him against the wall.

Dorin darted back, and she swung at his lower leg. It connected, but he skipped a step and shook it off. The cursed man kept countering her moves. There was no way he was merely a manservant. She swung again, and he grabbed the staff and yanked her close. He ripped the charm from around her neck.

"There, that was giving me a headache." The shadows disappeared as he shoved the necklace into a pocket.

Tits! She let go of her staff and drew her dagger. His eyes gleamed with a fierceness, yes, but excitement and mirth lingered in his gaze as well. The corners of his lips twitched, as though threatening to grin. Wait…

He tossed the staff to the side and drew his own dagger. The skinny blade glinted cruelly in the dim light of the alley. The kernel of a thought that had tried to grab her attention vanished. The animals behind her grew restless, stomping and neighing. Help would come soon, drawn by the horses. She only needed to keep him here and stay out of his reach. Betony circled him, planning three different ways to take him down.

"I don't want to hurt you," Dorin said.

"Then it's a good thing I showed up." A bitter voice from behind sent shivers along her spine.

Betony whirled to confront the other man from the Fiddle. Realization slammed into her. The ambassador's captain of the guard. A man she'd only seen from a distance, a man who set off alarm bells the first time his eyes lit upon her. The man who had laughed at the idea of a child's death.

Behind him, the ambassador stood calmly in the shadows, allowing his underlings to fight his battles for him. He was the ranking member of the delegation, and all of this would fall on his head.

Hatred stole into her heart. These men dared to threaten the Lorean royal family. *Her* family.

"I don't have time for this." She gripped her blade and hurled it at the captain, trusting her training and the balance of the fairy-wrought steel.

Lorant twitched aside at the last second, and her blade skittered off into the dark, leaving a red line of blood on his cheek. His brows drew into a scowl, and he pulled his own dagger from a sheath at his belt, the faint ringing setting her teeth on edge. She was in a fight not just for her life, but for her nephew's, and perhaps even her realm's.

"Bitch." Lorant stormed toward her, his murderous intent blazing.

Betony had enough. Though her gifts ran toward the healing, she was trained to draw upon her faerie heritage in battle, as well. She opened herself to the magic, calling the wind, the ice, the animals. Her staff lifted into the air and flew toward her outstretched hand. The ice on the buildings began to coalesce into sharp lances. And the horses pulled wildly at their reins, squealing in their urgency to lend their aid.

"Fuck," Dorin muttered behind her. "I'm so sorry, Princess."

His warm body pressed against her back, and his arm snaked around her neck. She struggled against him, but his other arm wrapped around her waist, pinning one of her arms. His leg hooked hers. Her free hand clawed at the arm blocking her airway to no avail, and she couldn't move her free leg without putting more weight on the fulcrum.

The desperate need for air drove every other thought from her mind. The wind quieted, her staff and the ice fell to the ground, the tinkling almost musical, and the animals stopped trying to break free of their bonds to come to her aid.

She gasped, but to no avail. The world dimmed, then faded to black.

Chapter 12

S hit. A hundred times shit.

Dorin let go of Betony, and she crumpled in a heap at his feet.

"Now I can finish the bitch," Lorant snarled, stalking across the alley and drawing his blade.

Dorin glared at him, letting the icy touch of his anger stretch over the last few feet between them. "Touch her and I will feed your balls to you before I tear out your heart with my bare hands."

Lorant hesitated, which is all Dorin had wanted. He had a plan. It was an awful plan, and so many things could go wrong. But it was a plan.

"Gentlemen, there is little need for such violence." Vedel stepped into what little light remained and held the blade Betony had thrown at Lorant. "There is, however, a need for haste."

"What is she to you, anyway?" The guard's familiar sneer returned.

Good question. An object of his desire? Yes, given his dreams. A dance partner? Also yes. A small glint of joy in his dreary days? Fuck yes. But he went with the explanation Lorant's walnut-sized brain would understand.

"A hostage."

A cruel smile spread across Lorant's face, and threads of misgiving wrapped around Dorin's gut, making what Dorin had to do next even harder, but there was no other choice. He trusted neither of these men to keep Betony alive.

He reached into the secret pocket of his jerkin and pulled out a small black pouch with an embossed silver crescent moon. Digging through the accouterments of his trade, Dorin found the vial of sleeping draught. Or killing draught. It all depended on dosage. There wasn't enough to kill her in this small ampoule, but there should be enough to keep her asleep for several hours. He knelt next to Betony and dribbled a few drops of the sleeping potion in her mouth. She choked a little, but slipped further into unconsciousness as it did its work.

A sly glint shone in Vedel's eyes as he straightened his jerkin.

"I knew there was more to you. Manservant, my ass. Only a midnight man carries a pouch such as yours. Only a midnight man would see through a fairy charm."

"A midnight man?" Lorant scoffed. "They're tales told to children."

"Keep telling yourself that," Dorin spat. He'd rather keep his hands free of blood from this debacle, but slitting Lorant's throat would bring him an inordinate amount of pleasure. He brandished his dagger.

"They aren't just tales, Lorant, but few have met a midnight man and lived," Vedel said thoughtfully. "Consider yourself beyond lucky."

"I guess Kalman didn't trust you as much as you thought, old man." Lorant wheezed out a chuckle.

"Enough!" Dorin tucked the pouch back in his secret pocket. "I have a plan."

Time slipped away, and he needed to hurry before someone came to investigate the commotion the horses had caused behind the tavern. He collected her staff and ran his fingers over it. There was a button in the middle. He pressed it and pushed one end against the wall. It collapsed into the central cylinder. He repeated the motion on the other end and tucked the weapon under his belt.

"Why do you get to devise the plan?" Lorant demanded.

"Because you and the ambassador made a shitshow out of this assignment, and it seems it's up to me to pull your asses out of the fire." Dorin slipped his cloak off and wrapped Betony in it, then hefted her in his arms. She was so pale, so limp, but her breaths were even. Zovog would have a laugh when Dorin tried to explain *this* at his final judgment. He carried her to the nearest horse. "We have a reliable witness who overheard you and the ambassador planning to abduct a toddler, the second in line to the Lorean throne. We can't kill her—that would bring the wrath of Lorea and Faerie to Fuartir's shores. So I am taking the only option left. I will take her to the chief, and she'll be a hostage we can trade

71

for concessions."

Lorant looked…dumbfounded. Maybe surprised. Definitely pissed over how he'd spoken to them. His half brothers had colored Lorant's impression of him. Rodric and Illes had low opinions of Dorin's capabilities. But even they did not realize he was a midnight man.

"Jani has done exceptional work keeping your secret," Vedel said, his expression smug. "But what happens when she wakes? She's fae and has magic. If you delay your departure, I have something in my medicine chest that should help."

Dorin's heart stopped beating for a long instant. He reached into the secret pocket again. It was still there from yesterday, the bracelet he'd pulled from the chest.

"I found the zelizka, Ambassador. Care to inform me why you felt it necessary to bring it into Lorea, where magic is allowed and encouraged?"

The ambassador merely shrugged. "I always come prepared. Perhaps a lesson you would benefit from. But if you have it, you know what to do."

If it would even work. His training suggested it should, but few fae and fewer fairies stepped foot in Fuartir. Only one way to find out.

"But what do Vedel and I do?" Lorant bit out.

"Act normal." Dorin draped Betony across the horse's withers. The animal snorted, but when the princess didn't move, it settled. "Take the other two horses back now. Provide a cover story. With any luck, they won't learn she's missing until morning. When they finally realize things aren't as they seem, I'll be far from the city."

"A cover story. I doubt that's going to fool them?"

Dorin spun on the thick-headed guard. "I don't need it to fool them for long. Tell them you saw me and the princess kissing and sneaking off on this horse. Again, when they realize you're lying, it will be too late."

"It's your neck on the line."

By Zovog's scythe, Dorin wanted to slice away the smug look on Lorant's face. It would make a truly horrendous mask.

"It's all our necks. If you don't lie well enough, they'll know you were part of it. And if they catch us, I am not going down alone. Do you know what happened the last time an ambassador threatened a member of the royal family?"

Something finally got through Lorant's self-centeredness. He shook his head slowly, fear replacing the smirk.

Dorin opened his mouth to reply, but it was Vedel who answered.

"She's rotting in a prison in the Calcolo Mountains. The Loreans aren't big enthusiasts of executions."

Glaring at the two men, Dorin had one more warning for these two egotistical fools. "If you even think of touching a hair on the young prince's head, you will have a long line of sword-wielding royals out for your blood. And if they don't end your miserable lives, I will. Once they learn she's gone, give them this to prove we have her."

He pulled out the necklace Betony had been wearing and gave it to the ambassador.

"Give me all the money you have on you. Getting her to our ship in Nimel won't be cheap."

Lorant sputtered a protest, but Vedel pulled out a heavy purse and handed it to Dorin, along with Betony's knife. The blade seemed to vibrate in his fingers, and a note thrummed through his mind. Dorin quickly pocketed the little blue knife. Grumbling, Lorant tossed a purse at Dorin's feet. Alet help him, Dorin hoped his warning was enough.

"You better hope this works, you ass-licking bastard," Lorant growled out. "Because if it doesn't—"

The ambassador held up a hand and quelled Lorant's rant with a glare. "Enough. If it weren't for Dorin's quick thinking, we'd be dealing with much, much bigger problems. Either getting expelled in the middle of winter or facing the mercy of a grieving king. This is…better. Another word from you, and I'll tell King Rowan this was your idea."

That shut Lorant up. He huffed off to gather their two horses.

"May Alet grant you luck and Zovog forget you exist." Vedel followed his captain.

Dorin hefted the purse at his feet and tucked both in his pocket, shivering a little as a breeze blew down the alley. He mounted his horse and tapped its sides with his heels. They moved off in a normal walk as Vedel and Lorant mounted their horses and rode in the opposite direction. Not at all like men in the middle of a kidnapping plot. Nothing to see here. Everything was fine.

He shifted the cloak to better cover Betony and prayed to Zovog that if there were guards at the docks, they were too tired to pay attention. There was one chance at making this work.

He went straight to the docks. Avora wasn't a port city but did a fair amount of business via river barge. It was the quickest way to the port of Nimel, and he knew just the unscrupulous barge pilot to ask for a lift. Hopefully, Conrad was at the docks tonight. If not, he was fucked.

The streets had quieted since their arrival at the Fiddle and Drum, but there was still enough activity his passage should go unnoticed until after the fact. The crowd thinned as he approached the docks, but his god must have heard his prayer. Only a single guard was stationed at the docks, and he barely glanced up as they passed.

Dorin looked along the line of barges and empty berths. There she was, the *Blenny,* about halfway down the quay. He'd been keeping Conrad busy with missives to Jani and procuring smuggled goods from Fuartir. The man liked his money and would do anything for a few extra coins. But perhaps it would be wisest to avoid mentioning they'd be smuggling a princess, especially since Conrad was Lorean.

He halted the horse and dismounted. The windows glowed with light, and smoke came from a small stovepipe sticking out of the cabin on the barge.

"Ho, Conrad," he called as quietly as he could.

A quiet clattering greeted his words, and a moment later, Conrad opened the door.

"That you, Dorin?"

"Yes. Got a job for you. How soon can you leave?"

"Any time. I'm in and out all hours, and I pay good coin to avoid questions."

Dorin wanted to avoid questions like the spotted plague. "That will work."

"What's the cargo?"

"Me and a…guest."

Conrad smiled knowingly and clicked his tongue. "Understood. Can't take the horse, though."

Gods damn it, of course he couldn't take the horse. And if he let the horse go, it would head straight to the castle. As good as his plan was— and it was shit, but the only plan he could come up with that would keep Betony alive and his father happy—he hadn't thought everything through. In fact, his concern for the princess had driven almost every other thought out of his mind.

Time was all he needed. Time to escape to the Fuartiran ship in Nimel.

"Know someone willing to stable it while I'm away?"

"It'll be at least four days round trip, going to Nimel. Cost at least two gold coins."

"I can cover it."

"And the journey, with food for two, cost ya five."

Robbery, but Dorin couldn't protest, and Conrad knew it. "Deal."

Dorin handed over seven gold coins. Conrad walked on the deck of the barge and opened a trapdoor into the shallow cargo hold, then sauntered to his cabin.

"I'll finish my dinner while you…unpack. Look carefully at the bulkhead at the stern. I'll take the horse to the stables for you as soon as I've eaten."

Dorin loved sneaky smugglers. "Much appreciated."

"Ta!"

Conrad did exactly as he said, closing the door behind him and making more noise with his dishes. Dorin lifted the still-sleeping woman off the horse. He carried her into the cargo hold, his head almost brushing the beams above. He inspected the mentioned bulkhead and found a slightly discolored spot. A door cracked open when he pressed it, revealing a hidden room.

There was a small cot, a pisspot, some bottles of liquor, and a few waterskins. If everything went to plan, they'd be in Nimel in a day and a half.

Dorin pulled out the sleeping potion. He dribbled a little more into Betony's mouth. Though he didn't have a lot left, it should be enough to get them at least half a day down the river. He found some rope in the cargo hold and returned to the little cabin. Before he tied her up, he pulled out the thin, black leather strap studded with iron discs.

He tied the strap on her wrist. The zelizka gave off a faint hiss as it touched her skin, and the knot melded together. It wouldn't come off until a cleric removed it. He'd taken it to keep anyone from using it, and just look at him. In case he was wrong about the sleeping potion, he tied her wrists and ankles together, too. He would answer for his sins when Zovog collected him, be it in an hour, a month, or many years from now.

Dorin tucked the cloak around her. She seemed so fragile, and he wanted to do nothing but protect her. He tried telling himself that was exactly what he was doing. If he hadn't kidnapped her, Lorant would have killed her. And despite his protests, Vedel would have let him.

He'd been wrong. It wasn't a hundred times shit. A thousand was more like it.

The barge pulled away from the dock, and the bell at the city gate rang once, signaling midnight. Dorin settled his back against the bulkhead and dozed off.

Chapter 13

A sickly sweet taste lingered on her tongue as Betony regained consciousness. She pried her eyes open to a dimly lit room. A musty smell invaded her nostrils, and whatever she rested on rocked gently beneath her. Or maybe whatever he'd used to keep her unconscious was messing with her balance. She tried to sit, but coarse rope bound her hands and feet. She wiggled uselessly for a moment.

Fuck this. She winced. Rane was the princess who swore at the drop of a hat. But desperate times…

Betony reached for her magic, but it wasn't there. Instead, something burned on her left wrist, above where the rope bit into her skin. Panic lanced through her, mixing with the betrayal she shouldn't be feeling, roiling in her belly. Acid threatened to overpower whatever he had dosed her with.

"Tastes like shit, doesn't it?" said a familiar male voice from the far corner of the room.

She turned her head and found the owner of the understatement. The memories faded in. Right, Dorin, the so-called manservant. No manservant she'd ever met could have done what this jackass had. May Veitha's hounds piss on his shoes.

"Want some water?" he asked.

She turned away without a word. Betony wanted nothing from him besides her freedom. To think she'd liked him, found him intriguing. She obviously had the worst judgement when it came to character.

His feet scuffed on the wooden floor as he approached.

"Touch me, and I will hurt you," she croaked. How she was going to hurt him trussed up like a pig remained to be seen, but she would find a way.

"I know you will." He kneeled next to her.

Was there a touch of amusement in his voice? What precisely about this mess was amusing to anyone?

A waterskin sloshed next to her ear, and he returned to the far corner of the room. The sound of it made her dry mouth crave the water within. Suddenly, she could think of nothing else.

"It's not dosed with anything. Just water."

She turned over, scooted until her back touched the wall behind her, and used it as leverage to sit. Betony grabbed the skin with her tied hands. Bringing it to her lips, she used her teeth to pull out the cork and spat it towards her abductor. He snorted as she drank, washing away the foul taste in her mouth. The sensations in her belly were another matter.

"Better?" he asked once she drank her fill.

Betony bit back the curses that came to her tongue. No telling what this man was capable of. He'd kidnapped a princess of Lorea. She needed to stay on his good side.

She nodded and kept her angry words to herself.

"I apologize for the necessity of this trip. Vedel spoke out of turn, and Lorant is an asshole of the highest order and refuses to use one iota of the intelligence given him by the gods. Unfortunately, Fuartiran culture tends to reward rash thinking."

"You're not a manservant." Her voice was more her own now that she'd had some water. "So, who *are* you? Is your name even Dorin?"

He blew out a breath and sunk onto his haunches. "Yes, my name is Dorin, and yes, I am a manservant. But I'm also something more. Chief Kalman of Clan Fher ordered me to accompany Vedel to gather information on Lorea and do whatever else I could to further plans to build an alliance with your country."

"And kidnapping one of its princesses seemed a good idea?"

Dorin's lip quirked up. "No. No, it did not, but Lorant would have killed you and the ambassador would have let him. None of this is my first choice. What I would have preferred was Vedel keeping his fucking mouth shut, and Lorant not to be a bloodthirsty beast desperate for recognition. But no one has ever cared what I preferred, so here we are."

"Where are we?"

He pressed his lips together and shook his head. "Not going to give you more information than you need."

The Dorin she'd known in Avora was shy, mumbling conversations with an accent so thick, it was often difficult to understand. This Dorin seemed composed, calm, imperturbable, and he spoke clearly, with only a hint of the Fuartiran accent she was used to from the ambassador. And smart. He wouldn't allow her any advantage to escape. She would have to be on her toes and take whatever chances presented themselves. She could expect no more kindness from him.

"Will you tell me where we're going?"

"No."

She had no idea how long she'd been out. The only thing she knew was she was on a boat. It could be anywhere from the Tivra River that ran past the capital city of Avora to the middle of the Rhoheda Sea.

"What day is it?"

He shook his head again. Idoya's tits! He was good at his job.

"What's to keep me from screaming for help?" she asked.

"Nothing, but there's no one to hear you."

"Liar." He wasn't piloting the boat, so there had to be *someone* to hear her.

"There's no one to hear you who *cares*, Princess."

She thunked her head against the wall behind her. No, she was on a boat. It was a bulwark, right? Or a bulkhead? Betony cared little about boats, only dealing with them when necessary. Usually a barge down the river to Nimel to see off the newest warship or an occasional afternoon spent sailing with her fairy friends in the bay of Sinkala. The subtle rocking pointed more to the former than the latter, but she couldn't be certain.

An urgent matter started making itself known. "I have to pee."

Another snort. Glad she amused him.

"Yeah, I figured this was coming. I'll give you a choice. I can help you, or you can give me your word you won't escape, and I will untie you and give you some privacy."

"How do you know I'll keep my word?"

He stood again and leaned against the wall. "You're fae, you spent a significant portion of your childhood in the Faerie Court and nearly all of the last seven years. If you don't keep your word, I'll eat my cloak."

"I'd enjoy seeing that," she muttered. But he was right. If she gave her word, she'd keep it. "Fine, you have my word I will not try to escape while using the facilities."

Maybe she'd find a way around it. Or maybe she should focus on not exploding from the pressure building inside.

He walked the few steps over, untied her legs, but left her wrists bound.

"Excuse me." She shoved them in his face.

"I've seen you fight. You can maneuver a chamber pot with your hands tied. I am not fool enough to give you all your freedoms."

"When you die, I hope Veitha roasts your balls in front of you before he eats them."

He laughed then, a full-throated belly laugh that did things to her insides she'd rather not contemplate at the moment. It also rang a small bell in her memory. She'd heard the like before, hadn't she? Whatever it was remained elusive to her drug-addled mind.

"I am not worried about *your* god," Dorin said before he left, shutting the door behind him. She heard the lock turn. There were no windows and no other exits. *Fine, he wins this round.*

She used the chamber pot to the best of her ability. The Veitha-cursed cur was right. She was agile enough to maneuver it how she needed. Bet pulled up her pants and stumbled to the bed.

"I'm done."

Could she kick him, slip out before he could react? She was done using the chamber pot, so had she fulfilled her promise? If she did escape, she had no idea how far from home she was, nor in what direction. Were they still on the river or had he drugged her into unconsciousness all the way to Nimel? She could be facing the open ocean with no escape.

He opened the door slowly, her own staff in his hand. Betony growled at the man. The audacity of not only disarming her but trying to use it against her.

"I'm keeping my word." She passed that off as the reason she'd growled.

"I have occasionally been wrong about someone's character. No need to take unnecessary risks."

"At least let me keep my legs free!"

He barked out a laugh. "No way in the underworld. I've seen you fight, remember?"

Betony bit the inside of her cheek to repress the smug grin threatening to form. Why was it such a compliment coming from him? She should hate him—and a part of her did—but she still found him intriguing, maybe even more so now than before. She needed to start thinking and stop feeling.

She kept silent when he wound the rope around her ankles once more. What would be the point? The rope was snug but not terribly uncomfortable. This was not the first time he'd tied up someone.

When he finished, he resumed his seat as far from her as he could get. He wasn't afraid of her, so the only reason to do so would be to prove he meant her no harm. Well, no further harm.

Dorin said nothing else, merely leaned his head back and closed his eyes. The small lantern next to him was the only light in the room, and the flame was low. There was barely enough light to see anything other than vague shapes.

The silence got to her, an eternity of listening to the creak of the boat and his soft breaths. If he was sleeping, she was going to be a pain in his ass and keep him awake.

"What's this?"

She held up her wrists. A black leather band studded with iron discs was on her left wrist. It was tight, almost tight enough to cut off circulation. And it tingled unpleasantly.

"That is a zelizka to keep you from using your magic. They're common in my homeland. Once on, only a cleric can remove it. Glad to see it's working. I wasn't entirely sure it would work on a fae-born."

"I thought the people of Fuartir didn't have magic."

He narrowed his eyes at her, his hands clasped over his knees.

"No, we have magic but believe it should only be used to better the community. All those with innate magical gifts are given a choice when they reach adulthood—serve one of our gods or bind your magic away. Until then, they wear those bands, so they do not accidentally injure someone or themselves."

Bind their magic away. Betony swallowed the bile rising in her throat. It was...*monstrous*.

"That's cruel."

"No, it is necessary. Too many would use their magic to usurp the rightful chiefs, they would use it to gain power over others. Chaos would reign, and everyone would be at risk. The clerics of Alet and Zovog are trained for years in the proper control and use of their magic, and everything they do is to benefit their communities. Can you say the same of the fairies? Or of the humans in your kingdom who learn to use magic? If I recall correctly, Prince Nevar's stepmother is in prison, at least in part for the misuse of magic. Wouldn't a band such as the one you're wearing be a kinder consequence?"

She couldn't say he was wrong, but something was off with his arguments. Her mind still hadn't recovered from the drug he gave her, so she let the matter drop.

Speaking of which…

"What did you give me?"

"A sleeping concoction."

She raised a brow, the question unasked, but he answered anyway.

"According to the cleric who prepared it, mostly poppy syrup, with some extract of valerian and chamomile. A little magic to make it work faster and last longer."

Yes, that would do it. She kept a similar concoction in her medicine chest but added the magic herself. It was a popular tonic in the apothecaries of Avora, and the hospital had a ready supply, but…

"I'm lucky I'm not dead. Too much can kill someone."

"I know what I'm doing, Princess. Why don't you get some more rest?" He closed his eyes again. "We still have a ways to go and there's nothing to do on this Zovog-cursed boat."

It wasn't the best idea, but it seemed to be the only idea. Betony wriggled down and got as comfortable as possible with her bound limbs. She waited for sleep to find her. If she were to have any chance at escape, she needed rest so he couldn't catch her.

Chapter 14

The room was surprisingly warm, and as usual, the peaceful sway of the river barge lulled Dorin into a doze. A strange scratching woke him.

Betony rubbed her bonds on the edge of the cot. She was so focused she failed to realize he was awake. He watched for a moment. She scrunched her face in concentration, her eyebrows drawn nearly together. Her movements were quick and efficient as she rubbed the rope between her wrists. Even in this light, even after a day confined in this cramped space, she was gorgeous. And she was still fighting.

It would make his life hell, but he couldn't help but admire the fuck out of her.

"Don't make me pull out the irons," he bluffed. "They're not very comfortable."

She startled and turned a fearsome glare his way. With her bright hair wildly escaping her braid, he caught his breath at her ferocity. Surely not even the god of death held such menace in their gaze. The princess stopped and schooled her expression into regal serenity.

"None of this is *comfortable*, Dorin," she said.

"I've already apologized, but it was this or death."

Dorin released his hands from where they'd been clasped around his knees. He stood slowly, his feet tingling as his circulation returned. Bouncing on his toes to hurry the process along, he pressed his hands to the beams overhead.

Betony eyed him disinterestedly. "You done?"

"Almost." He bent side to side at the waist, finally banishing the kinks left from his little nap. "There, now I'm done. Are you hungry? Need to use the facilities again?"

"Food and privacy would be appreciated," she ground out, not breaking eye contact.

Good for her. She didn't care if it made him uncomfortable.

"Same promise as before?" he asked.

She nodded.

"Nice try. Say it."

Betony rolled her eyes. "I promise not to try to escape while you grant me privacy to use the chamber pot."

"Excellent." Dorin allowed a wide smile, only half fake, to spread as he knelt next to her and untied the ropes on her ankles. "I'll go get food."

He took the ropes with him and locked the door. Dorin climbed the ladder and pushed open the hatch. The dawn was breaking over the bow of the barge, a golden light stretched its fingers high into the sky. The sleeping draught had worked better than he'd expected, and she'd slept most of yesterday. It had been over a day since he'd seen daylight, and after the dim room, the sight dazzled him. Whistling, he strode to Conrad's cabin, a small boxy structure toward the stern of the shallow, long vessel. The man opened the door before he reached it.

"You're in a good mood," Conrad said. "Your 'guest' cooperative?"

Dorin did not like the implications of the barge pilot's words, but he could do little to persuade him nothing of the kind was happening in his secret room. Not without telling him the entire story. And while Conrad might turn a blind eye to human trafficking, kidnapping a princess and the shit that was going to come his way because of it was too much. Plus, Loreans loved their royal family. Dorin was starting to figure out why—they were kind people who genuinely cared for their subjects and worked hard to serve them. All bets were off if Conrad discovered his "guest" was Princess Betony.

"We could use a little food," he said, choosing to ignore the comment.

Conrad stood aside, gesturing Dorin in. "Got some bread and cheese, a bit of jam. Won't be long. Should be there by mid-morning."

"I'll need some help transferring my guest. Do we need to worry about inspectors?"

The smuggler pressed his lips together, looking displeased by the question. "Depends on how busy the port is. Lorean shipments are spot inspected—a random draw. If it's busy, it's unlikely they'll inspect a barge from the capital. Even if they do, a couple gold coins could delay the inspection until after nightfall. One way or another, I'd rather not draw attention to my…less than transparent business activities."

"Thank you. Guess we'll see when we arrive."

"Guess we will."

Dorin took the food back to the room. He unlocked the door to discover Betony pacing the room like a caged wildcat. She stopped and glared at him. If she had her magic, he'd be regretting all his decisions leading to this moment. Hell, he did regret some of them. But not the dance, not the kiss. And not saving her life.

"I have food. Sit and I'll share."

She sat. He tore off a hunk of bread and slathered some jam on it. She took it and nibbled delicately. They ate in silence for a while.

"Will you tell me where we are or where we're going yet?" she asked after the silence became oppressive.

"Nope, sorry."

He liked watching her stew, trying to work it out. Of course, one answer made the most sense, but if he didn't confirm or deny any of her guesses, it meant she had to prepare for every possibility. That gave him the advantage should she try to escape.

"How much longer?" she tried next.

He merely smiled and ate his cheese. She stared at it and licked her lips. With that simple action, he wasn't thinking about the cheese, or her obvious attempts to extract information from him, or his role in this whole debacle. No, he was remembering how she tasted after drinking mead. Why did she make his thoughts veer where they had no business going?

"Do I get some cheese?"

Grateful to be distracted, Dorin broke off a chunk and passed it to her. Betony nibbled that, too.

"There's plenty more," he said. "You can take bigger bites."

"I'm a princess. What did you expect?"

He shrugged. What had he expected? "I don't know what to expect from royalty. We don't have that notion in Fuartir."

Not yet, anyway. His father was working hard to change the whole of

Fuartiran politics.

"Then what does the ambassador expect to accomplish without a central government?"

Dorin knew she'd catch on as soon as he'd said it. "Peace and trade. Fuartir is not so different from other countries in that. And the clans do have a governing body, the Witan. Each clan chief has a seat. They decided Clan Fher, my clan, could lead the diplomatic mission."

Decided was a stretch. His father had strong-armed, bribed, and coerced the chiefs not already on his side. Kalman had *plans*, and he wouldn't let the democratic process stop him. Dorin wondered if the other chiefs realized where this would eventually lead. Not his problem. His only concern was ensuring his clan came out on top. That *Kalman* came out on top.

Clan was everything, a lesson taught by his mother and the priests who trained him after her death. And frankly, for the good of Fuartir, Kalman was the best choice. He might be bloodthirsty and power hungry, the same as all clan chiefs, but unlike the others, he was pragmatic. Fuartir couldn't reasonably take on the combined power of Lorea, Faerie, and Teruelle. Since Kalman couldn't beat them, he wanted to join them.

"You expect me to believe the Fuartiran Witan, well known for squabbling and trying to keep any single chief from coming out on top, simply 'decided' Fher would lead the mission? Seems…unlikely."

Yes, Princess Betony was as sharp as his dagger.

She licked her fingers, sucking down every last crumb of cheese and bread. Her bright pink lips pursed sensually, and Dorin had to drag his thoughts away from the ideas trying to distract him from his duty.

"Unlikely or not, it's true. So the chief sent the ambassador before the cold weather set in. A little before you arrived, hoping we'd stay the winter to persuade your father to ally with Fuartir. It would give Clan Fher more honor and influence."

"Why are you telling me this?"

Why indeed?

"Bored, I guess. And it's not like you can tell anyone."

"What if I escape?"

He snorted. "Won't be happening, Princess. Speaking of which…"

He held up the rope to bind her ankles again. She scowled, and he wished it didn't have to be this way. What could have happened if Lorant and Vedel had kept their speculations to themselves? Perhaps, someday, he could have revealed himself as Chief Kalman's son and earned a chance to dance with her again. Kiss her again.

Betony complied, but loathing shone from those emerald eyes, as bright as the noon sun. Too late for what-ifs. The best he could do now was keep her alive and return her to her family in one piece once his father had what he wanted.

"I am sorry, Your Highness, but if Ambassador Vedel has any hope of succeeding on his mission, this is how it must be."

"You should stop apologizing. You're not actually sorry. If you were, you'd let me go and face the consequences of your actions. If my nephew comes to any harm because of this…"

"Did I not mention that Vedel, though pompous and conniving, is a very skillful diplomat? He may speculate, but he lacks the balls to see anything through."

"Lorant doesn't. He was ready to kill me."

He stepped back and lowered himself to the deck before leaning his head against the wall. "And thus we find ourselves in this predicament. Lorant is a bully and a coward, and if I'd had the time, I would've taught him a lesson he wouldn't soon forget."

"You expect me to believe that?"

"Believe what you want."

"Fuck. You."

"Fine."

Dorin hid his surprise at her cursing—from everything he'd observed, the princess rarely cursed. He closed his eyes and ignored her. The sooner Betony accepted her position, the sooner she accepted he wasn't there to hurt her, the better. The rest of the morning went by in silence, and whenever their gazes met, he could sense the resentment in her heart. Not how he wanted to end his mission in Lorea.

More noises from outside snuck into the room. Shouts, bells, the splashing of other boats. Thank Alet, they were nearly in Nimel.

He wished he had enough of the sleeping draught to transfer Betony to the *Zovog's Revenge*, but he didn't. He'd need to leave her alone on the barge with Conrad while he fetched some potion from the apothecary and informed the captain of the *Revenge* to ready his ship.

Conrad minded his own business for the most part, but if Betony made a stink, they would have the harbor guards over them like flies on horseshit. The only way to prevent such an event would make her hate him even more.

He pulled out a fine linen kerchief from his jerkin and some more rope he'd found the last time she slept. She eyed him warily.

"Don't fight me and you won't get hurt. I promise after today, you'll have more freedom of movement."

"I am not letting you tie me up even more. If you want to, you'll have to earn it."

He sighed. "Fine, if that's how it has to be."

Dorin struck quickly, as he'd been taught. Had she been free, it was likely she could have evaded him, but she was tied hand and foot. Before she could scream for help, he pulled her to him, shoving the scarf in her mouth. She drew back and tried to butt him in the head, but he saw it coming and leaned to the side before she made contact, her forehead glancing off his jaw. Hurt like a kick in the balls, but he was still conscious, so he'd call it a win.

Betony chewed at the scarf, trying to dislodge it. He flipped her to face the wall. She kicked out ineffectually with her bound legs, and he snaked an arm around her neck again.

"Calm down," he hissed in her ear.

She answered with a jab with her elbows toward his gut, bringing them up quickly with as much strength as she could. He intercepted the blow and tightened his grip. As soon as she lost consciousness, he let go.

Fuck, he hated this. Hated himself for making her feel helpless. Hated Vedel and Lorant for putting him in this position. Hated the voice in the back of his mind telling him he was better than this. He was not. His father had made sure of that. In the end, Kalman would finally have the leverage he needed to secure what he wanted most: a crown. And Dorin would have the empty satisfaction of serving his clan and his chief.

Dorin pulled the scarf from her mouth, looped it around her head, and tied it securely, gagging her. He quickly tied her feet to her hands. He waited quietly, stewing in his own self-loathing, until she regained consciousness. Tears of fury, and probably pain, sprang to her eyes and dribbled over her cheeks. The sight would haunt him in his nightmares.

"I'll be back soon," he said. "You'll be safe here."

If looks could kill, he'd be facing Zovog right now, awaiting his judgment. Thankfully, they couldn't. He wasn't ready to meet the god of death just yet. The judgment would not be in his favor.

He slipped from the cabin and headed to the deck. Conrad greeted him with a grand gesture at the harbor.

"You're in luck, my friend. I've rarely seen it this busy in the winter, but the weather has been mild so far. People are trying to get the last shipments out before the storms come. Not enough inspectors to worry about little ole me. Do what you have to."

Dorin touched his fingers to his temple in a salute and hurried off the boat. Thanks to his unexceptional looks, no one gave him more than a passing glance. First stop was the apothecary, where he fed them some nonsense about a wife he didn't have who was having trouble sleeping. He tucked the sleeping draught into his pocket and went to find the *Zovog's Revenge*.

As a raider, the *Revenge* had sent landing parties to several Faerie and Lorean port towns since his father had commissioned the ship four years ago. The flagship of Clan Fher, it became the vessel to carry the Fuartiran ambassador. Unlike the northerners, the Loreans played by rules. When the *Zovog's Revenge* had arrived, full diplomatic privileges were extended, and the captain and crew had free rein in the harbor city of Nimel. The worst that could happen, and had happened, was if a sailor was caught doing something illegal, they would be confined to ship and no longer welcome in Nimel.

There it was, at the farthest berth. Her mainsail was furled, though he could spot the brilliant blue stripes on the edge to indicate its diplomatic status. Shallow of draft, with oars as well as sails, the ship was about thirty paces from bow to stern. And captained by the most ruthless and efficient sailor Dorin had ever met.

"Ho, the *Revenge*!" he called from the end of the gangplank.

A sailor appeared and leaned over the rails. "Can I help you?"

Alet's rainbows, it was nice to hear the cadences of his homeland.

"Tell Captain Mertok that Dorin, son of Piroska, wishes to speak with him."

She shrugged as if to say "your funeral" before disappearing once more. Most of the sailors were lodged in the city, with a rotating schedule for a skeleton crew onboard. Captain Mertok would not leave his ship for more than a short trip. His people skills were often shit, but the man was nothing if not dedicated.

Soon enough, Dorin spotted the blond head of the captain. He peered over the side of his ship, and a smile split the bushy beard streaked with gray.

"Dorin, good to see you. Come aboard."

Dorin hurried across the gangplank, and Mertok clasped his forearm in greeting.

"Thank you, Captain."

The older man slung an arm around Dorin's shoulders and led him aft to the captain's cabin.

"What trouble brings you to the *Revenge*?" he asked.

"Trouble?"

The captain chuckled. "I got a bird from Vedel yesterday to prepare for sea the moment you showed. What disaster can I expect to visit *my* ship?"

Dorin smiled wryly. It's not as if he planned on lying to Mertok, but he had wished to avoid telling him the whole truth until they were far enough out to sea that the temptation to throw him overboard was gone.

"I have an…unexpected guest who needs to return to Fuartir with me. The nature of their identity is sensitive, and I'd prefer to give you all the details once they're secured onboard."

Mertok glowered, but Dorin held up a hand.

"If you need to know everything right this moment, I'm prepared to share it with you but need your word nothing gets to the crew."

Rumors on ships spread like fire, and neither was good for the morale of the crew.

"There's already rumors. With the message, I put them all on notice. Fuck their wenches, fuck their swains, and pay their debts. We'd be sailing soon. I can decide on the best perfume for this shitshow if I know what the fuck is going on."

Dorin sighed. There was no help for it, but it meant the Loreans would soon learn the Revenge would be leaving—without the ambassador. Speed was more important than stealth at the moment.

"I have a high-ranking hostage to take home."

"Well, that's a stinking cluster of whale shit. I assume it was your brilliant idea."

The color flushed on Dorin's cheeks. "Killing them would have had the Loreans dropping an entire decomposing whale on Clan Fher, while

Faerie would have sent the fires of the underworld, and Zovog only knows what the other clans would have done to us for fucking this up so bad. I went with the choice that gave us all a chance at survival, both literally and politically."

He didn't tell the captain the mere thought of harming his hostage sent waves of nausea through him and froze him dead, a reckless position for a well-trained assassin. Caring about Betony would only put her in more danger and risk a mistake on his part.

"Aye, I suppose that's the case. What do you need from me?"

"When can you sail?"

Mertok lifted a brow. "I forget you aren't a sailor, as often as you've joined me onboard. We have oars and a shallow draft. I'll need to tell the harbormaster if we want any shot of returning to Nimel. However, if we leave at night, it might look…suspicious. Between now and mid-afternoon would be fine, or at first light."

Dorin considered. He would have an unconscious woman to transport, and there would be less chance of discovery at night. But time was not their friend. The longer they waited, the more likely Betony would be discovered missing.

"As soon as possible, then. Have two of your men use a dinghy to meet me at the barge named *Blenny*. It's busy in the harbor today. They should go unnoticed. I have enough sleeping draught to keep them out until we're at sea."

Dorin stood, and Mertok followed suit.

"If they're discovered, if you're discovered, I don't know you. Good luck," the captain said. "See yourself out."

Dorin strode out of the cabin, over the gangplank, and wove through the crowds around the dock. He took the most direct route to the *Blenny* but waited until the dockworkers looked away before sneaking on board. Yes, time was of the essence, but he wasn't one to take unnecessary risks. Betony was where he left her.

"Once more, Princess, I apologize."

She started and turned to glare at him. Some part of him was glad the gag kept her from hurling curses at him. Another part was heartbroken. In another life, they might have been able to build on their dance at the ball, which wasn't even a fortnight ago.

He pulled the vial out of his pocket. Her eyes grew wide and she shook her head vigorously. She wriggled and squirmed, trying to put as much distance between them as possible. But it was hopeless. Dorin wasn't a sailor, but he knew his knots. He wasn't a warrior, but he knew how to physically subdue someone. He wasn't a doctor, but he knew the draught would do its job.

He used the dropper the apothecary had been so helpful to provide and slipped in enough potion under her gag to knock her out until the *Revenge's* sailors showed up. She glared at him through a sheen of tears until the draught took effect. Without the magic supplied by the clerics, it took a few moments. He wrapped her in his cloak and covered her hair with the kerchief for good measure.

Any hope he fostered to have something more with Betony was dashed on the deck of this barge. She would never forgive him. Worse, he doubted he'd forgive himself.

Chapter 15

The world came slowly into focus, Betony's head pounding after being forced into unconsciousness several times in quick succession. Her mouth tasted like cotton steeped in half-fermented fruit. Again. That shadow viper! If she ever had the chance, she would kick him in the balls then force feed him his own vile concoction.

The first thing Betony noticed was the gag was gone. Thank Idoya. Being tied didn't bother her as much as it should have. It meant he viewed her as a threat. But the gag…Betony hadn't ever felt that helpless.

Speaking of being tied up—the rough ropes on her ankles and wrists were gone as well. The abomination of a bracelet was still there, still forming a wall between her and her magic. Betony gave it an experimental tug, but the blasted thing stayed put.

She sat and looked around, shaking out her hands and tapping her feet to get the blood flowing. Who knew when she'd have to make a sudden move? This was not the same cramped, dimly lit room. Probably not even the same vessel. Bright sunlight poured into the cabin, and instead of a flimsy cot, she sat on an honest-to-goodness bunk built into the bulkhead. Blue velvet curtains partitioned the bed from the rest of the room, but they were drawn back, held with fine silk tiebacks. A small table was bolted to the deck and four well-made chairs surrounded it. A lamp swung from the ceiling, unneeded in the bright day. Maps were rolled up and stored on shelves built into the same bulkhead as the bed. A few leather-bound books were next to them.

The busy sounds of the harbor had been replaced by the calls of crew, the creaking of ropes, the splash of oars in the water, and the screech of gulls.

Veitha's hounds, they were at sea. They must be headed to Fuartir, possibly the home port of Clan Fher. It only made sense. She should have tried harder to escape. Her chances of going anywhere while at sea were slim to none, but if they were still using oars, she might have a chance.

She scrambled out of bed, rushed to the door, and tried to open it. Locked, of course. She stepped on the bed and peered out the window above. The lighthouse of the Nimel harbor was a stone's throw away, but no one walked its ramparts. If she could wriggle out the window, there was a chance she could swim to shore. She slid her fingers over the window, but the latches were on top, and it was hinged to only crack open. Maybe she could break it? As small as she was, she doubted she could fit through, but she had few options.

She hopped off the bed and explored the room further. A ceramic carafe sat on the table. She pulled the stop free and sniffed. Water. She drank it. If more of the sleeping draught was in it, she was in trouble, but her mouth tasted terrible, her head ached, and her throat burned from thirst. Her shoes were on the deck beside the bed, a fresh pair of socks nestled on top. A coat was draped over one of the chairs in the center of the room. Besides the carafe she held, there was nothing that could break the window, and it was doubtful even the carafe could accomplish the task.

Betony had to try. She moved toward the bed but froze when a knock sounded. A key turned and the door opened. Dorin walked in carrying a tray of bread and cheese, and the frigid breeze he allowed in pebbled her skin. On impulse, in a fit of rage and desperation, she hurled the carafe at his nose. If she could knock him unconscious...

He twitched aside, almost as if he'd expected her to do this, and a tight grin crossed his lips. The carafe hit the side doorjamb and bounced back into the cabin, spinning as it came to rest at her feet. It didn't even have the decency to break. She resisted the urge to kick it.

"I brought food." He closed the door behind him but did not lock it.

Bet merely stared at him as he rested the tray on the table. At the very least, he deserved to feel like shit for kidnapping her. Maybe she could hurry this along and get on deck before her chance at escape was too far behind them.

"You have the run of the ship," he continued, unfazed by her silence, "as long as you don't interfere with the crew. We should be at sea for five to eight days, depending on weather conditions. This isn't the best season to travel the Roheda Sea."

She gave him nothing. If she didn't respond, maybe he'd go away. He stood there quietly, looking her over for a moment.

"I *am* sorry. You'll be treated as an honored guest, I promise. There are strict rules governing hostages in Fuartir, and the chief has every reason to ensure your safety."

Still nothing. What if he stayed? She could try to take him out, but he'd bested her twice. Twice! And it would bring unwanted attention. The crew would notice if he never came back out, and there would go her chance.

Betony breathed—in through her nose and out through her mouth—and gave Dorin her coldest, most pissed-off fairy stare. He flushed and broke eye contact.

"Well, if you need anything, just ask for me." He strode out but left the door unlocked. Who would be foolhardy enough to escape now? He hadn't studied the Lorean royal line hard enough, apparently.

Finally. The sight of the bread and cheese had her mouth watering, and another carafe of water was on the tray. She put aside the temptation of food. Nimel was fast disappearing into the winter mists. If she did nothing, she was doomed to travel to Fuartir and face whatever fate awaited her there. Dorin could make all the assurances he wanted. The last time she trusted him brought her to this moment. It wouldn't happen again.

She climbed on the bed and judged the distance. Yes, if she left now, she could make it, barely. Even with her control over her magic blocked by the bracelet, it was still there. The creatures of the sea would respond when she called. They wouldn't let her die. She hoped.

Betony stretched. It was at least a mile back, a long swim in the best conditions. These were not the best conditions. The seas were choppy, and she was not looking forward to the icy winter water. She eyed her shoes, the socks, the coat. She couldn't swim with those, but if she left the cabin without them, they would know something was off.

Slipping on the coat, Betony left the buttons undone. She skipped the socks and shoved her feet into the shoes before she walked out of the cabin as calmly as if this was an afternoon pleasure cruise.

A few heads turned toward her, but they quickly resumed their tasks.

Men and women worked alongside each other on the ship. About half the crew were stowing the oars, most of the others raising the sail as they cleared the harbor and made their way out to the open sea.

Betony had little time. With each passing moment, her homeland grew further away, and her hopes of escape narrowed. But she had to catch them off guard. She strolled the deck, trying to look vaguely curious. Between their tasks and her boring behavior, the crew quickly ignored her.

She still felt eyes on her. Betony made a show of examining the sail. There, in the corner of her eye—Dorin stood at the bow of the boat, watching. Pretending she hadn't noticed, she strolled to the stern. There was no commotion behind her.

Betony stood a few feet shy of the railing at the back of the ship. She kicked off her shoes and dropped the coat to the deck. She ran the last few steps and launched herself into the air.

A shout went up just before she hit the freezing water, then she heard nothing except the pounding of her heart as her body fought the current, the wake of the ship, and the cold trying to kill her. Needles of icy pain stabbed into her entire body as she worked with the currents and broke the surface, sucking in the sweet air.

Betony didn't look behind her before she swam for the harbor.

Chapter 16

*H*is feet flew across the deck, but he was too late. Dorin watched in horror as Betony dove off the end of the ship. He dropped his jacket as he ran, and once he reached the railing, he fumbled at the laces of his boots.

"Ready the dinghy!" he shouted at the nearest sailor. The woman stared at him, mouth agape. "Do it, or I'll have your hide for my next pair of boots."

She ran off, and Dorin dropped his boots to the deck, ignoring the shouts and scrambling sailors behind him. He sent a quick prayer for protection to Alet and another to Zovog as an extra safeguard. Surely, one of his gods would listen.

"You're mad!" Mertok called. "The water is as cold as an old whore's twat."

He glanced back at the captain. "We all need a little madness in our lives." And the gods knew, he'd had plenty of it since he snuck into the ball.

Dorin jumped.

The icy water closed over him and sapped his will to live for an instant. Pain lanced through him as he bobbed up, facing away from the boat. The next swell pushed him higher, and he saw Betony swimming for the harbor. Arm over arm, kicking his feet as hard as he could, Dorin followed her and tried to ignore the cold. His longer limbs and his long practice in the sea soon had him gaining on her.

Betony had to hear him closing in, but she didn't increase her speed. Her pace was slow but steady and she was pointed arrow straight at the harbor. Dorin dug deep and pulled on his trained strength, endurance, and speed to catch up.

When he could touch her heel, he slowed. It was too cold to have a conversation, and he was too winded by his exertion, but he had to say something.

"Do you have a death wish?" he gasped, fighting the cold, the wind, and the waves.

Smarter than he, Betony said nothing, merely continued swimming for the harbor. Surely she realized the game was over.

Alet save me from foolhardy princesses.

The slap of oars in the water and the voices of the sailors told him rescue was at hand.

"It's done, Princess."

Dorin grabbed her ankle, and a scream like a wounded animal skipped across the waves. She kicked and thrashed, and the sound issuing from her mouth knifed his ears and created shivers that had nothing to do with the frigid water. He might be saving her life, but he was destroying her heart and her spirit, two things he greatly admired.

The dinghy drew alongside them, and rough hands pulled them out of the water. Curses greeted Betony's thrashing. A sailor raised his fist, but before the blow landed, Dorin had his blade out and pressed to the man's throat. No, not his blade. Hers. The blue one that seemed to vibrate in his hand and in his mind.

"Reconsider your actions." He made eye contact with each person on the little boat.

The sailor lowered his fist. A tall, burly woman had wrapped her arms around the trembling and keening Betony, locking her in but not harming her. All other movement ceased.

"This woman is under my personal protection and the protection of Chief Kalman. Every effort will be made to treat her as an honored guest. If the need arises, restrain her in the most humane way possible. Do I make myself clear?"

"Who the fuck are you to give us orders?" asked the obviously brainless sailor who'd tried to strike Betony.

"Shut up, Chaba," hissed the woman holding Betony.

Dorin slowly bent down, putting the dagger a finger's width from the man's nose, his white-hot rage pushing away the tremors threatening to take hold from the cold. Chaba froze as if confronted with an ice bear, some bestial part of him sensing he was in extreme danger.

"Question me again, and I'll take your tongue," Dorin hissed quietly.

All color left the man's face, and he swallowed and tried to put distance between them.

"Good, you seem to have a drop of sense. Should you have any further objections to my orders, take it up with the captain."

Chaba shook his head.

"Excellent. Get us both blankets and row to the ship as though your lives depend upon it."

The woman had already wrapped Betony in a blanket as best she could, and held a hand over her mouth, dampening the eerie noise still coming from her. An itchy gray wool monstrosity that the ship called a blanket was draped over his shoulders. Dorin pulled it tight, gritting his teeth so his chattering didn't reveal how fucking cold he was, and knelt in front of Betony.

He took her ice-cold fingers in his. "Hush now."

The noise stopped and her eyes focused on him. They were empty, sad and broken, as they gazed at the harbor city behind them. He couldn't stand it. He kidnapped her, restrained her, drugged her, and hauled her out of the sea and her last chance to escape. What could he do, what could he say, that might bring some life back to those once-brilliant eyes?

Ah, he had just the thing. He coated the words with a strong dose of patronizing bullshit.

"Good girl."

Faster than a striking lynx, her fist connected with his jaw, and he fell to the bottom of the boat.

"F-f-fuck y-y-you," she said.

Sniggers rolled through the crew members.

"Sorry, sir, won't happen again." The woman clamped her large hand around Betony's wrist.

Dorin laughed as he rubbed his jaw and crouched. Betony's eyes widened in surprise as she tried to twist out of the woman's grasp. They gleamed with fury, with outrage. With life. Thank Alet.

"What's your name?" he asked the sailor.

"Signe." A flicker of worry flitted across her face.

"Signe, if I were a betting man, I'd wager your next raid's bounty that was the first of many punches she's going to throw at me on our journey home. I'd be disappointed if she didn't."

A half-grin replaced the worry. The dinghy bumped against the hull of the *Revenge*. Dorin returned his attention to Betony.

"Are you going to climb the ladder they're about to throw down, or are we going to do this the hard way?"

Her gaze darted to the water as a crew member caught the ladder. He'd underestimated her desperation to escape and her abilities once. He would never do so again or may Zovog curse him and all his progeny.

"Hard way it is." Dorin grabbed the coiled rope and cut off a length with the odd blade.

Before she could kick out, he had her ankles tied once more. She twisted in Signe's grasp, but he grabbed her wrists and tied them too.

"I am going to carry you up the ladder. If you move too much, you'll fall into the water, and this time you won't be able to swim. I don't feel like another ice bath and your little stunt has made you no friends on the ship. Do we understand each other?"

She clenched her jaw but nodded. He slung her over his shoulders and carried her up the ladder. Signe was the last out of the dinghy before it was hauled up.

"Signe, can you bring some dry clothes and hot beverages when you have a chance?"

"If I can't, I'll send someone."

"Thank you."

Dorin continued to his small cabin on the other side of the ship, away from the captain's quarters. Betony had lost the privilege of privacy, and he'd seen how she'd been eyeing the window in the cabin. If anyone could figure a way out, it would be her.

The tremors in her body shook through his own. Only his continued motion kept his shivers at bay. He slammed open the door and dumped her on the bunk in one corner.

Shaking a finger at her, he said, "Stay."

The look on her face was priceless, a cross between wanting to stick out her tongue and putting on a mask of royal indifference. He bit his cheek to keep from grinning. A smile would only make what had to happen next more difficult.

He shut the door and hurried back to her. Betony trembled from head to toe and her teeth chattered as she drew her legs to her chest and wrapped her arms around them, desperate for any warmth she could keep.

"We have to get you out of these wet clothes or you're going to freeze. I apologize for the indignity, but I won't let you die."

"S-s-stop ap-polog-g-gizing."

Surprisingly, she didn't fight him. Betony seemed barely able to control her body and those were the last words she uttered. Her rigid muscles almost vibrated as she tried to control the shivers. Her lips were blue and all the color had left her usually rosy cheeks. Dorin sliced through the ropes on her wrists and whipped the tunic off her, keeping his eyes on his own hands and her face. As soon as he dropped the tunic to the floor with a wet squelch, he covered her top half with the blanket.

He left her hands free and hoped it wouldn't bite him in the ass. He doubted it would—she shook so hard, she wouldn't be able to stand straight, let alone walk across the deck.

Dorin freed her ankles and yanked her breeches off in a swift move, trying like hell not to notice the pale, smooth flesh of her thighs as he whipped them across the room. He threw another blanket over her and started stripping down himself. There was little room for modesty on a ship, and if he stayed in these clothes any longer, he'd risk hypothermia, too.

Betony squeaked and looked away, her body still rigid with the cold.

His clothes joined hers on the floor in a big, wet pile. Dorin opened his trunk, pulled out an extra set, and dressed quickly. The best part was putting on warm woolen socks. He wiggled his toes.

A knock sounded.

"Come in."

Signe strode in, carrying a steaming, fragrant carafe and an extra set of clothes.

"Thank you. Her shivering is bad. Can you help her dress?"

The large woman nodded and handed him the carafe. He sipped it. Ah, spiced grog. Perfect.

"I'll be outside, Princess. If you don't give the kind Signe any trouble, I'll share this with you when you're dressed."

He shut the door behind him. No protests arose, no clattering from a scuffle.

Dorin watched the port of Nimel disappear over the horizon. It had been a long shot she'd make it to shore when she jumped. Now it was impossible. He heaved a sigh of relief. His mad plan had actually worked. He'd kidnapped the princess, saved her life, and gotten away with it. All he'd lost in the process was his self-respect. And hers.

A few moments later, Signe emerged.

"She's dressed," she said.

"I owe you one."

"I know. I'm keeping score."

Dorin smiled, then slipped into his cabin. Betony sat on the small bunk, leather-clad legs pulled to her chest, bright red socks on her feet, and the blanket wrapped tightly around her. The edges of a blue wool tunic peeked out. She still shivered, but her jaw was clenched so tight her teeth no longer rattled.

"Here, have some. It'll warm you up." He handed her the grog.

She pushed it away.

"It's not dosed with anything. Just grog." He sipped again, and the warmth of it flowed down his throat and out to his extremities.

"I don't want anything else from you," she said through clenched teeth.

"Listen, I don't want you dead. You don't want you dead. In fact, if you die, it will throw both our homelands into war, as your father will rightly seek revenge. Neither of us wants that. Drink the damn grog."

She snatched it from him and guzzled some, coughing as the strong liquor burned her throat.

He couldn't help himself. "Good g—"

Betony kicked his shin before he got the last word out. Between the socks and her trembling, it landed a glancing blow at best, but he shut his mouth anyway.

Note to self, do not call her a good girl. He rubbed his jaw where she'd tagged him earlier.

She took another drink and managed not to cough. She passed the carafe to him and scooted back. No longer shivering, she wrapped her arms around her legs. Some color had returned to her lips.

"It's too late to try that trick again. Until we're close to our destination, we'll be too far for you to swim to shore safely. I understand your desire to go home and that you do not want to be here."

"You understand nothing," she mumbled before yawning.

He softened his tone but kept his face neutral. "You need rest after your little adventure. The captain graciously allowed you his cabin, but you repaid his kindness by jumping overboard. You'll stay here with me so I can keep a closer eye on you."

"You're sleeping on the floor."

"No shit. Only way to make sure you stay in this room. And it's called a deck on a ship, Your Highness. Now rest."

She glared at him once more before turning over. When her breathing evened out, Dorin went to the quartermaster and procured an extra bedroll, but he wasn't tired yet. His nerves still jangled from Betony's dive overboard. He walked to the stern.

"Not thinking of jumping again, are you?" Mertok asked. "If so, let me lower the dinghy first."

Dorin chuckled. Mertok could be an ass, but the captain of *Zovog's Revenge* owed a debt to Dorin's mother. Since she was dead, he owed it to Dorin. They'd developed a…friendship was the only word that came to mind. As soon as the debt was repaid, all bets were off. Betony's antics today erased a part of the debt.

Dorin hoped she'd see reason and not toss the only card he held overboard.

"No. The princess and I have come to an arrangement."

"Outstanding," Mertok said, his voice becoming steel, "because if she endangers my crew or my ship again, you and I will have the sort of discussion that usually doesn't go well for the person on the other side of my desk."

"Yes, Captain." Dread filled Dorin's gut much the same as it had when he watched Betony jump overboard.

Mertok clapped a hand to Dorin's shoulder before going about his duties.

Dorin had known this was a bad idea from the beginning, but the idea of harm coming to Betony was abhorrent. Though every action he'd taken had been to protect her life, he'd done nothing but hurt her. He was her worst enemy, and she hated him. The night of the masquerade was a faded dream of a moment, one that would never happen again. It was time to stop thinking with his heart and, to be honest, other parts of his anatomy, and start thinking with his head.

No more pining. No more wishing. No more gentleman. It was time for the midnight man to take over.

Chapter 17

etony didn't sleep.

Her body was too sore, her mind too busy, her heart too broken. She'd had one chance, and she'd blown it. She was stuck on this ship, at the mercy of the man who'd kidnapped her.

Though his mercy seemed particularly merciful, he *had* threatened to drop her back in the ocean.

She said nothing when he returned a bit later. The soft rustle of a bedroll unfurling, the thump of boots hitting the deck, and a small groan all made her think of the brief glimpse of his well-muscled chest a few minutes ago. He might be the enemy, but he had a body worthy of the best fairy warriors. So what was he?

Betony waited for his breathing to slow before she turned over. He lay right in front of the door. Not like she'd leave—where would she go? They were decidedly too far from shore. They may have been too far from shore when she jumped, but she had to try.

"It's as much for your protection as it is to keep you confined." His eyes were still shut.

How—

Giving an exasperated huff, she turned back over.

"Some of my fellow Fuartirans don't care for fairies, even if their magic is bound."

"I'm not a fairy," she muttered.

"Might as well be, as far as they're concerned. The distinction between fae and fairy matters little in Fuartir."

This irked her more than it should have. Her entire life, she'd been neither fairy nor human, straddling the boundary between the two. Her parents had protected her for as long as they could, then sent her away. It still stung, though the years taught her it had been for the best. The fairies hadn't judged her for her differences, yet she never was truly one of them either.

"Why?" Betony turned over again and sat.

"Why what?"

"Why do your people hate fairies?"

Dorin groaned and ran his hands through his hair. "It's late, Princess, and I'm fucking exhausted. I dove into an ocean in the winter to save your lovely ass, and I'd really like to sleep."

"I was perfectly willing to pretend you weren't here. You started this conversation." She tapped his foot with hers. The room was tiny, and there was barely space for two as it was.

"I didn't want you to hurt yourself trying to escape. Again. Now I'm wishing I'd let you find out the hard way."

She nudged his foot again. "No, you aren't."

He pulled his foot back and glared at her. "You don't know what I'm thinking."

"I can guess."

"Fine, then guess," he ground out and begrudgingly sat up, keeping his back against the only exit.

Crap, he'd called her bluff. Well, the worst that would happen was that he'd declare her insights wrong and laugh at her.

"You kidnapped me when others would have killed me. You treated me with respect even while kidnapping me. You keep apologizing. And you jumped into the ocean to save me. You care what happens to me. You say it's to avoid a war, but I believe it's something more."

He leaned his head back with a soft thump. "I'm a fool, that's why."

Betony bit her cheek to keep from smiling. He didn't deserve her smile.

He kidnapped you, drugged you, and dragged you back to the ship when you tried to escape. He is not your friend. But he is a fool if he thinks you're giving up.

She tried to channel her mother's best queenly expression. "You have my gratitude."

"Fuck your gratitude. Believe it or not, I'm trying to ensure my chief gets what he wants without our countries going to war. He may be a bloodthirsty warlord, but if anyone can convince the other bloodthirsty warlords to sit down and make a country, it's Chief Kalman. When he makes that happen, he will have earned the title of king."

"Brilliant job so far. Your ambassador threatened the life of a child and you kidnapped a princess."

He rubbed his face. "Don't remind me. I'm making the best of a bad situation. And speaking of which, this will all be easier with a good night's sleep under our belts. We'll talk more about my poor life choices tomorrow. And your own might come up, too."

"What poor life choices? I was abducted," she snapped, unwilling to admit she'd also trusted the wrong man.

"You were outside the castle without a guard, one of the worst choices a royal can make. And you trusted me. I have no idea why."

Betony clenched her jaw to keep from sticking her tongue out at him like a child. But she was so tempted, not the least because the scoundrel was right. If she hadn't gone out without guards, if she hadn't trusted the simple manservant he pretended to be, none of this would have happened.

"Goodnight," she ground out, flopping on the bunk and turning her back to him.

"May Alet send you sweet dreams and Zovog miss your pillow tonight," he said softly as he nestled into his bedroll.

His blessing settled over her, bringing an odd sort of comfort, and Betony finally drifted off.

He was gone when she woke in the morning, the bedroll neatly stowed at the end of the bunk. She found another coat hanging on a hook and her boots waited by the door. Shoving her feet into the boots, she slipped on the coat and walked out into the bright day. She stayed close to the cabin, avoiding the sailors scurrying to and fro.

Dorin stood at the stern, next to a big man with a bushy beard. From his lack of activity, Betony assumed he was the captain of this vessel. Every other person moved with purpose and speed, but not those two. They must be plotting her fate.

She didn't want to talk to either of them. Turning away, Betony walked to the bow, drawing her hands within the overlarge coat's sleeves to stave off the cold. After her swim, she had no desire to be that cold ever again.

There was nothing in front of them other than the rolling blue waves of the Roheda, and the sharp scent of salt water filled the air. They were far enough from land no gulls cried. The only sound was the splash of water against the hull, the calls of the crew, and the creak of the ship. For the first time since she'd been sent to live in the Faerie capital of Neraida, Betony was truly alone.

Two sets of booted feet clomped on the deck behind her.

"Princess Betony of Lorea, may I present Captain Mertok of the *Zovog's Revenge*?"

There was something in Dorin's tone, something familiar she couldn't quite place. Betony wished she could ignore him, but years of training in both the Lorean and Faerie courts had her turning for the introduction.

The captain pulled off an elegant bow. "Your Highness, welcome aboard. I wish the circumstances were more…genial, but I hope you are comfortable."

This was no occasion for overt courtesy, but a captain was king on their ship, and Captain Mertok could make her life difficult if he chose to. She dipped her chin slowly, acknowledging the courtesy.

"As comfortable as I could hope, given the *circumstances*." She kept her voice neutral. "You have a fine ship, captain."

He beamed as though she'd called his wife beautiful. The ship was likely even more important to him than any spouse, child, or god.

"Thank you, Your Highness. She's fast and sturdy and does her job well. She'll have you in Cseobar within six days. You have the run of the ship as long as you don't interfere with my crew and their work. I have a few books in my cabin should you need to occupy yourself. Dorin can fetch them."

Books. The few she noticed in her brief stay in the captain's cabin did not seem promising entertainment for six days. She'd be bored by sunset.

"I appreciate the offer, but may I ask to be of more use to the crew, especially since I put them at risk yesterday?"

He cocked an eyebrow. "What do you have in mind?"

"I'm a fair hand with a needle. If you need clothing or sails repaired, I'll make short work of it."

Rane had hated anything to do with a needle and thread. Ebon would have blown through the captain's books in a day or two at most. But Betony had loved the feel of the needle in her fingers, the soft texture of the embroidery silk, the satisfaction of punching a hole in fabric over and over, until a work of beauty took the place of her unexpressed emotions. No silk here, but fixing something, anything, would give her a purpose while onboard. And she needed a better outlet for her anger than hitting Dorin again.

"Aye, that could be arranged, and the crew will appreciate it. Few have any skill, and there is little opportunity to mend clothing. Dorin will introduce you to the quartermaster and get you started. Please join me for dinner tonight."

"I'd be honored," she responded, the polite words out before she could stop them. Her mother had trained her well, as had her time with the fairies. They were all sticklers for manners.

Mertok chuckled as he sketched a bow once more and returned to tending his ship and crew. Dorin stayed.

"I wasn't expecting that," Dorin said.

"What did you expect?" She turned back to the view from the bow.

He joined her at the railing. "Silence, maybe. More swearing, definitely."

"I don't swear."

He coughed, and she glared at him. He looked innocent, too innocent.

"Usually," she allowed. "Besides, it would have gotten me nothing. This way, I stay busy and he sees I am useful."

She refused to rely solely on Dorin's assurance he would protect her.

"Beautiful, courageous, and smart."

She snorted elegantly. Rane always complained it was unfair Betony could snort elegantly.

"Flattery gets you nowhere. What will you be doing to pass the time?"

Why was she engaging him in conversation? He was her captor, not her friend. And yet, a lifetime of manners and his gentle way with her had blurred the line already. Not to mention her inexplicable attraction to her abductor. This did not bode well for the next several days, let alone for her indefinite stay in Fuartir.

Keep it civil, keep it impersonal, and keep looking for an opportunity to escape.

"Mending clothes and sails. Where you go, I go, Princess."

"Well, then, lead the way. I have no idea what a quartermaster is, nor where to find such a being."

He offered his arm. Once again, her training kicked in, and she took it. His arm was warm and muscular, and she had to shake off the feeling they'd walked like this before.

Chapter 18

hree days passed. The mending had been done, the sails repaired, and Dorin's fingers hurt from all the needlework.

Betony didn't even seem to notice. Day after day, she bent over the smelly clothes and the thick sailcloth and sewed. Her stitches were fine, neat, and straight, while Dorin's were…passable. She had him work on the sails while she handled the crew's clothes.

"A sail doesn't care as long as it holds," she'd said.

She earned thanks from most crew members and a sweet treat from the cook.

As surreptitiously as possible, Dorin watched Betony as she worked. She hummed, too, soothing melodies he missed whenever he was away from her. He continued to sleep on the deck between the bunk and the door to his tiny cabin—their tiny cabin.

The morning of the fifth day since they left harbor dawned cloudy and windy, ill weather for making it home by the next day. The ship rocked, and even many of the seasoned crew members looked a bit green about the gills. Dorin left Betony asleep in the cabin and stumbled across the deck to the captain's quarters. He knocked.

"Come," Mertok said.

Dorin stepped in. The captain held a steaming mug and dunked some travel bread into it to soften.

"Good morning, Captain."

"Bah, nothing good about this morning. This storm came out of nowhere. We'll be lucky to pull into the harbor by tomorrow sunset. And I have a bad feeling about it. Smells like a Zovog-cursed squall."

The air seemed to leave the room. It was early in the season for a Zovog-cursed squall. True to its name, it was a bastard of a storm. Every Fuartiran had at least a distant relative lost to one of these. The only thing that killed more Fuartirans than other Fuartirans was the storm-tossed sea.

"Anything I can do to help?"

"Besides praying to Zovog? Keep your princess in the cabin, especially if you want her to live."

His princess. Not likely, but the thought sent a thrill up his spine despite the dire situation. The last thing Dorin wanted was for Betony to be a sacrifice to the god of death and thunder. At least a couple of the crew were destined for the waves.

"Of course, Captain."

"Excellent. Grab some bread and drink from the galley and hunker down in your cabin."

Dorin took his leave and did just that, procuring enough for Betony, too. The skies darkened further, the clouds low and ominous, and the winds whipped through his coat as he crossed the deck again. The howling woke her when he opened the door to the cabin.

She sat up and rubbed her eyes. "What's going on?"

His heart skipped a beat. Betony was a fierce, capable fighter, but when she woke in the morning, she looked like any other woman: vulnerable and soft and oh so fuckable.

"Squall." He pushed aside the thoughts and answered her gruffly. She didn't want him, rightly so. He was here to see her safely to the port of Cseobar and ensure she was returned to her family. Nothing more. "We have to stay in the cabin. Crew's going to be busy and we'll be in the way. Brought you some food, but if you're going to puke it back up, best to set it aside until the waves die down."

She looked at the bread in his hands and slowly shook her head. "I already feel it. Give me the mug. Something warm sounds good."

He put the bread on the small table and handed her the mug. She sipped it and he leaned against the door. The howling wind snuck in through the cracks and the shouts of the crew were barely audible.

"How long until it's over?" she asked after a few uncomfortable moments.

He laughed. "Over? Princess, it hasn't even begun."

As if to reiterate his point, the crashing boom of thunder rattled the air and shook the ship. Betony squeaked and her eyes widened in the dim cabin. With only the storm-cast light coming from cracks around the door, it was almost dark as night.

"Why aren't you out there helping?"

"I'm a manservant, not a sailor."

She arched a brow at his statement but chose only to challenge the last half. "But don't most Fuartirans know how to sail?"

He sighed and slowly dropped to the floor. It was going to be a long day, and he might as well get comfortable.

"Don't most Loreans know how to farm?"

Another crash and ship dipped drastically.

Betony bit her lip. "Yes, but we're not all farmers. I mean, I'll help out in the kitchen garden, maybe volunteer in the orchard at harvest, but it's more fun than work."

"Same here. It's helpful to learn many skills, and I could help in a pinch, but right now, the experts are at work. If they need me, they'll come get me. The best thing I can do is make sure you're safe and stay the fuck out of the way."

"Okay," she said as the ship dipped again.

A trickle of water snuck under the door. Shit, he was going to be wet and miserable. He scooted away.

"You should sit next to me." Betony scrunched up at the far side of the bunk, knees to chest, and drew a blanket around her. "At least put your bedroll here so it doesn't get wet."

"Are you sure?" He peered at her. Was this some sort of trick?

She rolled her eyes and pulled the blanket closer.

"I wouldn't offer if I wasn't sincere, Dorin. You should know that about me by now. If you want to spend the storm soaking wet only to have a wet bedroll to crawl into once it's spent, that's entirely up to you."

Arguing with her would be pointless. He could choose to be relatively warm and dry, or wet and miserable. He'd spent enough time in his life wet, cold, or otherwise miserable, so the bunk it was.

"Thank you."

He placed the bedroll between them and sat much as she did.

"What's Cseobar like?" she asked after he got comfortable.

Dorin peered at her. Was she fishing for information to better plan her escape? And how in the underworld would she escape from Cseobar? There was nowhere else to go except another clan, and that would be a disaster for her. The other clans had no incentive to keep her alive and well. In fact, many of them had an incentive to do just the opposite.

Another boom of thunder caused her to jump. She tucked her toes under the blanket and rested her forehead on her knees.

"I don't like thunderstorms," she said in a small voice after the echoes died off. "Can we light the lamp?"

"No. It's too dangerous." It would be far too easy for a lamp to tip over in a storm and start a fire. If light wasn't needed, the lamp stayed out.

"Then could you talk to me, keep my mind off it? If you don't want to tell me about your home city, tell me about your gods, or your parents, or anything. Please."

She used a corner of the blanket to wipe under her eyes. Oh, Alet help him, she was crying. If there was one thing he couldn't abide, it was a woman crying in fear.

"Like the fairies, we have two gods." He settled into the storytelling cadence he was taught as a child at his mother's feet. "Alet, the god of light and life, and Zovog, the god of thunder and death. Zovog forged the world as we know it, and Alet graced it with life."

"So Alet is…Idoya?"

"Not quite. Our gods are neither male nor female, though have aspects of both. Most Fuartirans pray to Alet for the everyday things: happiness, good fortune, enough to eat, that the chickens lay and the bread doesn't burn. Alet sends pleasant dreams, the calm in the midst of a storm, and rainbows after."

"You tell the story well." She quirked her lips.

Dorin squeezed his legs tighter. He rarely talked about his mother; he'd found at a young age mentioning the hero of Cseobar was a quick way to rile people. His father wanted to pretend she hadn't existed, and the rest of the community venerated her.

"My mother taught me. She was a cleric of Zovog but knew all the stories."

"Knew?"

"She died a long time ago."

"I'm sorry."

Nothing anyone could do, then or now. But Betony's simple words of sympathy were more than most people ever said to him, even as a child, and a warmth grew deep in his belly.

"Zovog is nearly Alet's opposite," he continued, unwilling to examine the strange sensation sharing his mother's stories with her caused. "They send the nightmares, the storms, and collect the dead after. We pray to Zovog to stave off famine, to ease the passing of the sick and injured, and to call the winds to our raiding vessels. But we do not pray every day. No one wants daily attention from the god of death. Instead, we have community rituals and sacrifices to appease them."

Betony shivered. "Sacrifices?"

He smiled at this. "Chickens mostly, the occasional goat or sheep. The clerics' families eat well at rites."

A small snort escaped her. Dorin had never heard someone snort in such a refined manner, but he took it as a sign his stories were helping. Another boom of thunder shook the ship. Her shoulders tensed under the blanket, and she shrunk back from him. More water trickled in, a nice wet layer under the bunk.

"Once upon a time—" he said.

"Seriously, a fairy tale? I am not a child," she snapped.

"Do you want to learn more about my culture, or would you rather face the wrath of Zovog in silence? Besides, all the best stories start with 'Once upon a time.'"

She said nothing further, but her gaze met his. A sheen of unease and a hard determination rested in the emerald depths of her eyes. Alet, she was beautiful, even in her fear. But this woman could not be his, as much as he might want her. He'd broken her trust by not only kidnapping her but pretending to be something he was not. Perhaps this small offering of a story might help.

"Once upon a time, when the world was newly forged, only Alet and Zovog walked the shores. The god of life paused frequently, and wherever they lingered, new plants sprung from the earth. But this made inspecting their new creation slow, and Zovog grew impatient and angry. Zovog called down the lightning, burning the plants Alet had brought into being."

Betony's head rested on the wall behind her, and her eyes were closed.

"Go on," she said when he paused for too long, wondering if she was listening.

"'Why have you destroyed my creation, Zovog?' Alet asked, tears welling. As they fell, a raging river formed and washed Zovog out to sea. But Zovog was a strong swimmer and paddled back to shore quickly. They called another bolt of lightning, striking the sand at Alet's feet. 'You are too slow and there is much to see,' Zovog said."

The rhythm of the story flowed through him, echoing his mother's voice from all those years ago. This had been the story she'd told the night she'd died, before she'd sent him to the safety of the chief's compound. Ever since, he'd left the room whenever someone else tried to tell it, but the words came easily, as though no time at all had passed. As though his mother still lived through her words.

"Alet picked up the fulgurite. It sparkled in the light, sending rainbows into the sky. 'We created this world together, Zovog, but now we must create separately. Look at what you have wrought in your anger, while trying to destroy what I have wrought in my joy.'

"Zovog took the rock from Alet and heated it in their hands, creating a scythe sharper than anything made since. 'Then you will create all the living things you wish. But know each one has an ending. Nothing will live forever except the two of us. What you sow, I reap, so create carefully.'"

A tear escaped the corner of Betony's eye, but she didn't wipe it away. These had been his mother's last words, and he realized after nearly twenty years she had been imparting a final lesson. She had known where her duty lay, and she had faced it. Every living thing had an ending, and through her connection to Zovog, she knew hers approached.

The rest of the words stuck in his throat, thickened by his mother's gift. Betony opened her eyes and dashed away the tear. He swallowed and waited for her reaction. If she asked him to continue, he had no idea what he'd tell her.

"Thank you. I needed to hear a tale like that. You're a good storyteller."

"I'll tell my mother when we meet in the afterlife."

She reached out a delicate hand, and it hovered over his for an interminable moment. The corners of her lips twitched, but her half smile vanished when the door to the cabin crashed open. Two crew members dragged in an unconscious Signe.

Chapter 19

Betony's heart beat like a frightened bird's, and she snatched her hand back, grateful for this interruption. Her training kicked in and she jumped up to see to her patient. Whatever foolish thing she'd been about to do would have to wait, thank Idoya.

The blood streaming from Signe's head and shoulder was pink instead of red, the rain and waves mixing with it until it barely resembled blood.

"Here, put her on the bunk."

Her bare feet splashed in the water, the cold sending a shiver through her. Dorin scrambled away, wedging himself in a corner. The tiny cabin was nearly impossible to move in with five people standing when it was made for two at most. The sailors deposited Signe on the bunk.

"Are there more injured?" Betony kneeled in the icy water to examine the woman.

"Nothing too bad, but she took a boom to the head and was unconscious. She almost got washed overboard. Captain told us to stow her somewhere safe. We gotta go."

They didn't wait for any response and tromped out as quickly as they'd tromped in.

Dorin slammed the door shut behind them. "What can I do to help?"

Betony used her blanket to dry the wounds as best she could. They were not as deep as she'd feared, and now that Signe was out of the rain, the bleeding slowed.

"Pass me the mending supplies and light the lamp."

Dorin tossed her the roll of thread and needles, and she almost missed it in the dimness. She tucked it under her arm as the scrape of a flint and steel lighter had her gritting her teeth against the mind-flaying sound. He let out a grunt of triumph, and light soon filled the tiny room. Betony poked and prodded Signe's wounds. A couple of stitches on the forehead should close the wound, and the one on her shoulder was long but shallow. A simple bandage would do. Things could have been so much worse. Now they had to hope she regained consciousness. She pulled out a slightly curved needle and found the thinnest thread she could.

"Do you have some liquor in here?" she asked.

He grunted and rummaged around in a trunk, then passed her a bottle of golden liquid. She poured a little over the wound on Signe's forehead.

"Hold the lantern close," she ordered.

The light moved closer, and his presence loomed over her shoulder, comforting and supportive. She shook away the feeling—it was beyond ridiculous to feel anything of the sort about her captor—and quickly took care of the stitches.

Just in time, too. Signe's eyes fluttered open as Betony snipped the thread.

"What? Where?" The woman's head twisted side to side. She touched her forehead, but Betony pulled it away.

"You need to keep your hands off—I'll apply some salve once the storm's over. I need to clean and bandage the wound on your shoulder. Hold still, please."

Signe nodded, and before Bet could ask, Dorin gave her some toweling.

"Thank you," Betony said, both surprised and impressed.

He muttered something in return, but she couldn't make it out over the howl of the wind and Signe's harsh breathing. She soon got the woman patched up. Signe stood, but the ship rocked, forcing her down to the bunk.

"You shouldn't go back out." Dorin moved in front of the door.

"What, are you a healer of Alet now?" Signe snapped.

"He's right," Betony said. The woman's glare focused on her, but Betony held her ground. "You took a blow to the head, strong enough to knock you out for a while. If you go, you could pass out again, or your vision might be messed up enough you can't perform your duties."

"If they need you, they'll come looking. But listen, the storm is dying."

Betony blinked. In the flurry of activity around Signe, she'd paid no attention to the thunder or the wind. Some part of her was glad for the distraction of a patient. The ship was still rocking, but not nearly as bad, and the water covering the deck hadn't deepened in a while. As she listened, the howling wind seemed to find a softer voice, and no thunder cracked the relative quiet. In fact, she could hear the voices of the crew once more. The shouting was purposeful but not panicked.

The tension she'd been holding since the first boom of thunder bled away. Betony heaved a sigh and sat next to Signe on the bunk.

"How much longer until I can assess the injured?" she asked.

Signe turned to her, eyes narrowed in suspicion. "Why would you help us? We're keeping you here against your will."

Dorin merely stood there against the door, but she felt his gaze upon her, the question hanging thick in the air.

"That would be his fault, not the crew's," she said after a pause, hooking a thumb in Dorin's direction. He snorted but didn't dispute her claim. "And, well, it's what I'm good at. I swore an oath to Idoya and Veitha to heal any who need it, whether they be poor or rich, friend or enemy."

"You are Alet-avowed, then. My thanks, and I thank Alet for the blessing, too." Signe extended her hand with a solemn expression.

Betony took it in friendship and grinned.

"I'll check with the captain. Both of you, stay here," Dorin said quietly.

She twisted to look at him. His tone was off, but his back was to her and he slipped out. She had Signe perform a few small tasks to ensure her faculties had returned. Betony missed her magic now more than ever. A simple touch would have told her everything she needed to know, and a few murmured spells would have fixed whatever was wrong with her patient. But there was a reason the fairy healers focused on both magical and non-magical healing. One could not always rely on magic.

Dorin returned in short order, his face a neutral mask, and Betony glimpsed a sliver of blue sky over his shoulder. Thank the gods.

"The captain says we're almost clear. There are a few injuries, including a couple crew members with broken bones and a few wounds need stitching. But we didn't lose anyone."

"It truly is a miracle from the gods," Signe said. "Can I go help now, healer?"

"Yes," Betony replied, "but if you feel dizzy or lightheaded, sit and send for me. You should be better in a day or two, and someone should take out the stitches in seven days."

Signe hurried out, and two crew members carried in a third whose leg was pointing in the wrong direction. Betony got to work, and the hours passed. Another crew member had a broken wrist, and she spent some time cleaning and stitching deep wounds on legs, arms, and hands. She gave Dorin a list of ingredients for a salve, and he fetched them from the galley and the quartermaster. He watched with a bemused expression as she mixed it.

Before long, the seas had calmed, and she and Dorin went to each crew member she'd treated and spread the salve. The chill breeze and the setting sun finally drove them back inside the cabin. Betony felt every one of the hours she'd spent healing the crew deep in her bones.

She collapsed on the bunk, leaning against the wall, exhausted. Yet the excitement and terror still coursed through her veins. She stared at the ceiling as Dorin grabbed his bedroll.

"What are you doing?" she asked. "The floor is still wet."

"Deck, and no wetter than anywhere else on the ship. I'll be fine."

Betony found the words escaping her before she could stop them. "I'm not sleepy. You can sit next to me for a bit."

He peered at her, and he must have been wondering why she offered. So was she. Why was she offering him any sort of respite? He'd knocked her out more than once—and once should have been enough. He'd kidnapped her, put her on this Idoya-cursed boat in the first place, and had proudly announced she would be hostage to his chief's machinations.

And yet…

He'd kept her safe and distracted during the storm. He'd helped her heal the crew. He'd offered her the courtesy due her station, but never made her feel other for it. And there was something about him, something familiar, something she desperately wished to trust.

With a deep sigh, he placed the bedroll next to her and sat on the other side of it.

"Why are you nice to me?"

Betony chuckled wryly. "You know, I was just asking myself that very question."

"Talking to yourself is never a good sign."

She slowly turned and glared at him, but he was beyond unperturbed by the daggers her imagination sent his way. It was no fun. He looked at her out of the corner of his eye and grinned impishly.

Betony fought the urge to reciprocate, but her expression softened despite her efforts.

"And what did you say to yourself?" Dorin asked after a long silence.

"Still undecided. You don't deserve it."

"I don't, I truly don't. I keep going over that night, if there was another choice I could have made." He ran his hand through his hair, and it stuck up in clumps. It would have been funny if not for the corded muscles in his neck and the anguish in his eyes. The gold specks seemed to dull with it.

"You could have left me alone." The rancor she once harbored was missing from her voice. "You could have accepted the consequences and left in disgrace. Or you could have run and told the ambassador and his crony to do the same."

But he couldn't have, not really. Betony knew the burden of duty, the burden of expectations. She was a Lorean princess, after all. The expectations of her family and her position were hammered into her from the time she was born. And her stay in Faerie only reinforced what she'd already learned. Duty came before everything. Only when fate interfered, only when duty intersected with personal desires, did joy find the Lorean royal children. It had worked for her sister, it had worked for her brother. Surely Idoya's blessing was not generous enough to grant Betony her heart's desire.

"I could have." He leaned his forehead on his drawn-up knees, muffling his voice. "But then I wouldn't be the man I am. As much as I like you, as amazing and beautiful and kind as you are, my duty lies with my clan and my homeland. And though Kalman is a ruthless clan chief, he is the best man to lead the other ruthless clan chiefs. I've met all of them, and they make him seem a wolfhound more than a wolf."

Fate did not intervene, and both Idoya and Veitha had left her to her own devices. On a foreign ship, her magic stripped away, she was alone. One person had shown he cared, had risked a great deal to ensure her safety, but she was not his responsibility. He'd made clear where his loyalty lay. At least he was honest with her.

Betony sighed. "I understand."

A strange expression crossed his face, and he gulped, his throat bobbing.

As if he'd read her mind, Dorin tentatively held out his hand. "Do you trust me, Princess?"

Betony glanced at it and returned her gaze to his. There was something familiar in his soft eyes, his firm jaw, and the slight smile gracing his lips. Did she? Was there actually a choice?

There's always a choice. She could choose not to trust him. It was the safer bet, the easy option. Trust no one, wait for a chance to escape, and take it. But she couldn't do it. A feeling deep in her heart told her to trust this man, despite his desperate, misguided choice. That he valued her welfare as much as he valued his own life.

Tentatively, she placed her hand in his. He gripped it firmly, and shivers of longing traveled up her arm and lodged in her gut, spreading out like butterflies in a meadow.

He knelt at her feet, his expression as solemn as his words. "I will defend you to the death, and your fate will be my fate until you are returned to your family. By Zovog's thunder and Alet's rainbows, I swear it."

His voice resonated through her and his eyes glittered in the light of the lantern, the brown lightened by magical specks of gold. And she knew exactly what it was about him, why he'd been familiar, why she trusted him despite all evidence to the contrary.

Dorin had been the man behind the mask the night of the ball.

Chapter 20

The languid heat from Betony's touch almost caused Dorin to miss the strange spark in her eyes after he vowed to protect her, to share her fate until he could see her safely home. He swore it using the strongest oath he knew, one he'd rarely heard anyone swear. Breaking it would dishonor him and his entire clan. But more importantly, breaking it would mean leaving Betony to whatever fate his father decided or losing her forever.

Lose her? He didn't have her to begin with, but the thought of a world without her in it sent dread through his heart.

"What?" he asked.

She shook her head, but a small secret smile played on her lips.

"Do I have something on my face?" Dorin wiped his other hand down his face, loath to let go of her.

Betony seemed unwilling to break the contact, too. She squeezed his hand gently, and he loosened his grip, but she stayed where she was.

"No. I've never had anyone swear an oath to protect me before. It's a bit…"

"Gallant? Noble? Brave?"

Her nose twitched, as it always did when she was amused. "I was going to say arrogant, but sure, gallant will do."

She nudged his shoulder and a giggle escaped her, its musical nature infectious, and soon he chuckled. As if in a trance, he tugged her closer. His other hand floated up on its own accord and grazed her cheek. Dorin breathed her in, and under the sea water and leftover fear was a sweet herbal scent that was all Betony. His lids grew heavy and his focused slipped to her plump, kissable lips.

Enough of this madness. He had to put some emotional distance between them, otherwise, he wouldn't stop unless she told him to. And the look in her eyes said she wasn't going to do any such thing. It was up to him to stop this in its tracks, before either of them did something they later regretted.

Kissing Betony was the worst idea he ever had. Right up there with kidnapping her in the first place.

He tucked a loose curl behind her ear and smirked. "You think I'm gallant."

Her nose crinkled again and a tinkling laugh filled the space he'd put between them.

Dorin pulled back and leaned against the wall. "It's late, and you must be exhausted. Come here."

He held up his arm and moved the bedroll to the other side. Once more, the strange spark returned, and she considered him for a moment.

"It's cold, and you're still damp. You'll sleep better if you're warm," he said when she didn't move.

"So will you." Her mouth twitched mischievously.

"I never said I was being completely altruistic, Princess. If you recall, you invited me to sit with you. I'm happy to take the deck."

His legs bunched under him as he prepared to rise, but she scooted over and nestled under his arm, resting her head upon his chest. She sighed as though this was exactly what she'd wanted all along. Dorin relaxed, and with a dexterous flick of his wrist, he unrolled his bedroll and covered them both, ensuring neither of them would be cold this night.

"Goodnight, Dorin," she mumbled, closing her eyes.

He waited until her body relaxed into asleep. "Goodnight, Betony. May Alet send you sweet dreams."

Before long, he slept too. And Alet sent him dreams of Betony's soft skin and silky hair and quiet moans.

He woke, hard as a rock, with the very dream woman Alet saw fit to tease him with still snuggled next to him. Or maybe Zovog was tempting him toward his death, for surely that would be his fate should he follow through with such fantasies. Dorin bit his lip and tried to imagine anything besides waking the sleeping princess and bedding her. Fish guts—fish guts were nasty. Mertok's bearded face. Decidedly disagreeable, at least to him. The smell of bilge water.

His erection receded and Dorin breathed a sigh of relief. He gently extricated himself from Betony, allowing her to slump on the bunk, covering her with the blanket. He slipped into the bright sun of a clear sailing day. The crew was dashing about wildly, calling out instructions and responses to orders. It was organized chaos, the way the best run ships usually were.

Dorin dodged the busy sailors and found Captain Mertok in his cabin, poring over a map.

"Morning, Captain," he said.

"Dorin. How's our guest?"

"Asleep."

"She deserves it. I'll thank her before we arrive in port."

"Did the storm set us back?" Dorin peered over the captain's shoulder.

"A little. We would've been there tonight, but now it looks like before midday tomorrow."

Not bad, and a testament to both captain and crew. He had enough time to prepare Betony for what to expect. Zovog's scythe, even he wasn't sure. Clan Fher had never taken a foreign hostage before, and neither fae nor fairy had ever fared well in Fuartir.

"Get some chow from the galley, and both of you should join me for dinner tonight."

"Thank you, Mertok."

The captain waved him away, and Dorin collected some breakfast from the cook. But when he returned to the little room, Betony wasn't there. He deposited the food on the small table and went looking for her.

She stood at the bow, peering at the horizon. If he squinted, he could fool himself into seeing the peaks of the Szerhil mountains.

"How much longer, after the storm?" She did not turn around.

"Tomorrow."

"What happens then?"

He rested a hand on her shoulder. The muscles under his palm relaxed slightly, and Betony leaned into his touch. Dorin stepped closer, and her hip grazed his. He expected her to flinch, but she merely looked at him over her shoulder, brows furrowed in worry.

"Let's talk over some food," he said. "I'm famished."

Biting her lip, Betony nodded slowly. He removed his hand from her shoulder, but she reached out as though to stop him. Dorin hurriedly turned toward the cabin and walked away. If she wasn't strong enough to realize whatever was trying to spark between was a bad idea, it would be his responsibility to ensure they maintained proper boundaries. Without them, heartbreak would be the least dire outcome.

She sat on the bunk, and he handed her the bread and tea the cook had given him. Betony picked at it, but some made it into her mouth. It would have to do. Dorin sat on the stool at the end of the bunk.

"By now, I'm sure Ambassador Vedel has informed King Rowan you are in our custody. Negotiations for what the chief wants will proceed. Once he is satisfied with the agreement, he'll release you."

"I understand the idea of being a hostage, Dorin. But what happens to me? As you have mentioned, Fuartirans aren't often welcoming to fae-born."

"When we dock tomorrow, I'll escort you to the chief's manor. You will be an honored guest who cannot leave without an escort, as much for your safety as to keep you there. As long as you don't try to escape, it shouldn't be too different from your usual life."

Her jaw clenched, and the bread crumbled under her grip. She seemed as if she wanted to throw something at his head, and Dorin didn't blame her in the least. He'd brought this on her, and he deserved no forgiveness for his actions. In the end, he wouldn't have done anything differently, anyway. How could he? Duty demanded he put the interests of Clan Fher above all else.

"Fine, but this won't go how you hope. Lorea won't be bullied." She shoved the bread in her mouth and washed it down with the tea.

If she ever turned her anger on him, he'd be fucked.

"Lorea may be too strong to be bullied, but is your father?"

Betony straightened and put aside her teacup. "My first trip to Faerie at thirteen, I begged my parents to let me stay in Lorea. I'd known nothing else. Unlike my sister and my brother, I was rarely allowed out of the castle. Although they were kind about it, they told me in no uncertain terms I didn't have a choice. By treaty, the royal children of Lorea spend two months every year in the Faerie Court from the age of thirteen until they turn twenty-one. At the solstice ball after I turned eighteen, I danced with a boy my age. We moved to the gardens where things got…heated. I lost control of my magic, the magic that lets me talk to animals, and the hounds nearly attacked him. I was sent to Faerie for as long as it would take to gain control of my magic. For my own good, as well as the good of the realm and my people. Don't talk to me about sacrifice or what my parents would or wouldn't do for Lorea."

Dorin froze, bread halfway to his mouth. He'd thought she went because she wanted to go, because she would be among kindred spirits, not because her parents forced her to go. Alet forgive him his stupidity, they were more alike than he assumed. He saw a privileged princess and believed she would never understand sacrifice or duty.

"I'm sorry," he said.

His father had proven willing to sacrifice him for the good of Fuartir many times over. He was useful to his clan, but the only person who loved him had died when he was eight. It hurt to admit his father didn't care about him at all, but Dorin did himself no favors by denying the truth.

Betony blinked, but some of the tension left her, and she stopped strangling the last of her breakfast.

"What did I say about telling me you're sorry?" she grumbled good-naturedly, lifting the teacup again.

"To not to, but I mean it. My life hasn't been easy, but that doesn't forgive assuming your life has been."

"I'm not going to hold you to your vow."

"You don't have to. I will protect you, Betony, you just need to trust me."

She smiled, half wry, half amused. "You know, the villains in the stories always say that."

He snorted. "Do I look like a villain?"

Betony bit her lip, drawing his attention to the perfect bow. He remembered how she tasted, how she'd felt, in his dreams. The tight hold on his control threatened to loosen. He was a hairsbreadth away from kneeling at her feet, freeing her lip from her teeth with his thumb, and kissing the breath out of her when the mischievous smirk returned.

"Ask me again tomorrow."

Her words broke the spell she stitched around him. A spell without a single hint of magic, but perhaps all the more powerful because of it.

Beyond relieved, Dorin laughed, and her musical giggle threaded into his heart, his soul.

Chapter 21

*A*gainst all reason, Betony had wanted Dorin to kiss her last night. She wished she'd had the guts to close the gap herself and kiss him first, repay him for the night of the ball. The gentleness, the heat of that moment still drifted through her dreams, both awake and asleep. For an instant this morning, she thought he might try again.

Last night had been a fluke, of course. Nerves, fear, and relief mixing into the perfect storm of need—the need for connection, for kindness, for a kiss. At least, almost. This duty-bound more-than-a-manservant had more in common with her than anyone she'd ever met. Their circumstances were different, but deep down, there was a kindred bond between them.

It wouldn't happen again. It couldn't happen again. He had his duty, after all, as he'd made abundantly clear. And she had hers escape.

Betony made the rounds after breakfast, ensuring her many patients were healing adequately. She mixed a fresh batch of the salve and reapplied it as she changed bandages. No sign of infection. The two with broken bones rested comfortably in the crew quarters in the hold, and those she'd stitched up seemed to be taking the care needed to keep the wounds closed.

But her mind drifted to her revelation of the night prior. Her mystery lord at the ball had been Dorin. The unforgettable eyes, the firm yet graceful body. The voice that had made her insides twist and turn in a way that should have been uncomfortable but warmed her instead. How had she not put it together? Sure, the accent was different—he'd spoken like a Teruellan at the ball—but the voice was the same. All the more obvious now that she'd finally figured it out.

Admittedly, she had been preoccupied the last several days with trying to escape. And mending to keep her mind off failing to escape. And a storm. And—

"…milady? Betony?" Signe's voice finally cleared her mind of her whirling thoughts. "Is everything alright?"

"I'm sorry, what were you saying?" She finished applying the new bandage and started packing her supplies. "My mind wandered for a moment."

"Ah, yes, Dorin." Signe snorted a laugh.

"No! No, there is no reason for me to think about Dorin. Why…why would I be thinking about *him*?"

"I don't know, but you're protesting an awful lot for *not* thinking about him."

"Hmmph." Betony wished she had a better comeback, but she must be wearing her thoughts on her sleeve for Signe to mention it.

"That's not a denial." Signe stood and stretched.

"How's the head?" Betony asked, hoping to distract the other woman.

Smirking, Signe allowed her to change the subject. "Aches a little, tender where the boom hit, but no blurriness or double vision."

"Excellent. You should be fully healed by the time those stitches come out."

Bet turned to leave.

"The way Dorin looks at you…he's thinking about you, too," the sailor said, almost as though talking to someone else.

Betony nodded and slipped out of the hold. Dorin looked at her, thought about her. What was she supposed to do with such information? It changed nothing and only further muddied the waters. There were two Dorins, as far as she could tell. The first had been a gentleman at the ball, the man who had comforted her in the midst of a storm, the one who had vowed to protect her. And the other was the pawn of Chief Kalman, the man who had kidnapped her, the man who would allow his clan to use her to further their ambitions. She feared the first was the more dangerous.

Which one would win in the end? And did she even want to be around to find out?

The day passed quickly, and once the sun set, she and Dorin joined the captain in his cabin for dinner. A whole roasted fish graced the middle of the table, surrounded by herbed potatoes and carrots. A short voyage meant food stores hadn't been depleted, and they'd eaten well, but this was a work of art. Her stomach rumbled at the rich scents in the air.

"Please sit." Captain Mertok pulled out a chair for her.

With as much elegance as she showed in court, Betony sat and gently unfolded her napkin before laying it on her lap. Dorin sat next to her, and Mertok poured a golden wine into the goblets on the table.

"Teruellan white," he said. "Hard to come by in Fuartir, but I bought a few bottles for special occasions while in Nimel."

"Thank you," Betony said as Mertok served her some fish and vegetables.

She waited until both the captain and Dorin had loaded their plates before taking the first bite. The delicious tang of citrus melded with the savory, smoky fish.

"I didn't know your cook was this good," Dorin said after his first bite.

Betony was too busy to speak, eating as fast as she could while still seeming polite and ladylike.

"I don't want him to get poached by another ship. And the crew doesn't care as long as the food is unspoiled and hot more often than not."

She sipped at the wine, which perfectly complemented the meal. She needed to accept the idea that the northerners weren't barbarians. They appreciated the finer things in life as much as any other people did. Perhaps they raided, but they also practiced diplomacy. And when faced with a choice of killing someone or kidnapping them, one particular northerner chose mercy. While it may have been for political reasons, she couldn't stop herself from hoping something of the personal affected his decision too.

"Are you both ready for tomorrow?" the captain asked.

"Yes," said Dorin.

"No," said Betony.

She glared at him, and he shrugged with a smirk on his lips. His very kissable lips. Dear Mother of All, she had to stop thinking of him like that. He was her kidnapper and her protector, which was complicated enough. She'd be mad to add "lover" to the list.

Captain Mertok chuckled and drank more wine. "Guess it doesn't matter. It's coming whether you're ready or not. She's tiny. Will you be able to find furs to fit?"

"'She' is right here," Betony protested. "And I'm not tiny."

She was barely taller than some pixies in their full form, but she was not about to admit anything to the captain. She liked Dorin, and Mertok had been nothing but courteous to her, but she didn't trust him. Despite her protests to the contrary, she did trust Dorin. Likely she'd succumbed to his charm, but he'd seemed beyond sincere when he'd vowed to protect her.

And his eyes. And the kiss at the ball, said the annoying voice in the back of her mind.

Fine, yes, lust played no small role, Idoya help her.

"Yes you are, Princess, but I'll find something appropriate to keep you warm." Dorin said it matter-of-factly, but the gold flecks in his eyes lit up like the sparks from a fire.

The double meaning had her warm in places that hadn't been warm in a long time. She should stop flirting with her kidnapper, she really should. But Betony didn't want to. Unlike her sister, she wasn't known for living dangerously. She'd played by the rules her entire life, trying to be the obedient daughter.

And what had playing by the rules earned her? Confinement to the castle as a child, banishment to Faerie as an adult. She had a chance for different choices in Fuartir. Maybe she should follow her instincts and add "lover" to the list after all.

"…isn't that right, Princess Betony?" Captain Mertok asked.

She'd missed the first part of his question. She glanced at Dorin hopefully, but all the help he would give her was a playful smirk, as if he knew exactly what his words had done to her.

"Yes, Captain, that's right," she said to avoid an overly awkward silence.

Apparently pleased, the captain continued on about some of the ports he'd been to. All legitimately, of course. They polished off the bottle of wine, and the captain unveiled a pancake torte covered with a rich orange sauce. It was the most decadent thing she'd eaten since the night of the ball. The memory had her sneaking glances at Dorin, who seemed ignorant of the effect he had on her. Bastard.

"Why don't you go to the cabin?" Dorin said after she'd swallowed the last bite of dessert. "The captain wishes to discuss something of an official nature. I'll be there shortly."

"Thank you for a lovely dinner, Captain Mertok. I wish we could have met under better circumstances."

He rose and gave her a graceful bow. "As do I, Princess Betony. Thank you for tending to my crew. If I do not have the opportunity to say so tomorrow, goodbye and good luck."

She bowed back and went to her little cabin. Their little cabin.

Bet kicked off her boots and sat on the bunk, tempted to wait for Dorin. Oh so tempted. Instead, she pulled the blanket over her and closed her eyes before she did something reckless. Sleep claimed her quickly.

Betony woke to the calling crew and Dorin rolling up his bedding.

"We're almost there." He tossed the roll into the corner of the cabin. "There's some warm water in the carafe if you want to wash. I'll wait outside."

There was also some bread and cheese, but Betony first poured some warm water on a cloth and did what she could to wash away days' worth of sweat and dirt in the cold. It wasn't much, but it would have to do.

"I'm done," she called out as she pulled on her boots.

Dorin returned and sat at the table, chewing mechanically on the bread and cheese. Betony braided her hair and snagged her portion. She nibbled at it, but it tasted like dust. Today, she would meet the man truly in control of her fate, Chief Kalman. No matter Dorin's vow, if his chief ordered her imprisoned or harmed, what could he do?

He stared at her, as though taking a last look. She still hadn't told him she'd figured it out, that he was her mysterious dancing partner from the masquerade. That she trusted him because of it. Idoya only knew why. He'd lied to her then. Hadn't he? Ridiculous. She was not going to be one of those flighty nitwits who fell for their captors in the fairytales. She was Betony of Lorea—princess, warrior, healer.

"What?" she asked after his long stare started to get on her nerves.

Dorin blinked, a blush coloring his cheeks as he looked away. "Sorry."

"Afraid things won't go the way you planned?" Betony prodded, unable to keep a hint of acid out of her voice.

"Something like that."

"*Something like that.* My life is on the line, and that's all you have to say?"

He leaned against the door. "I will protect you, Betony. I swore it, and I keep my promises."

A thrill ran through her. Was this the first time he'd used her name without her title? It might be, and she liked it. A lot. There she was, being ridiculous again. He was not her lover, never could be. Let it go.

"But—"

He leaned forward, his gaze dark and his jaw set. "Are you doubting my word? Because if you are, this conversation will take an entirely different turn, and I doubt either of us will appreciate where it ends up. Doubting an oath sworn to both Alet and Zovog is not conducive to good health in Fuartir."

She swallowed. It wasn't just the words, but his dangerous look. Most of the time, Dorin seemed a perfectly nice man. Polite, gentle, honorable, noble, even. She liked that Dorin. The look on his face now was the opposite of all those. His words were cool and measured, but there was a hard edge to them. And something told her he'd be less than polite and gentle should she challenge him. There was a dangerous streak Dorin hid well, but that streak did things to her insides. Warm things, pounding things, wet things.

"No, I don't doubt your word."

The dangerous thrum in the air subsided. She missed it, wanted to grab hold of it and stoke it higher. What was wrong with her?

"Then do you doubt my ability?"

Betony tore her gaze away and looked at her feet. A shuffling sound came from the far side, and Dorin knelt next to her. His finger nestled under her chin, and he lifted her head until her eyes met his.

"I have spent most of my life training with blades, poisons, and all manner of weapons." The gold motes shone brightly in the daylight. His voice threaded through the space between them, insinuating itself into her mind, wrapping her fear up with a little bow and stowing it far from her conscious thoughts. "I have become a weapon myself. The only way harm will come to you is over my dead body."

She closed the gap between them and kissed him. At first a brush as gentle as sunlight's caress on a warm spring day. He froze for an instant before kissing her back. He cupped her cheek in his rough hand and deepened the kiss. She gasped as all the passion from the ball, all the temptation from the night after the storm, crashed into her. She opened beneath the firm pressure and lost all reason. As they devoured each other, she wanted nothing between them. No space, no clothes, and definitely no more lies. She wanted this weapon of a man as hers.

And somehow, she would make it happen.

Chapter 22

D orin didn't let himself think, didn't let himself consider the consequences, didn't let himself hesitate. He could kiss her forever. Soft moans escaped her as he dipped his tongue in, her sweetness pouring into him, yet a searing flame danced under the candy layer. He'd let it burn him if it meant he could kiss her every day. Her softness yielded against him, and the desperate desire to taste every inch of her threatened to overwhelm him.

He broke away and leaned his forehead against hers, whispering, "I'm sorry."

Her fingers grazed his jaw. "I'm not."

He looked at her, truly looked. Her eyes blazed with desire, her lips parted, and her breaths came fast. She untangled their joined hands and brought his to rest above her heart. It thumped wildly beneath his palm, and he couldn't take his eyes off his hand so close to her breast. If he spread his fingers, he would brush against the soft flesh, rub the—no, he couldn't have her, so it was pointless to imagine.

"That was one of the best kisses I've ever had," she said shakily.

Oh, he could go again, show her that was only the beginning. But it was a bad idea. Beyond bad. It could lead to something neither of them was ready for.

"Only one of?" He sighed dramatically, breaking the tension. "I must be out of practice."

Someone pounded on the door, and they jumped apart.

"We're here," Signe called.

"Thank you," he said as her booted feet moved away. "Are you ready?"

"Would it matter if I wasn't?"

He gave her a wry grin. "No, but I doubt this day will go as poorly as you fear."

He hoped. There were at least a dozen ways the day could go poorly. He stopped himself from thinking of a dozen more that might happen tomorrow.

Dorin held out his other arm to Betony. She rested her hand on it, and he led her out of the cabin. The smell of home assaulted his nose. Fish and salt and horse droppings, and the faintest hint of evergreen from the pines dotting the bustling city.

The crew of the *Revenge* darted and dashed about, securing lines and stowing barrels. Captain Mertok was already on the docks, talking with an official, probably the harbormaster. Betony's head swiveled as she tried to take it all in. Her nose wrinkled at the smells, and her eyes widened at the sheer size of the city before her.

"I thought it was a village," she murmured so quietly he was certain the words weren't meant for him.

"It was, once. Thanks to Chief Kalman, it's grown. Not quite a Nimel, but in another decade or two, it might be."

She looked up at him, and a tremulous smile played across her lips. He wanted to kiss her again, reassure her, but this was neither the time nor the place.

Signe lashed down the end of the gangplank and turned to them.

"Best of luck to you both," She stepped close,

She passed him Betony's staff. He'd given it to Mertok for safekeeping, and now he tucked it in a hidden pocket of his cloak where it joined the small blade he'd kept close on the voyage. Betony's gaze followed the movement, and a hint of the old animosity crept into her expression. The resentment disappeared when Signe held out a small wooden disk to her. About the size of a gold coin, the disk had an image of the *Revenge* expertly carved into one side.

"I owe you," Signe said, "as do many on board. Wounds could have festered, and you set those broken bones as good as any Alet-avowed healer. People will walk without limps and have fewer scars to scare off the lads and lasses. This is a debt chit. Should you need anything, find me or any member of this crew. If it's in our power to help, we will."

Betony took it, her expression sober. She bowed formally to the sailor. "I was only doing my sworn duty, but I'll treasure this and hope I never have to use it."

A smile crossed Signe's windburned face. She stepped away, and Dorin led Betony over the gangplank and onto the dock. Mertok looked over and touched the brim of his cap, the only goodbye they would get.

"Stay close," Dorin said in her ear to be heard above the noises of the dock.

She gripped his arm tightly enough he might have bruises and allowed him to lead, weaving and dodging through the crowded docks. The streets were slick with mud, but wooden boardwalks lined them, keeping their feet dry and relatively clean. Even in the six months since his last visit, new storefronts lined the path to the chief's compound. A few new houses had popped up on the next street over. Children played in small parks around the stands of pine trees, and the altars to Alet were filled with small offerings.

They passed the temple of Zovog, two clerics standing guard outside. One stared at Betony's hair as they passed, but the other raised a hand in greeting. An old friend of his mother who had become a mentor when he was sent to train with them.

Past the city center, the houses decreased in size, and the road inclined, leading to a wooden wall on the top of a rise. Two sentries stood guard on either side of the gate. The one on the left moved to intercept him.

"Welcome back, Dorin, son of Piroska. Chief Kalman awaits you in the hall."

Of course he did. One of Captain Mertok's first actions would have been to send word of their arrival. Zovog's scythe, the harbormaster would have seen the *Revenge* and sent word. And Vedel would have sent a message via pigeon as soon as Dorin had left Avora.

The sentry eyed Betony with suspicion but didn't question her presence. As he'd suspected, as long as she was accompanied by someone familiar, someone they trusted, she would be safe.

Dorin acknowledged the greeting with a hand over his heart and led the way to the hall, though anyone with sight could have found it. The large wooden building was 150 paces directly behind the gate. It was as large as the main hall in Avora Castle.

"There is one more thing you need to know about me before we present ourselves to the chief," he said once they were far enough from the sentries. The enclosure was busy with servants and guards dashing to and fro, and no one was near enough to hear them.

Betony merely squeezed his arm.

"I'm bastard-born," he muttered, waiting for her gasp of scorn. Nothing. He chanced a glance her way. Polite curiosity was the only emotion he could see.

"So?"

"What do you mean, so?"

"I mean, it doesn't matter. Not to me. Not to most Loreans."

She focused her attention on all the activity surrounding them, dismissing his concern. At least, he hoped it was the activity and mere curiosity. She could be planning her escape. He would have to reiterate tonight in no uncertain terms why escape would be a horrible idea. It had absolutely nothing to do with how much he would miss her.

They arrived at the massive, intricately carved wood doors. On one was a depiction of Alet with a rainbow over their head, standing on a small isle surrounded by animals. On the other was Zovog, clouds with lightning framing their head and a scythe slung over a shoulder as they stood on a pile of skulls.

"What if I told you the chief was my father?"

That earned him a gasp, and her lips thinned. Before she could say anything else, he opened the doors and led her into the building. Long tables lined the hall, making an aisle down the center. Chief Kalman and Lady Rahel waited at the far end, seated on elaborate thrones. They weren't nearly as grand as the Lorean thrones. No velvet or gold leaf, but they were beautifully carved and painted. His father's was bloodred with carved wolf heads on the arms. His stepmother's was a creamy white with lynx feet and furred armrests.

His half brothers stood behind his father, and his half sister behind Lady Rahel. The women's eyes widened at the sight of Betony, gazes flicking to her brilliant lingonberry hair. But sinister gleams flashed across his brothers' faces. Interest and lust, yes, but their matching gray-eyed stares sent tendrils of dread circling his gut. If nothing else, he needed to keep Betony as far from Rodric and Illes as possible.

"Greetings Chief Kalman, Lady Rahel." Dorin dropped to one knee.

He didn't bother telling Betony she should. She was a fucking princess and outranked his father, for now. She could bow, curtsy, or completely ignore them and be well within her rights.

"Why isn't *she* kneeling?" Gizi whispered harshly to her mother, glaring at Betony.

It was a familiar expression these past ten years. In the months immediately after his assignment as Jani's assistant, sixteen-year-old Gizi had taken advantage of his desperation to connect with at least one family member. He helped her sneak out to meet with a boy she was interested in until his father found out. He was given ten lashes for aiding in the corruption of a young lady of standing. Gizi had looked on and smirked, then returned to pretending he didn't exist. The woman she'd become was just as indifferent to others' suffering.

"Hush," Lady Rahel said.

The chief's gaze darted briefly to his wife and daughter, and he cleared his throat. That shut them up. No one would get away with embarrassing Kalman in front of actual royalty, not when he desperately desired to be counted in their ranks.

"Rise, Dorin, and introduce your...companion," the chief said.

His father was better at politics than he had any right to be, considering he was the clan chief in a country that had yet to form a centralized government and relied more on brute strength than gentle words.

"I present Princess Betony of Lorea, our honored guest," Dorin said. "I am sworn to protect her until she is reunited with her family."

Betony snorted, and though protocol might have her bow here, she did not. "I believe he meant to say hostage, Chief Kalman."

Lady Rahel and Gizi gasped, and his half brothers' hands went to their swords, their expressions of interest morphing into scowls of disapproval. Dorin tensed, waiting for his father's reaction, but kept his hand from his blade. Such an action would only escalate the situation and force him to defend Betony.

But Chief Kalman's response surprised him. He smiled, his white teeth peeking through his magnificent bushy beard, and soon his booming laughter echoed in the hall.

"Good, I hate pretense. I would bid you welcome, Princess Betony, but you do not want to be here, and we do not wish you to stay longer than necessary. You will, in fact, be treated as an honored guest while you are with us, as is the custom in Fuartir. For your own safety, I bid you stay within the walls of the manor. Should you want or need to leave the premises, an escort will be arranged for you."

"Thank you, my lord." Betony bowed, a brief one, but a bow, nonetheless. Kalman beamed. "May I send a letter to my father to assure him of my safety?"

"Of course, but I must insist a member of my family or staff read it before you send it."

She nodded, as if she had a choice, but she couldn't refuse this request.

"Excellent," the chief continued. "In the meantime, Dorin will show you to our guest house and ensure you have everything you need to make your stay comfortable. He will also have main escort duty, as this situation is entirely his responsibility and he is apparently gods-sworn."

His father's glare meant there would be an uncomfortable conversation later. What else could he have done? The Loreans would never forgive the murder of a princess. They might not forgive her kidnapping either, but it was at least possible.

"It is our custom for honored guests to join me for dinner at the high table each night. I look forward to seeing you later."

He waved them away. Grateful for the reprieve, Dorin finally rose and led her out. Taking a hard right, they walked to the back of the hall.

"Why didn't you tell me earlier?" Betony snapped in a low voice.

"I don't go around announcing the fact. It would create more problems than it would solve. But I thought you should know. I'll be happy to answer other questions later, but there are too many people here. And…there's someone I'd like you to meet."

He poked his head into the pit house kitchen set about twenty paces from the wooden hall for safety. An older, round woman with snowy hair looked up, and a beautiful smile broke out on her face.

"Dorin!" She wiped her floury hands on her apron and bustled over. "Alet, I haven't seen you since before midsummer. Where have you been?"

She hugged him tight, and some of the tension of the day vanished as Dorin squeezed her back.

"Hello, Delia. It's good to see you."

Her gaze went to Betony, standing quietly beside him.

"And who is this lovely young thing? I've never seen hair that color. How on earth did you get it that way?" She spoke too quickly for Betony to respond, but grabbed her hand and led them further into the kitchens to a small table on one side. "Sit, sit. I'll fetch you both something to eat."

Delia rushed off before Betony answered even a single question or offered her thanks. They sat on the stools and waited for Delia to return.

"Delia is the head cook," Dorin said before Betony could ask. "And she's brilliant enough Rahel wouldn't fire her even though she has always treated me with kindness."

"Oh," was all Betony managed to say before Delia returned with a tray of dried berries, bread, and a little sliced meat.

She slid onto a stool and stared at Betony. "Well, girl, I don't have all day. Are you going to answer my questions or not?"

Betony blinked and her nose twitched. "My name is Betony, and I was born with my hair this color."

Interesting—she introduced herself without a title. Perhaps that was for the best. Her station and position as a hostage would soon make the gossip rounds, but he liked her lack of pretension.

"Oh, you must have some fairy ancestry." Delia glanced at Betony's wrist, taking note of the magic-suppressing bracelet. "Chose the ordinary life, I see. Well, probably for the best. Can't get married and settle down as a cleric, can you? And you seem the type…"

Dorin cleared his throat and caught Delia's attention. He subtly shook his head.

"Look at me, prattling on. What do I know about types? You'd never guess I never married. Helped my sisters raise their children, though. And tupped a few handsome men in my time. How about you, Betony? Tupped any handsome men lately?"

"Delia!" Dorin's cheeks flamed suddenly, but Betony's silvery laughter drowned out his protest.

"I like you, Delia the cook." She leaned forward and patted the older woman's hand. "And please call me Bet. All my friends do."

"Lovely! Well, Bet, come see me anytime you're hungry. Or anytime you want me to point out the men worth tupping. You can always start with this one here."

"Oh dear Alet, help me," Dorin murmured while Betony shook with laughter.

Delia patted his cheek, gave Betony a quick hug, and hurried away, yelling at one of her underlings. Dorin's ears burned, and he wasn't sure he'd live this down. One fae princess and the only person who gave a shit about him had negated years' worth of training as a midnight man.

Betony ate quietly, but he felt her eyes on him, and the smile never left her face.

"Come on, let me show you the rest of the compound," he said when she finished.

Chapter 23

*I*t was strange, watching Dorin interact with his family like they were nearly strangers. There had to be more to the story.

As much as her own family could annoy her, how they felt about each other was never in doubt. With only a few exceptions, they treated each other as family first. She grew up knowing her parents loved her, even if they didn't always know what to do about her and her talents. And Betony actually liked her brother and sister.

But Dorin behaved as any trusted staff member would have to his liege lord. The icy disdain coming from all five members of the chief's family could have frozen the hottest tea in a flash. Though a little hurt he hadn't shared his parentage with her earlier, perhaps given the nature of their relationship—or lack of one, as seemed clear—it was understandable.

Delia, on the other hand, had been a breath of fresh air. She radiated kindness, and everything about her body language showed she loved Dorin. Betony liked her just for that.

Dorin continued the tour. Besides the large hall and the kitchens, there were four more longhouses, two on each side of the Great Hall. The stables were next to the main gate, with a small pit house on the other side.

"The small building is the bathhouse. Have you ever had a steam bath?"

Betony shook her head.

"I'll make sure you have some privacy and arrange one for you. The chief and Lady Rahel live in the longhouse to the right of the Great Hall." He pointed at the most elaborately decorated building. "Gizi still lives with them and will continue to do so until she's married, if the chief ever allows it."

He pointed at the house furthest from the first. "The heorthwerod live there, warriors pledged to my father, headed by Rodric and Illes. They fight and hunt all day and drink all night. These men are interested in proving themselves any way they can. And my brothers don't like hearing *no*. I suggest you stay far away, if possible."

"I didn't like how your brothers looked at me. As if I was a horse they were trying to decide if they should buy." She understood a little better how Rane must have felt when she had to consider who would be her consort. Thank Idoya Nevar came into her life when he did.

"I didn't like it either," he muttered.

Betony wasn't sure if she was supposed to hear that, but a warm satisfaction chased away the coolness left by the memory of their calculating eyes on her.

"What about the other two?" she asked when he lapsed into silence.

Dorin pointed to the longhouse on the other side of the hall. "That one is for the unmarried higher staff—the chamberlain, the cook, the head groom, and Lady Rahel's maid. I also sleep there when I visit. The last one…well, I guess that's yours now. Usually, some of the lesser staff rotate in and out, as most of the servants live in town but don't want to travel if they're needed well into the night."

"I don't want to put anyone out."

"It's common practice when we have emissaries from the other clans or wealthy merchants visit. The chief is powerful and wealthy, but not the same way as King Rowan. We can't justify having a building just for the times we have honored guests. The servants will be fine. They'll either make the journey into town each night or sleep in the Great Hall."

"I don't like it." An understatement. She hated it, hated that her comfort was more important than the people who served the chief and his family.

"You don't have to like it, but that's how things work here. You should have the house to yourself until spring. We don't receive many visitors in the winter. Hopefully, we'll resolve this mess quickly, and you'll be able to go home as soon as the winter storms die down. Let's go get you settled."

They walked into the last longhouse. The doors had simple but elegant carvings of vines and flowers. Someone had started a fire in the hearth in the middle and laid fresh rushes on the floor. Though dimly lit, enough light came through the oilskin windows and the fire to find her way around. If only she had her magic, she could conjure a fairy light to see better.

A roughly hewn table with two benches for a total of six people sat in front of the hearth, and at the far end was a small washing station. Six built-in beds lined the walls, two on either side of the hearth and four on the opposite wall. A tall, thin man with white hair stood next to the table.

"Greetings, Princess Betony," he said. "Welcome to Cseobar. I am Jani, chamberlain to Chief Kalman. I am at your service for the duration of your stay. Lady Rahel and her daughter will be by with some clothes shortly. Should you need anything, you only have to ask any servant. Dorin, please come see me when Her Highness is settled for the day."

Jani bowed and left before Dorin could say another word. The older man's voice had been calm, but Dorin swallowed and paled.

"Is everything okay?" Betony asked.

"Yes," he said, but he didn't take his gaze away from where Jani had stood.

Betony touched his arm, and this seemed to pull him from whatever spell the older man had cast.

"Claim whichever bed you want," he said. "When Lady Rahel and Gizi arrive, take everything they say with a grain of salt—they may come off as kind and genteel, but either of them will cut your heart out and feed it to the dogs if given a chance. I've been gone for a while, so I'm not sure which way the political winds are blowing. I should have more information after I meet with Jani. Trust no one but me and Delia."

He turned and took a step toward the doors. He was the only person she knew here. When he left, she would be truly alone. Delia had been kind, but she was the cook—she'd be too busy to spend any time with Betony. She did trust him, at least enough to believe he had her best interests at heart, despite everything that had happened.

"Dorin," she called.

He froze midstep. His foot came down, and he turned to her. The light hit his face, and she saw the family resemblance to his brothers then, but there was no cruelty in his features.

"Thank you, and you are welcome here any time."

It wasn't all she wanted to say. She wanted to beg him to stay, to not leave her alone among strangers, possibly hostile strangers, but it was all her pride and honor would allow her to say. She quickly squashed the part of her that wanted him to hold her, kiss her, and chase away the fear. It wasn't his job, not yet. Somehow, she had to convince him it could be.

He bowed, as elegantly as he had at the ball almost a month ago, and grinned. The smile warmed her like sunshine on a summer day, like hot tea on a cold night, like…

"I'll see you at dinner."

Dorin left before her longing got the better of her.

She studied the four beds across from the hearth. Each was built into an alcove with curtains for privacy. Besides different colored curtains, they were the same size with a drawer underneath for storage. The one with green curtains was already made with linens and furs. It would suffice.

Betony had nothing to unpack, no books to read, no embroidery to work on. She was in desperate need of a bath after all the days at sea, so she walked over to the washstand. A silvered glass mirror in a wooden frame hung on the wall above it. Lorean work, with a motif of stylized hazel trees she'd seen in many a noble's house, likely spoils from a raid.

Tucking a few locks that had escaped her braid behind her ears, she splashed water from the plain pottery ewer into the glazed porcelain bowl, also Lorean made, if she had to guess. A similar green glaze was a specialty of potters from Avora. She used a cloth and some of the softly scented soap—pine, maybe—left for her and washed away the sweat and dirt from her journey. The smell of the soap reminded her of Dorin, and she missed him all the more.

She sat on the bed and let her thoughts wander. How was she going to get out of this mess? She didn't have her magic. A quick tug on the bracelet was a stark reminder of her powerlessness here. Her quarterstaff and blade were in Dorin's possession, and despite their recent kiss, she doubted he trusted her enough to arm her. At some point, she would pen a letter to her father, but he knew of her situation and was surely putting together some sort of rescue. She could call in her boon from Hyssop, but again, without magic or uncensored letters, how?

No matter how she looked at the situation, it seemed hopeless. All she could do was wait for it to play out. She hated feeling helpless.

Betony flopped on the bed and stared at the ceiling until a quiet cough brought her out of her funk. She sat up, and Lady Rahel and Gizi waited inside the doors.

"Your Highness, we didn't mean to disturb your rest," Lady Rahel said.

If that was true, they would have left instead of announcing their presence, however politely. But she needed clothes and didn't need enemies, so she played the diplomat.

"Please come in. I was merely thinking," Betony said. It wouldn't do to tell them she plotted her escape.

Gizi was nearly a copy of her mother. They were both on the tall and lean side, with intricately plaited auburn hair piled on top of their heads. Pale skin, rosy cheeks, round faces. The only difference Betony spotted was in their eyes. Gizi had blue, while Lady Rahel's were a greenish hazel.

Gizi carried a few dresses over her arm, and Lady Rahel had a fur-lined blue cloak over hers.

"I brought some dresses from when I was a girl about your height." Gizi placed the dresses next to Betony on the bed. One was a rich red, the color of bricks in Avora, and would contrast horribly with her hair. Another was a light blue. Though lovely, it would show every stain from the mud of winter. The last was a deep brown, plain and serviceable. "Mother will send a seamstress over later to take them in at the bust."

"Thank you," Bet said.

Now she understood what Dorin meant. A more diplomatic or kind person would merely mention getting the dresses fitted. Betony had come to terms with her body ages ago. She was more pixie-sized than anything else. Her parents were about average, her sister, too. Ebon was a bit taller than their father, but Betony had always been small, some might say dainty. She never had much extra anything on her, but small breasts and narrow hips hadn't kept lovers at bay, especially in all her years living in Faerie.

Lady Rahel laid the cloak on top of the three dresses. The hem was frayed and the fur a bit worn, but Betony wouldn't demand a new cloak from her captors, nor the lady's finest. Once the hem was shortened, it wouldn't matter.

"The seamstress will bring some underthings and stockings," Rahel said. "I need to be off. I wish my sons were available to entertain you while you wait, but they're out hunting. Gizi will keep you company."

"Thank you for your hospitality, my lady." Betony hid her relief the two men had been too impatient to wait around to "entertain" her. Their ideas of amusement would likely end in her having to hold Dorin to his oath or enforcing her boundaries herself.

Rahel curtsied and left. Gizi wandered the longhouse aimlessly, poking into various containers, trunks, and drawers. There was nothing to be found. Betony came to Fuartir with nothing but the clothes on her back.

Gizi eventually settled at the table in the middle of the room. Betony walked over to join her.

"You should ask at the kitchens for some tea and a kettle," Gizi said. "It's our custom to offer a beverage to guests."

The rebuke was clear in her voice. Idoya help her, the woman was acting like a girl still in pigtails. Betony wouldn't be accused of being impolite, not from one of her captors.

"I'll remember to bring tea the next time I'm taken hostage, then," she said, perhaps with a bit more bite to her words than was strictly polite.

"You do that," Gizi replied absently.

"Do you happen to have some embroidery thread and a needle?"

"Ugh, I hate embroidery! It is so boring."

Great, Gizi hated one of the things Betony loved. There was nothing like creating exquisite designs out of thread, meant to be worn by herself or the people she loved, to push away the stresses of the day.

"What do you do to pass the time?" Bet asked. Maybe they would have something in common.

"Follow Mother around, learning to manage my own household one day. Join some of the more influential families for tea or dinner. Visit the temples and go to market. Flirt with the sailors when no one is watching. Hawking, riding."

The only interest they had in common was riding, though Betony would guess for vastly different reasons. Gizi likely did it to escape, while Bet did it for the pleasure of the animal's company. None of Gizi's other pastimes were wrong, by any stretch of the imagination, but none of them were things Betony chose to spend her time on. Queen Beatrice had to force her to learn how to manage a large court. Socializing, including flirting, had always been challenging. She'd found friends in Faerie, but elsewhere, relationships were difficult to find and hold on to. And her connection to animals made hunting them difficult.

"Oh" was all Bet said, and she was saved from saying anything else by the arrival of a nervous middle-aged woman carrying a sewing basket.

She curtsied clumsily. "Lady Rahel sent me to alter some dresses."

Betony smiled at her, trying to ease her nerves, but Gizi snapped at the poor woman.

"You're supposed to call her 'Your Highness.'"

The seamstress's face paled and her lip trembled. "Oh, I am—Um, I mean…"

Betony rose and put her arm around the woman's shoulders. "You don't get many princesses here, so I take no offense. What's your name?"

"Hilde, Your Highness."

"Thank you for coming so quickly. I hope to wear one of the lovely dresses Gizi provided tonight at dinner."

Gizi preened in her chair, as Betony had hoped. They were serviceable dresses, but lovely wasn't the word Betony would use. Not yet, anyway. Give her a needle and thread and she could change that.

"Gizi, please excuse us. I'll see you at dinner," Betony said.

Happy her dresses were apparently up to a princess's standards, Gizi left with a smile. The annoyance of dealing with her bled away, and Bet turned to the seamstress.

"Now, you and I have work to do."

Chapter 24

*A*fter Dorin left Betony, he went straight to the longhouse to drop off his belongings and wash, but Jani waited for him.

He shouldn't have been surprised, but he was. His thoughts swirled around one person lately, a person who was not Jani. Leaving her had been difficult. Everything about her body language had screamed "stay." He'd wanted nothing else, but duty called.

"Start talking, Dorin. This…situation is far from ideal, and I need to know what happened so I can run interference with the chief."

Dorin tossed his things on the spare bed and sat at the table in the middle of the longhouse. They had the space to themselves. He poured some tea and told Jani everything that had happened leading to today. The chamberlain listened, shaking his head at Dorin's more rash decisions.

"I have a question for you," Jani said when Dorin finished, fingers folded in front of his mouth. His face was carefully neutral, but his piercing gaze examined him carefully. "How will King Rowan react to the kidnapping of his daughter?"

Matching his mentor's expression and mannerisms, Dorin's heart thundered in his ears, so loudly he wondered if Jani could hear. His palms sweat, and he blinked.

"The King of Lorea is a thoughtful man, not prone to rash actions. He'll be outraged but won't send an entire fleet after us. But I wouldn't be surprised if a ship lands within a few days with a small contingent to ensure the princess's safety. Queen Beatrice follows her husband's lead. Who you really need to be concerned about are her siblings and her godmother."

"Why?" Jani frowned.

"Lady Hyssop is a powerful fairy, both magically and politically. I did not have the pleasure of meeting her, but from every story I've heard, she is a force unto herself. She fears nothing and no one." Dorin shivered at the thought of an indignant fairy as fierce as rumors held Hyssop to be. "The crown princess is known for her rashness and she adores her sister. And rumor suggests her brother is somewhere in Fuartir. Between them, they could mount an effective rescue mission with little effort."

"Very well. I'll suggest an increase in patrols. Anything else I should know?"

Yes. If anything happens to Betony, I'll rip your throat out myself.

"No."

Jani seemed satisfied with his answers. Dorin didn't tell the chamberlain Betony herself could become a threat. He didn't tell him it wasn't only the oath that bound him to her. He didn't tell him he was falling for the princess.

"Good."

Jani strode out of the longhouse, giving Dorin some time alone to unpack and wash. The sun was low on the horizon, but he'd just stripped off his shirt when his father stormed in.

"What were you thinking?" Kalman demanded with a hint of rage.

Of course, that was the exact question he'd been asking himself since he first saw Betony run from the tavern.

However, what he said was, "That your hopes for the diplomatic mission would die if the princess told her father what she overheard. And killing her would end all hope for Fuartir to form an alliance with Lorea for the foreseeable future."

"Not that!" He waved dismissively. "Your vow to protect her. You break it and you'll bring dishonor to the entire clan. I could have left you to the elements, but I made you into a weapon instead, something to serve the clan. You should be more grateful, Dorin. Your self-righteousness will be your undoing, and gods help you if it becomes mine as well. You brought her here, so she is your responsibility. Whatever shit flows from this is yours to deal with."

And the chief left with as little announcement as his arrival.

Grateful. Dorin supposed he was. No eight-year-old wanted to die. But he'd gone from a beloved son to a student of death to a servant with hidden talents. It wasn't the life his mother would have chosen for him, but it was the life he had. At least it had brought him into Betony's path.

Dorin splashed some water on his face, pulled on a clean tunic, and hurried to the Great Hall, barely in time for the feast. He took his customary seat near the doors. The only reason he wasn't serving tonight was his vow to Betony.

As usual, few people greeted him. He was rarely in Cseobar and never for long. At most, he spent a few months at home in any given year. So little time that it no longer felt like home. If he was honest, it hadn't felt like home since his mother died.

The hall quieted and heads turned to the doors. Dorin followed their lead and had his breath stolen.

Betony stood in the doorway, the firelight of the torches casting shadows around her. She'd never looked more like a fairy. The shadows behind her mimicked wings, and an otherworldly glow surrounded her.

The deep brown of her dress showed off her hair, and it fit her as if it had been made for her. Though the dress was plain, with no ornamentation, she wore it like the princess she was. No other woman was as regal. Dorin glanced at the head table. Lady Rahel and Gizi wore matching scowls, and his stepmother drummed her fingers on the table in displeasure. It was a gesture he was more than familiar with.

Betony's gaze found Dorin, and her eyes widened. Her fingers made a subtle "come here" motion, but he tilted his head toward the dais. He was unwelcome there and wouldn't force the issue, but she needed to join the chief and his family. Their approval and how they treated her would set the stage for her stay in Cseobar. If the population knew she had their support, she would be safe. Or at least, safer.

Her jaw clenched, but she squared her shoulders and continued on her way.

His father stood as she approached, and the rest of those on the dais followed suit.

"Please greet our honored guest, Princess Betony of Lorea. She has the welcome of our hearth and the protection of our sword."

Dorin sighed in relief, and the weight he'd been carrying lifted from his shoulders. The chief had announced an attack on Betony would be seen as an attack on a member of his family. Kalman suffered no insult without repaying tenfold. She would be safe, at least from outsiders.

A smattering of applause greeted Kalman's words, but it grew louder with Betony's elegant curtsy.

"Thank you, Chief Kalman."

She stepped onto the dais and took the chair between his half brothers. Next to them, she was doll-like. They were big, as was his father. Not just tall, but well-muscled from hours spent at sword, spear, and wrestling. Dorin supposed they were handsome, if one liked brute strength over intelligence. And neither of his brothers ever had trouble finding women willing to warm their beds.

Rodric leaned his brown-haired head down to Betony and whispered into her ear. She laughed, and his gut clenched. Illes slapped Rodric on his back, and their laughter drowned hers out. Once more, her eyes found him, and she rolled them. Something inside released its clutch on his stomach, and he sipped his ale. She wanted to be there as much as he did, which was not at all.

The rest of dinner proceeded like this. Either Illes or Rodric would speak with her, and she'd laugh or speak politely. His stepmother looked on in approval, but his sister would glare at her, and his father had a scheming gleam in his eye. It had been in Dorin's best interest to anticipate his father's wants, ideas, and plans. And this dinner said more than a conversation ever could.

Chief Kalman didn't want the princess to go anywhere, despite his assurances earlier today. He was hoping Rodric or Illes would catch her eye. What better way to ensure the treaty with Lorea than with a marriage between one of his heirs and a princess?

With the support the King of Lorea would send for his daughter, both in dowry and in defense of Clan Fher, Kalman's ascendancy to the not-yet-existent throne of Fuartir was all but guaranteed. No one ever accused his father of being dull witted, and few ever underestimated him and lived to tell the tale.

Betony's physical safety might be assured, but if Kalman's machinations came to fruition, her future and her happiness were in grave jeopardy. He had to warn her.

"The clerics taught you better than this," Jani said from beside him. The older man had, as usual, snuck up on him. Few could, but Jani had the knack. "*I* taught you better than this."

"Than what?" Dorin snapped, though he didn't need Jani to say it. He knew, of course he did.

"Your every emotion is written on your face, Dorin. And from the direction of your stare, it has everything to do with our 'honored guest.'"

Fuck, these feelings he had for Betony were ruining all of his hard work. Dorin took three deep breaths and schooled his expression into its usual bland neutrality. He was lucky the gathering was so taken with the princess and the antics at the head table that the likelihood of anyone having noticed was virtually zero. While Jani could read him like a book, even Dorin's most obvious emotions were but mere flashes to others.

"Better," Jani said. "This has disaster written all over it. I still cannot believe you took a princess hostage."

"Lorant and Vedel gave me little choice."

Jani raised one eyebrow, a skill Dorin had always envied. "This may blow up in your face."

Dorin resisted the urge to tell Jani it already had. He hadn't meant to fall for the princess, but he had. And the best he could do for her now was to keep her out of his brothers' clutches and ensure she made it home safely. No matter what.

They ate the rest of the meal in silence, and people began to leave. Jani slipped out with the early crowd to see to the higher ranked lords and ladies. Those remaining milled about, starting and ending conversations, but all eyes eventually focused on the princess. She seemed unaware of the attention, but every once in a while would find Dorin. *Please*, she would mouth. But he could do nothing for her here.

"Chief Kalman, if you'll excuse me for the night, I'll see you tomorrow. I haven't slept in a proper bed in over a week, and I am tired," Betony announced when the crowd had thinned enough.

Dorin walked up the center aisle.

"I'll escort you," Illes said, beating Rodric with his offer.

His eldest brother's brows wrinkled in frustration, but before Rodric could protest or make a counteroffer, Dorin spoke.

"Her safety is my responsibility. I'll see her to the longhouse."

His family all turned as one, fixing their glares on him. Why the fuck had he opened his Zovog-cursed mouth?

Before anyone could protest, Betony had slipped through their grasp and linked her arm through his.

"Thank you, Dorin, that is most kind. A familiar face is just the thing."

None of them could protest if this was what Betony wanted, but he would pay for his interference. Some horrible prank, a drubbing in the practice field, a loosened saddle the next time they rode together. It would be worth it. The idea of either of his brothers so near to her bed filled him with horror and disgust.

Without another word, he led Betony out and to her longhouse. His brothers watched from the entrance to the hall. He wouldn't be able to linger, but at least he could assure himself she was alone.

He opened the door to the longhouse and walked in ahead of her, like a competent bodyguard. The place was empty, as expected.

"Goodnight, Princess." He turned to go.

She grabbed his arm. He glanced around the compound, but there was no one watching. He relaxed the smallest amount possible.

"Stay," she said, so quietly he almost missed it.

"I can't." His answer was as soft as hers. "If I stay, it's a coin toss whether my father or one of my brothers will kill me. They have plans for you."

"That's why I want you to stay. They're horrible, and I want nothing to do with them."

He pried her fingers from his arm and brought them to his lips before dropping them.

"I make no promises, but I'll try to return. In the meantime…" He checked over his shoulder and stuck his hand in his pocket. He held out her staff and her knife. The latter vibrated strangely, and a melodic hum filled his ears. He'd kept them safe all the way from Lorea, but now she needed them. Escape into the wilderness in winter would be a death sentence for someone unfamiliar with Cseobar and Fuartir, but she might need a means of protecting herself against the threats here in the manor. "You can have these back. Though the chief's words tonight guaranteed your safety from those outside, I would feel better if you could defend yourself against Rodric and Illes."

Betony crept closer, took the weapons from him, and tucked them away so quickly he couldn't tell where she'd put them. The hum disappeared, and she stood on tiptoes and kissed his cheek.

"Thank you."

Heat rushed through him, and he had to fight his every instinct to pull her close and kiss her properly. Passionately. Perpetually.

"I have to go."

He ducked into the moonlight before he lost the battle. She closed the door and her footsteps receded into the house. His stepmother had replaced his brothers, and she watched carefully as he walked to his own quarters.

"You're back early." Delia placed two cups on the table as he strode in and motioned him over. Now the feast was done, she could leave the cleaning to her staff and relax.

"What else am I supposed to do, Delia? Besides you and Jani, no one else speaks to me unless necessary."

"I thought you might spend a little time with our visitor. She seems to like you."

"Don't know why," he muttered.

"You're a good man, that's why. Even though you kidnapped her."

He flinched. He'd hoped Delia might not have put two and two together, but his luck rarely held.

"I had no choice."

She patted his hand. "I know, but why not get to know the girl better?"

Because I already know her as well as I know my own name. As well as I know my own breath. As well as I know my own heart.

But all he said was, "Because my stepmother has plans for the princess, and I don't want to draw even more attention to her. It wouldn't go well for her."

"See, I told you. A good man."

Dorin finished his tea and kissed Delia on the cheek. "It's been a long day. Oh, who am I kidding? It's been a long month. I'm off to bed."

"Goodnight, Dorin."

He crawled into his bed and drew the curtains, but he did not sleep. He pretended to. Anytime the scuff of a shoe approached, he let out a snuffle or a snore. He counted as his housemates entered and shuffled around the room as he'd been taught. Eventually, the longhouse quieted, and the last person settled into their bed with a creak. He waited until all the noises greeting his ears were soft snores and the rustle of furs. Then he waited a bit more.

Twitching back the curtains, Dorin scanned the longhouse. All the other curtains were drawn closed, and no one stirred. He slid his feet into his shoes and tiptoed out, the sliver of moon high overhead. He was truly a midnight man tonight.

He could still claim he was making his way to the latrines. Dorin looked at his father's longhouse. Only the dull glow of a dying fire lit the oilcloth windows and peeked from under the doors.

He glanced at the longhouse his brothers occupied. Boisterous calls floated in the night air, and their windows were brightly lit. But no one was outside to see him cross the courtyard to the guest quarters.

Keeping to the shadows as he'd learned during his training, Dorin crept silently across the cold ground. His tread was light on the wooden steps, barely a squeak escaping from their planks. But he paused with his hand upon the door.

This, this was truly madness. As much as he wanted to be with her, be near her, bask in her peaceful presence, he couldn't. Whatever was blooming between them needed to be nipped before it led to their downfalls. With a heavy sigh, he slipped back to his bed. Alone.

Chapter 25

A soft knock sounded, waking Betony from where she dozed at the table. She wiped off the drool from the corner of her mouth as the door cracked open, letting in a bright ray of sunlight and an icy gust. A young woman walked in carrying a tray.

"Good morning, Your Highness."

Betony rubbed at her eyes. She could have sworn someone was at the door last night, and she'd risen with her staff in hand to protect herself. But no one had entered. Too wound up to lie back down, she sat at the table and must have dozed off.

The maid bobbed an awkward curtsy and placed the tray on the table. On one side of the tray was a plate with a thick slice of buttered bread, a few slices of cheese, and a covered ceramic container. On the other side was a piece of parchment, a quill, and a small inkpot. Before she could look into the covered container, the young woman whisked it away and hurried over to the hearth behind Betony.

"Let me start a pot of tea for you," she said.

Well, that answered her first question. Betony picked up the bread and cheese and broke her fast. She wasn't hungry, but she should maintain her strength. An opportunity to escape could arise at any time.

"Would you care to join me?" she asked.

"Oh, oh no, I couldn't. Lady Rahel would…"

Betony turned around. The maid's expression said it all—Rahel would be most displeased and would take it out on the poor maid.

"That's fine." She was not in Lorea anymore, and the people here were not hers to befriend. With any luck, she'd be here a few weeks, maybe a couple of months, and she'd never see any of them again.

Not even Dorin? asked the maddening voice in the back of her mind.

She wanted him, yes, but was she willing to risk her future freedom? Instead of starting a difficult conversation with herself, she pulled the piece of parchment off the tray and smoothed it out. The quill and ink followed as she continued to nibble on her breakfast and stared at the blank page. How was she going to explain this to her father?

The maid placed a pot of tea and a mug in front of her.

"Do you need anything else, Your Highness?"

"No, thank you."

She bobbed another curtsy and hurried out. Betony sipped the tea, an herbal blend with a nice citrusy tang. It would be even better with a dollop of honey, but if she couldn't befriend the servants here, at least she could be no bother. With no further excuse to put off writing this letter, she dipped the quill into the ink.

Dear Father,

I am well. Kicking myself for my own boneheadedness, but well.

Chief Kalman has offered me the welcome of his hearth and the protection of his sword, which assures me of safety while I am under his roof. I have been given a place of honor and my own living quarters.

The voyage was trying as we encountered an early winter storm, but none aboard were lost, and my safety was a very high priority. I only had to deal with wet shoes and damp bedding. I was able to mend some of the crew injured while seeing us otherwise safely through the storm.

Please tell Mother I am sorry for the bother. Tell Rane to put down her sword and listen to Nevar. There is no need for war over me. And please pass along my greetings to my godmother. I may soon need to beg that favor from her.

Your loving, though abashed, daughter,

Betony

She looked over the missive. It did everything she needed it to—inform her family she was fine and was being treated well, called for peace, and put Hyssop on notice. If things took a bad turn, her boon from her godmother might yet make this situation salvageable. Chief Kalman should be appeased both by her praise and her disinclination for armed intervention.

Betony finished her tea and breakfast as she waited for the note to dry. The planks outside creaked, and another knock sounded, this one firm.

"Come in."

The door opened and Dorin stepped in, but he left it cracked. Her heart leapt at the sight of him.

"Princess Betony." He refused to meet her gaze.

He'd said he'd try to come last night. Obviously, he'd either been smarter than her and stayed where he belonged, or he'd been unable to sneak away. She held nothing against him. His political position was tenuous, and so was hers. They both should proceed with caution. Lots and lots of caution.

"Hello, Dorin. What's on the agenda for today?"

Confusion was written all over his face. "You're the princess. I'm here to offer escort wherever you need or want to go."

She blew across the letter and tested a patch. Dry. Folding the parchment, she rose.

"Getting approval for this is in order. I need to arrange supplies for my embroidery. Then…then I want to make some actual friends."

Betony strode out, not waiting for her escort. If he was going to play this like they were strangers, like they hadn't shared a toe-curling kiss, like she was nothing but another duty, another responsibility, she could play along.

"Friends? Princess, you're barking up the wrong tree if you think you'll make friends here."

She snorted. "No, it's the exactly right tree. You'll see. Now, where is someone who can approve my letter so I may get on with my day?"

Dorin hurried in front of her and led her directly to the Great Hall. The older man who'd greeted her in her quarters yesterday was directing the staff on cleaning and resetting the hall.

"Jani," Dorin said as they approached.

He turned, eyes widening at her presence. "Yes?"

Betony handed over the parchment, and he took it almost reluctantly.

"I've written a note to my father. I'm sure you'll want to look it over before sending, though I doubt I shared anything untoward."

He cocked an eyebrow at Dorin.

"I have not read it," Dorin said.

Jani unfolded the letter and scanned it. "Thank you, Your Highness. This should smooth things over and allow negotiations to proceed. Is there anything else I can do for you this morning?"

"Embroidery supplies, if you please. I like to keep my hands busy. Some brown and golden thread would be most appreciated, as well as any other colors that go well with the dresses Lady Rahel and Gizi provided."

"I'll speak with Hilde and arrange that for you."

"Thank you."

Betony turned and strode right back out, heading straight for the stables. Dorin's footfalls crunched on the snowy ground as he ran to catch up.

"Betony," he grumbled, and his low voice strummed a chord deep inside, setting her heart to thumping and her skin tingling. "Where are you going?"

"To the stables, obviously." There was nothing else in front of them.

"You can't...my father...no one will let you take a horse without a member of the chief's family to accompany you until you prove you can be trusted."

"Doesn't matter, I'm not going riding. I'm making friends."

She tried to outpace him, but his legs were longer than hers and he had no trouble keeping up. Fine. She'd woken on the wrong side of the bed— make that the table. Though she told herself she didn't blame him for not showing last night, obviously a part of her did and was taking it out on him now. It was not his fault. It was not her fault. It was this horrible situation.

A situation she'd brought upon herself by acting rashly. A situation he'd only made worse. A situation that wasn't likely to have a happy ending. But she'd try anyway.

"I don't understand," Dorin said as she slowed.

"You will."

They stepped into the warm barn, scented with fresh hay and the earthy smell of horses and their dung. It may not be her favorite scent, but it was real and smelled exactly the same as the stables in both Avora and Faerie. Some things were the same no matter in which realm she found herself.

Dorin remained close to the exit as she approached the first horse slowly, her hand out, and observed its body language. It remained calm and allowed her to pet its nose, even relaxing into her touch. As it did so, a cat twined between her feet and purred.

All the stress from the last week started melting away. Yes, her direct access to her magic had been blocked, but the animals still could sense it. She might not be able to talk to them directly, but they still trusted her, still liked her, still comforted her.

Another cat joined the first, and the horse in the next stall nickered softly.

"See, friends," she said without looking at Dorin hanging about in the shadows.

"I've never seen anything like it. How?"

"It's a gift. Along with my hair and healing abilities, I can talk to animals. They still sense I'm a friend even with your horrid little bracelet. I was trying to call for help when you pulled me out of the harbor."

She did look at him then, and he winced, but didn't bother apologizing.

"I'll wait for you outside." He slipped silently into the bright sunshine.

Betony greeted each animal, rubbing noses, scratching behind ears, and listening as the stable filled with contented purrs and snorts. Once all the tension bled from her, she made her goodbyes. Dorin escorted her to her longhouse.

Hilde waited for her with plenty of embroidery supplies. Betony happily pulled out the red dress, knowing exactly how to make this into a garment she could wear with pride. She worked all afternoon, only stopping once the sun went down and Jani collected her for dinner at the Great Hall.

No feast tonight, only the chief, his family, some of the servants, and the heorthwerod. She looked all over, but there was no sign of Dorin. Her heart fell. Had she hurt him earlier with her supposed indifference? She wasn't indifferent, not at all. But she hadn't yet figured out a way for them to be together that would be safe for him. Because she knew, without a shadow of a doubt, if anyone were to pay for their relationship, it would be Dorin.

Given an opportunity to marry into the Lorean royal house, Kalman would take it. But not with Dorin. It was clear Dorin earned only grudging respect for his services. And only for his services. None of his family saw him for who he was, only what he could do for them, for the clan, for

Fuartir.

But he was waiting for her as she exited the hall. He took her arm like a gentleman and leaned in to whisper in her ear.

"I have a surprise for you, Princess."

A thrill traveled along her spine, and heat pooled low in her belly. No, he couldn't possibly mean *that*, not with so many eyes upon them. For she felt them keenly. Rahel and Kalman, stepping out of the hall. Illes and Rodric as they stalked to their longhouse. Hostile murmurs from the werod. But Dorin led her past the guest quarters and toward the small building he had mentioned housed the bath. Delia stood outside with a wide smile.

"I'll return to escort you home." Dorin bowed and slipped off into the shadows.

The eyes that had been watching seemed to find other, more interesting things, and the weight of their stares lifted.

Delia slung an arm over her shoulders and pulled her inside.

"Dorin thought you could use a bath."

"Do I smell that bad?" Betony gave a half-hearted chuckle.

"Now, now. He's a kind and considerate man. He knows this isn't how Loreans bathe, so he asked me to show you the ropes. Every other day is for women, and he let word get around you'd like some privacy today."

They stripped off their clothes and hung them from hooks in the cool vestibule. Betony shivered, but Delia pushed aside the heavy leather curtain and led her into a hot, steamy room. A brazier glowed in the middle and benches lined the walls. The older woman used a small metal cup to scoop some water from a bucket next to the brazier and sprinkled it over the coals. Thick steam soon filled the room, and Betony began to sweat.

"There are herbs to throw on the coals to sweeten the air, and there's soap and washcloths, but it's best to let the sweat work for a bit. Here, sit."

And they did, letting the steam fill the air, letting it soothe the remaining aches in her muscles from the voyage. When she was finally ready, she grabbed a cloth and reached for some soap.

"Oh, Dorin bought the greenish bar for you at market today. He said you like rosemary."

Rosemary soap? For her? Betony blinked back the tears. Her mother loved rosemary. Pots of it grew all over the castle in Avora and there was a ready supply of rosemary soap.

She picked up the small bar and sniffed. Home, it smelled like home.

They finished and dressed, and Dorin waited for her. He walked her to the longhouse, accompanied by Delia until she continued on. Those who had watched them earlier seemed to mind their own business this time. Dorin walked her up the steps, opened the door, and after ensuring no one was in the house, stood out of her way. But as Betony passed him, she grabbed his jerkin and pulled him in after her.

She kicked the door shut and pulled his head down to hers. He didn't fight her, but he seemed unwilling to help her, either. Betony pressed her lips to his.

As soon as she did, Dorin's control broke. He pulled her close and clung tightly. She opened, and his tongue licked the edge of her lips. He groaned and his fingers dug into her hips. She wrapped her arms around his neck and held on for dear life as he nipped at her lower lip. He hardened against her belly, and he pressed her back until her thighs hit the table in the middle of the room. Her sudden stop seemed to bring him to his senses.

He lifted his head, pupils nearly obscuring his golden-brown eyes. His gasps were harsh and swift as his gaze raked over her, longing, passion, and regret taking their turns.

"I'm sorry," he said hoarsely.

Betony cupped his cheek. "Please don't be. I could never be sorry for kissing you."

"This is a bad idea. No, worse, it's a dangerous idea. You don't know what might happen if they found out."

She dropped her hand. "You're right. It's my turn to be sorry. You don't need to pay any more of a price for my recklessness."

He stepped away but shook his head. "Not me. You. I don't care what happens to me, but my father will look at this as an opportunity. Something he might be able to use against you, your father, your kingdom. I won't be the cause of any more of your misadventures. I can't be. I—"

Dorin ran a hand down his face but said nothing further.

"There are two of us here, and we both share responsibility for what happens between us," Betony whispered.

He turned his back on her and walked to the door. "That's not how anyone here will see it. Goodnight, Princess."

Opening it, he took a deep breath and stepped outside, pausing when she called out.

"Dorin, thank you. Thank you for the soap tonight. And the dance, once upon a time."

He pulled the door closed behind him without a word. It had only been a moment, but she already missed his touch, missed his warmth, missed *him*. She'd lost him in the last moment, and she wasn't sure she'd ever get another chance.

Chapter 26

*W*hat had he been about to say then, right before Betony had tried to take responsibility? He what? Loved her? Oh, gods, did he?

Dorin walked to his house. She knew who he was, who he'd been, back at the ball. When had she figured it out? Betony was clever, and he was no longer disguising his voice, though he kept to his natural accent. They seemed to bother her little, his lies. Of course, he'd lied about so many things, right from the start. His true reason for being in Lorea, his parentage, who he was. Now the only secrets he kept were his profession and his feelings for her.

He slunk into the longhouse and silently crawled into his bed, twitching the curtain shut behind him. He'd never been in love before, and the only love he'd felt in his entire life had been from his mother and Delia. Maybe he loved Betony, if love meant always thinking about someone, worrying about someone, doing anything to protect someone.

Fuck, he loved her.

Alet didn't bless him with sweet dreams that night. Nor did she bless him with sleep. At least Zovog didn't come calling.

He dragged himself out of bed and went about his day as best he could. First stop, the kitchen for some tea and a chat with Delia. If anyone could help him navigate these emotions, it would be his only friend.

But Betony was already sitting in the kitchen, despite his early morning.

"Good morning, Your Highness." He searched for the cook. "Where's Delia?"

"Gathering eggs, I believe. Would you care for some tea?" She gestured gracefully at the teapot beside her.

"I can get my own tea." Dorin walked to the cupboard where the cups were kept and picked one out.

"I've been serving tea since I was at least ten years old. I can certainly pour a cup for you." She gripped the pot like he was going to yank it out of her hands.

"I don't want to fight over who pours the tea, Betony."

She blinked, then smiled sweetly before she set down the pot and nudged it closer to him.

"Fine."

He noticed a basket at her feet as he poured his tea. A bit of red fabric stuck out of it.

"What's that?"

"A dress your sister was kind enough to give me." She checked for eavesdroppers, but no one was in earshot. "I think she picked the color on purpose to clash with my hair and skin tone."

He almost spit out his tea. Yes, Gizi would in fact do that.

"So," she continued, "I decided to embroider every last inch, make it something I'd want to wear."

"And you brought it to the kitchen?"

"The guest house doesn't have great lighting." She smiled sadly. "And...it's a bit lonely. The Great Hall is better, but there are too many interruptions. Here, I have company but everyone is so busy, they leave me alone."

Gods, his heart cracked at her smile, at her admission. If she stuck around long enough, Betony would make plenty of friends. But if she stuck around long enough, it would mean she wasn't home where she belonged. And it gave his father more time to fulfill his plans to corner her, trap her here. She deserved so much better.

Dorin finished his tea and washed his cup.

"I wish you good lighting and pleasant company. Should you need an escort anywhere or a familiar face, I'm available. I'll be in the Great Hall with Jani."

He left as Delia was returning with a basket full of eggs and a kind word for him, but she was busy and hurried into the kitchen. Jani waited for him, and they reviewed the happenings in Cseobar since his last visit, went over the accounts, and discussed the possible negotiations.

The days quickly settled into a rhythm. Dorin checked in on Betony each morning, usually at her longhouse, but sometimes he found her in the kitchen or the Great Hall. But always alone, or nearly so. At least, there were rarely people close by. But the cats took turns sleeping at her feet, the dogs often kept watch, what birds remained this far north perched outside, and he even caught glimpses of small whiskered faces as the mice and rats checked in on the fae princess.

His brothers were less than pleased with the attention he paid Betony. Or, more importantly, the lack of attention she paid them. Of course, they blamed him.

Dorin found honey on his usual seat in the Great Hall one night. The first time Betony wanted an escort for a ride in the forest with Gizi, he found his tack cut through halfway when he checked it before riding. It would have broken and left him in the snow if he were lucky. If he were particularly unlucky, he could have been severely injured.

Not to mention all the challenges by the heorthwerod. They had largely ignored him before now, seeing him as unworthy of a challenge. Since his vow to protect Betony had made the rounds, they came all too frequently and, in a warrior-based culture, a man never refused a challenge. The first day, three days after Betony's arrival, it was the newest recruit, a boy not even sixteen. Dorin had him on the ground within a few moments. The next day, it was one of Illes's friends, and it came to a draw. The day after, it was one of Rodric's friends, a burly man known for taking things too far, much like Rodric himself. He weighed twice what Dorin did and had at least a forearm's length in height on him.

Dorin left the training enclosure with a win, but by the skin of his teeth. Something told him if he'd lost the bout, he wouldn't be moving freely for weeks if ever again. He escaped with a knot on his head that almost knocked him unconscious, several large bruises, and a possible cracked rib. It hurt to breathe.

He limped into the kitchen to seek Delia's expert care, only to encounter Betony hard at work on her embroidery. In the last few days, the dress was nearly transformed. Golden and brown leaves curled over the bodice, with green vines swirling over the sleeves.

Betony looked up as he entered, and her eyes widened. She dropped her dress without a thought and rushed to his side.

"Dorin, what happened?"

"Oleg happened."

"Sit."

It was a tone he'd have to be a fool to ignore. He sat with a wince and a gasp. Her gentle fingers poked at the knot behind his ear.

"Ow."

"Where else does it hurt?"

Could he say everywhere? Because that's what it felt like.

"The worst is the head and my ribs."

With no preamble, she pulled up his shirt and poked until she found the tender spot. Somehow, with her gentle fingers trailing over his skin, it hurt less than it had a moment ago.

"Breathe," she commanded.

He did, gasping as his chest expanded and the pain shot through him.

"Again."

This time, it wasn't as bad.

"Okay, bruised not broken. Let me get some snow to reduce the swelling while the pain reliever tea brews. I think Delia has everything I need."

But she didn't have to fetch the snow. A kitchen maid ducked out as soon as the words left her mouth and returned momentarily with a cupful. Betony dumped it into two cloths and put one on his head. She grabbed his hand and squeezed, and suddenly it didn't matter he was injured. He wanted her. Wanted her kindness, her tenderness, her warmth, her breath, her body. Only the pain and the ice kept his body from betraying his desire.

She put that hand on the compress on his head, then repeated the action for his ribs. Their gazes locked for a moment, and he could see the same desire flare in her eyes.

Bad idea. Dangerous idea. Tempting idea.

A lazy, sultry smile twitched up the corner of her lovely, kissable lips, and she leaned in.

"What happened, Dorin?" Delia bustled in, and Betony spun away to gather the ingredients for her tea.

"I'm fine, Delia."

"I didn't ask if you were fine, I asked what happened."

He told her as Betony mixed some herbs and bark and other things that looked none too appetizing. She put it all in a pot and poured hot water over it. The smell was awful and only got worse as it steeped. She added a large dollop of berry preserves to the cup and poured the brew over.

"Drink." She handed him the cup.

He dropped the ice from his head, wrinkling his nose and frowning.

"It won't kill you, and I added the preserves to make it taste better. Do you trust me?"

He hated when his own words were thrown back in his face, so he returned the favor.

"Isn't that what the villains say?"

"Dorin!" Delia said with a gasp, but Betony only laughed, her silvery voice filling the kitchen.

"Yes, we do. Now, drink up."

So he did. It wasn't nearly as bad as it smelled, but he drank it as quickly as he could, given how hot it was. He flushed under Betony's gaze, and her lips twitched as she fought a smile or another laugh. When he was finished, he set down the cup with a thunk.

"Happy?" he said.

"Almost. You need to rest. If anyone gives you trouble, tell them I said so."

"What if you need me?"

Once more, heat flared in her emerald eyes, and they sparkled like jewels in the sunshine.

"I know where to find you." Her voice was low and husky and did things to his insides he didn't want Delia to notice.

"Good." Delia wrapped a motherly arm around him. "I'll see him to bed, unless you want the honor, Your Highness."

He was gratified to see the flush of pink across her cheeks and nose. Delia cackled knowingly as she led Dorin out and to their shared longhouse. She got him settled into bed and looked him over.

"You have it bad," she said with a thoughtful expression.

"I have no idea what you're talking about, Delia."

"Sure, we'll go with that." She smoothed his hair from his forehead and pulled up the blankets. "You should tell her before one of your lousy brothers lays claim." Delia had figured out his parentage in his first month at the manor, but she told no one.

"I can't. She isn't for me."

"Who says?"

He ticked off all the people who could possibly object to their relationship. "My father, his wife, my brothers, Jani, her parents, probably her sister—"

"What about the woman herself? Doesn't she get a say?"

"I kidnapped her."

"From where I stood, didn't look like that bothered her very much."

A bitter retort died on his tongue. Delia had a point. He hadn't asked Betony what she thought. And she'd requested nothing other than his company.

He sighed instead, a soul cleaning one that immediately cleared his mind. "Why do I bother arguing with you?"

"I have no idea. You'd think as smart as you are, you would've learned that lesson long ago. Go talk to her tonight. I'll make sure no one notices."

Dorin sat up and kissed her cheek. "Thank you."

Delia smiled and closed the curtains. He could hear her chuckle all the way out. Whatever Betony had put in the tea did its job. The pain ebbed and he drifted off to sleep.

When he woke, the soft murmur of voices and the squeak of bed planks told him the others were readying for the night. Feeling better, he waited as patiently as he could, trying not to let his thoughts spiral out of control. But two thoughts kept repeating, and as soon as he let one go, the other took its place.

What if she says yes?

What if she says no?

There was only one way to find out. The little light that snuck between the curtains dimmed, and the voices hushed. Soft breaths filled the longhouse. He turned back a corner of the curtains. Delia sat at the table in front of the hearth, still and quiet and focused on his bed. When she saw his movement, she nodded and placed a finger over her lips. He dropped silently to the floor and grabbed his shoes, then crept out, closing the door with barely a snick. Dorin slipped on his shoes, only a dull ache remaining from his injuries earlier. He kept to the shadows as he crept across the compound.

Even the heorthwerod's longhouse was quiet, for once, only a faint glow in the windows from a banked fire. Midnight in the compound was all still, the only movement coming from the guards at the gates as they paced, trying to keep warm. But their attention was focused outward, and he made it to Betony's quarters with none the wiser.

He leaned his forehead on the door, facing his decision, his fate. He could return to his bed—his cold, lonely bed—and no one would know. Not Betony, not his father, not Jani. Only Delia. And himself. He would forever wonder what might have happened had he found the courage to stay.

Dorin cracked open the door, its well-oiled hinges nearly silent.

A harsh swish of air blew past his face, and cold metal pressed against his neck.

Fuck.

Chapter 27

"*D*orin?" Betony dropped the tip of her staff to the ground. "I'm sorry. I-I didn't know it was you."

She grabbed his hand, pulled him further into the longhouse, and shut the door. He hissed in pain as the sudden movement pulled at his injury.

"Gentle, Princess."

Relief warmed her at the sound of his voice, but her words came out harsher than she intended, partly from the ebbing fear and partly from worry over him.

"What are you doing here? You're supposed to be resting."

"I was worried you might need me," he said with an impish grin, rubbing at the spot on his neck where her staff had poked him.

"I told you I knew where to find you. I thought it might be…"

"Who, Betony? Who did you expect?"

He pulled her close, and she let him. He was cold from outside, but his solid hold on her chased away the remaining chill of fear.

"Maybe your brothers. They were pestering me at dinner, trying to get into my good graces. Maybe…maybe your father. Or maybe your stepmother with a knitting needle. She doesn't seem to like me."

Dorin stroked her hair. "Oh, she likes you just fine. At least, she likes what she thinks you have to offer. Plans are afoot."

Betony peered at him, and what she saw on his face irritated her to no end. The smile he wore a moment ago was gone, replaced by a too-serious furrowed brow and a slight frown. His shoulders were tense too, and he seemed ready to spring away at any moment.

"What plans?"

He sighed. "I shouldn't tell you. My duty rests with my clan, but I cannot allow you to be a pawn in my father's grasp for power. They're hoping you might fall for Illes or Rodric, and if you don't, they're looking to force a marriage."

She snorted, and it turned into a giggle.

"It's not funny, Betony."

"Yes, it is."

She disentangled herself from his arms, but twined her fingers through his and dragged him to the table in the center of the longhouse. He grunted, trying to hide his pain, and she slowed her steps. She missed his embrace. It centered her, calmed her, and excited her all at the same time. That's why she needed a little space. Having her wits addled by his proximity would make this particular conversation more difficult. She sat on the bench and patted the spot next to her.

"Princess—"

"Don't 'Princess' me, Dorin, son of Piroska. We're talking royal weddings—who knows more on the subject? A princess of marriageable age, or a 'manservant' from the barbarian north?"

"Hey…"

But he'd relaxed a bit. His brow remained furrowed, but the frown was gone. There wasn't yet a smile to replace it, but she was working on it.

"Fuartiran custom is not Lorean custom. A Lorean woman, even a princess, cannot be married against her will, and divorce, while not common, is allowed under our laws, especially if any coercion is suspected. Even if forced into marrying one of your brothers, as soon as I step foot in Lorea, I have the law on my side."

"But they'll keep you here." His hand covered hers. It was cold, colder than she expected, as though he truly feared her marrying one of his cursed brothers.

"They can *try*." She grinned widely and pulled out the staff once more. "How long do you think anyone can keep me here if I truly want to leave?"

The furrow eased, and a gleam of hope twinkled from his eyes. "Not forever."

"Not forever," she agreed. "Let them play their games. Maybe I'll even string them along. Buy us time…"

"Us?" He latched onto that word, her little mistake. His voice dropped low, so close to the voice he chose at the masquerade. "What do we need time for?"

She licked her lips, and he watched avidly. Warmth pooled between her legs.

"You can't look at me like that," she said. *Idoya, please make him stop. I won't be responsible for my actions if he keeps it up.*

"Like what?" His grin was feral. He knew, and he was pressing her.

What was she going to do about it?

"Like you're about to devour me." The words slipped out before her mind caught up with her mouth.

His eyes flamed, and he twined his fingers into hers.

"Do you want me to?" he growled.

Her heart thudded so loudly she wondered if he heard it. Her mouth went dry. All she could do was nod before all the possible consequences came to mind.

Dorin threaded his free hand through her hair and pulled her to him, but paused when there was but a fingerbreadth between them.

"I need you to say you want this, that you want me," he murmured, his breath tickling her lips when she wanted his mouth on hers, his hands on her body, and her hands on his.

"I want you like I've never wanted anything in my life."

He closed the distance between them, and Betony sighed as his lips crashed into hers. She opened for him, and his tongue traced her lower lip. Small moans escaped her, and he swallowed them, humming against her lips. His tongue explored further and tangled with hers, driving all rational thought from her mind.

She pressed closer, rose on her knees and straddled him. The hard length of him pressed against her core, and it was his turn to moan. She smiled against his lips as her hands slipped under his tunic and stroked his abdomen. The muscles rippled beneath her touch.

Dorin broke the kiss with a gasp of pain. His eyes were wide, his black pupils swallowing the gold-flecked brown, and his cheeks flushed. He clasped her hands and pulled them away from his body. Her body burned at his touch.

"I'm sorry," she said. "I didn't mean—"

"Shh, I know. But this isn't why I came over tonight."

"It doesn't matter why. You're here now, and so am I, and this is what we both want."

"We can't—"

"Yes, we can," Betony insisted.

She twisted her wrists and clutched his in return. She guided them to her breasts. He seemed entranced, unable to stop her as she rested them on the cloth of her chemise. Dorin swiped his thumbs over the nipples pebbling beneath his touch.

"Touch me, Dorin."

He tore his gaze from where his hands teased her and looked into her eyes.

"Please," she pleaded.

A low groan rumbled from his chest. "Zovog will strike me down for this."

"No, they won't."

His hands drifted away from her breasts, and Betony held her breath. Dorin did not remove them entirely—they seemed weighted and trailed down her stomach until his fingers played with the hem of her chemise.

"How do you know?" he asked earnestly, never removing his gaze from hers.

"I won't let them." She stroked his cheek with a finger and smiled.

He returned the smile, but there was a wolfish quality to it, as though he was, in fact, about to devour her. Dorin grabbed the hem and bunched up her chemise, inch by inch, exposing her skin. He finally broke eye contact, drinking in her nakedness.

He pulled the garment over her head and stared, taking her in, but Betony didn't feel embarrassed. She didn't rush to cover herself. Instead, she felt cherished, admired, desired.

"Lie back, Princess," he said in a rumbling voice that had her instantly obeying. "It's time for me to feast."

The table was cool and smooth against her back, but she forgot it as his hand blazed trails over her belly. His fingers were lightly callused, and the contrast between their roughness and her smooth skin sent shivers along her spine. He worked his way to her knees and spread her legs apart, moving between them. Inch by tormenting inch, Dorin dragged his hands up to cup her small breasts. He grazed the skin on the underside of them, and a small whimper escaped her lips.

"You like that."

It wasn't a question, but she answered anyway. "Yes."

He brushed her nipples with his thumbs, and her back bowed in pleasure, forcing her breasts closer to him. He leaned over her and kissed a trail down her neck until his mouth fastened on one of her breasts. She clasped his head, and he hummed appreciatively.

His fingers skimmed along her side and across her hipbones until they dipped between her legs. He circled the nub of sensation but didn't linger. Dorin slid a finger into her slit. Her hips rose off the table, driving him deeper.

"Oh love, you're so wet for me," he said with a chuckle. He pulled his finger out, and she mewled in protest. He brought it to his lips and sucked it clean. "You taste divine. I want more."

"Yes," she whispered. "More is good."

His hands kneaded her breasts, and his tongue found the nub between her legs. He licked and nibbled and teased until she writhed on the table. He clenched her hips, pinning her.

Languid warmth curled through her, pressure built, and when a hand released her hip to slide down and slip a finger inside her, she exploded with pleasure, bucking against his mouth. He sucked and thrusted his finger until her spasms subsided.

Dorin gathered her in his arms and carried her to her bed. If he suffered for his actions, he gave no sign. He nestled her on the furs, then pulled his tunic over his head. Her gaze caressed him, taking in his lithe muscles. She licked her lips, anticipating another taste of him. But he kept his breeches on.

"What's wrong?" she asked when he seemed frozen in place.

"I want you, Betony. I want to bury myself inside you and make you come again, with my name on your lips. But I don't want you to suffer any permanent consequences. You're a princess, and you don't need a bastard child. Trust me."

She stretched out a hand and he took it. "First, Lorea has different views of legitimacy—any child I have, whether in or out of a marriage, will be loved and won't be disinherited. Second, I am fae, and like my fairy ancestors, I can only get pregnant when I want to. And now would be a very, very bad time."

He narrowed his eyes and pursed his lips as he ran his fingers over the iron-studded bracelet. "What about the zelizka?"

Betony smiled and tugged, pulling him off balance so he leaned over her once more.

"It's a physical ability, not a magical one. I can explain the mechanics if you want, or…"

An answering smile spread over his face. "Or?"

She brushed the hard length of him through his breeches.

"Or you can bury yourself in me and make me come again, *Dorin*."

He shivered as she lingered on his name, giving him a taste of what he wanted. Dorin didn't answer with words, but kissed her hard, devouring her once more, nipping at her lips, twirling his tongue around hers. Before long, she was moaning in pleasure and heat settled between her legs again.

Dorin peeled off his breeches, his hard length standing at attention, eager for her. He settled between her legs, kissing her neck. He clutched her close and teased her entrance with his tip. She lifted her hips, but before he could sheath himself inside her, he rolled them over so she was on top.

"Ride me. Take your pleasure so I can take mine."

When she didn't move for a moment, he added, "Please."

She lifted and grasped his hardness. He groaned as she seated him deep within her.

"Yes," he breathed. "Oh Alet, yes."

He bucked beneath her and she rocked back and forth. Dorin grabbed her hips and held her steady as she rode him to her pleasure.

Betony exploded, her skin aflame.

"Dorin," she gasped. She wanted to scream his name, but this would have to do.

He thrust up into her once more.

"Betony," he groaned as he came.

She collapsed onto him. He pulled the furs over them both and stroked her hair.

"Sleep now, love," he said.

And Betony closed her eyes and slept.

Chapter 28

The morning Dorin woke with Betony in his arms was the best morning of his life. He wished he could stay all day, but he needed to go before anyone discovered them.

He pulled her closer and kissed the hair above her ear. She groaned and turned in his arms. Her fingers grazed his scruffy cheek.

"I have to go," he whispered.

"Must you?"

"Yes."

He kissed her, holding himself to the softest brush when all he wanted was to devour her once more. She sighed but didn't protest when he let go. He crawled out of the bed and went to find his tunic and breeches. The light coming through the windows was barely brighter than the moon, a bluish pre-dawn awakening. Few people were awake this early, and those who were often had more important business to attend to than noticing who was sneaking out of the guest house. His stepmother and sister were rarely up before the sun was high in the sky, and his brothers had to be rolled out of bed by servants if they were needed somewhere before midday.

His clothes were where he'd left them last night, on the floor by the table. He picked them up, brushed them off, and dressed. Dorin looked back at Betony. She leaned on one elbow, watching him with a wistful expression.

"Will you return tonight?" she asked, and he couldn't help hearing a note of anxiety in the question.

"I'll try." Dorin fought the urge to go back to her, to kiss her once more, because it would only lead to other things, things that would doom them both should they be caught.

Betony dropped into the furs, and he left before he could change his mind.

It turned out he didn't return. Too many people wanted his attention, and when he lay down on his bed to pretend to sleep and wait for everyone else to settle for the night, he actually fell asleep.

But he made it the next night, and the night after. He buried himself in her warmth, forgot the world for a while, and snuck out before the sun rose. It felt glorious and dishonest all at once. Betony deserved someone who didn't have to sneak around to be a part of her life. She deserved someone who could point to her and say, "She is mine and I am hers."

He had to find a way to make it possible, foil his father's plans for her. Marrying her to the bastard wasn't good enough for Kalman's pride. Only his legitimate sons would do. Even if Dorin tried to marry her, Illes and Rodric would have his head out of jealousy.

But did she honestly want him as something other than a bedfellow? Despite being the bastard son of a hungry and grasping warlord. Despite being an assassin. Despite being the man who had kidnapped her. Did she want *him*?

Because gods knew, he wanted her. Now and forever.

Dorin would enjoy it while it lasted, for as long as it lasted. When this was over, when she finally returned home, he would let her go, because what else could he do? Dorin was no fit match for a princess.

He watched from his table as night after night she was seated between his brothers. As night after night, she fended off their poor attempts at seduction, their wandering hands, their leers. As night after night, her gaze lit upon him, and he burned for her. Just from a glance.

He would let her go when this was over. He would. But Dorin doubted he would survive it.

A few days after their first assignation, he found himself with a little free time in the afternoon. He wandered over to where his brothers practiced nearly every day. Their usual cadre of onlookers and admirers were there: off-duty guards, merchants' sons from the city, a few young women, too. And Betony.

It was the first time he'd spotted her there. She seemed to prefer being alone or in the kitchen with Delia. In the ten days she'd been here, she managed to finish embroidering the red dress his sister had saddled her with, found some lace to stitch onto the neckline of the blue dress, and wore the brown dress as if it were the finest silk.

Rodric faced off against another young man, one unknown to Dorin, and Illes stood by himself, waiting his turn against the next opponent. They carried blunted battle axes and swiped at each other. It was unlikely anyone would die, but many, many bruises were guaranteed, and broken limbs were a distinct possibility.

His brother got in a solid blow and knocked his opponent to the ground, unconscious. While Rodric paraded around the ring like an elk in rutting season, Betony rushed in to check on the poor sod lying in the mud.

She showed the same care as she had with Signe and the other sailors on the *Zovog's Revenge*, the same care she'd shown to him. A little jealous, he strode over and helped her move the man to a bench near the wooden wall surrounding the chief's compound.

"You, dogsbody, you don't belong here," Illes thundered. "Get off the field or prepare to defend yourself."

"Go," Betony muttered as she examined her newest patient. "I've got this."

He hated leaving her, but the only way to avoid drawing more attention to them together was for him to acquiesce. Dorin nodded and turned to go, only for Rodric to block him. His half brother thrust a blunted sword at him, a menacing sneer on his face.

"No, Illes, he shouldn't leave yet. Let's see what the son of Piroska is made of. Take the sword, Dorin."

"Don't," Betony whispered from behind him.

But he had no choice. In a warrior society, refusing a challenge would mean dishonor, and though his own honor meant nothing to him, Rodric had called him out by his mother's name, and her reputation as a warrior, as a savior, as a hero, couldn't be besmirched. He took the damned sword.

Illes approached and grabbed his brother by the arm.

"Reconsider, Rodric," Illes hissed. "Jani trained the prat. Who knows what he's capable of?"

"That is exactly what we'll find out."

Rodric gave no further warning. As soon as Illes let go, he charged. But Dorin expected it. His brother, while a brute on the battlefield and in the training arena, was predictable. Dorin stepped out of the way and readied his blade.

His brother spun and slashed, but Dorin blocked the attacks. Not without effort. Rodric was bigger than him, stronger than him, probably even better than him on the battlefield. Dorin's sword skills were more defensive, but he was faster, moved unpredictably, and, most of all, he was a survivor.

They traded blows, and Dorin gave as good as he got. Before long, they were both limping, and blood oozed from where fists had struck faces in their close encounters. Neither had the upper hand. They circled one another, occasionally lashing out with their blades.

Dorin sensed the presence behind him as Betony called, "Watch out!"

He ducked, and a broadax swished right above his head. Illes laughed, and Rodric struck. At least he tried to.

A wooden staff intercepted the sword stroke and parried it.

Betony shifted into Dorin's line of sight and stood in front of Rodric, leaving him to confront Illes. Tiny as she was, there was no way his brother could miss the hostility pouring off her. Betony pointed at Rodric.

"I thought this was supposed to be a fair fight. Two on one doesn't seem fair to me."

Her color rose, and her voice was as cold as the north wind now blowing.

Rodric swatted her finger aside with the flat of his blade. "What do you know of fighting, little girl? A battle isn't free from risk, and neither is this arena. I can't always control myself in the heat of battle."

Illes seemed more interested in the scene Betony was making than in fighting Dorin, but Dorin doubted it would stay that way. He didn't press any advantage his brother's distraction presented, neither did he lower his sword.

Betony narrowed her eyes and spun the staff slowly, getting a feel for it. The crowd stilled.

"I challenge you, Rodric," she called.

A few nervous chuckles skittered through the gathering. Rodric looked at her and laughed.

"Put it away, Your Highness. I don't wish to hurt you."

Dorin bit his cheek to keep from smiling. His brother was digging his own grave.

"If I'm so little, why are you afraid of fighting me?" Betony asked in her sweetest voice, the one Dorin had learned was her deadliest.

A few of the men oohed at her taunt. Rodric's ruddy face reddened even further.

"Hold your tongue, woman, and learn your place," he snapped.

"It's *Princess*, and I know my place. Do you?"

Rodric leered at her and grabbed his crotch.

"On your knees sucking this would be a start."

Dorin's grip tightened on his sword, and his blood rose. He'd always been an ice-cold fighter, leading with his mind not his gut. This must be the bloodlust he'd heard so much about. If he ever heard those words from Rodric again, he'd cut out the fucker's tongue. Illes flicked his gaze at Dorin and paled, as though he could read Dorin's mind and feared what he saw there.

Good.

Betony smirked, the staff still whirling lazily. "That tiny thing? I'd be afraid of hurting you."

Like a bull moose, Rodric roared and charged at her, brandishing his battleax. She easily dodged his attack and rammed her staff into his stomach. Dorin heard the whoosh as the breath left his brother's body and the subsequent wheeze as Rodric tried to suck in more air.

Illes chose that moment to strike, and Dorin couldn't watch Betony beat the crap out of Rodric while defending himself. And he certainly couldn't help her if she got into trouble. He needed to end this absurdity with Illes swiftly.

He parried the blow and spun out of his half brother's reach. Out of the corner of his eye, he saw Rodric turn and approach Betony more cautiously, spinning his axe in his hand.

Illes grunted and tried the same move, but once again, Dorin parried and spun. This time he kept low and swung the flat of his blade against the back of Illes's right knee. It collapsed beneath him, and his sword landed in the mud. As quick as a striking viper, Dorin hooked an arm around Illes's thick neck and pressed the vessels on either side. He held his blade to his brother's throat for good measure. Ille's eyes rolled into the back of his head, and a word escaped.

"Yield."

Dorin let go of his barely conscious brother and turned his attention to Betony's fight.

They circled each other. Winded, Rodric poked and prodded at her with the sword, and she easily blocked each blow. Sweat trickled down his brother's brow, while Betony looked as fresh as she had this morning after a night of lovemaking.

Rodric grinned, a cold, evil thing that sent pangs of fear racing through Dorin's body. He knew that look—his brother had a plan, and he believed he could win. Dorin dared a look at Betony once more. Cool, calm, collected Betony. He'd fought her. He'd seen how she moved. But could someone so small truly beat a brute like Rodric?

He ground his teeth and curled his hands into fists, the fingernails biting into the flesh of his palms. There was nothing he could do. It was one-on-one, and interfering would be seen as more than dishonorable, even with his vow to protect her. But he readied himself to rush in if it seemed Rodric would injure her.

Rodric inched closer to her but stayed outside the reach of her staff. With his height and long arms, he could still hit her without her being able to return the favor. Quicker than a cat with a mouse, he struck. Betony didn't even look surprised. In fact, if Dorin had to give a name to the emotion flitting across her face, it would be *satisfied*.

The princess ducked at the last second, and the blade sliced the air above her. She lunged toward Rodric, her staff low, and jabbed him in the balls. His brother howled in pain, and Betony swept her staff into first one knee, then the other. In an instant, Rodric lay in the mud next to Illes, and the end of the staff was pointed at his throat.

"That's a fair fight," she said.

She dropped the wooden practice staff and walked away.

Dorin never wanted her more.

"Bitch!" Rodric shouted, rising out of the mud like some sort of mythical monster.

Illes grabbed his ankle, and Rodric crashed back into the mud. Rodric kicked out at his younger brother, and soon the two were wrestling and trading insults. The crowd paid no attention as Dorin hurried out of the arena, the sight of the sons of the chief far more entertaining. Betony maintained her steady pace, leaving the two warriors looking nothing more than small children fighting over a sweet. He arrived at the opening as Betony did. She glanced at him and winked. It was quick, and he doubted anyone else saw. She continued walking, never looking at the chaos in her wake.

Dorin stood firm in the opening, in case Rodric escaped Illes, but he imagined the sway of her hips and her hair blowing in the breeze as she returned to her quarters. He ached to go after her, check for himself she was uninjured. He did not.

Instead, he guarded her retreat, though it seemed Illes had the situation under control.

"You need to calm down, Rodric. You can't go around calling the princess a bitch."

"But did you see—"

"Yes, I saw. She got lucky. Don't let her get under your skin. Can you imagine living with that all your life?"

The fight left Rodric. "No, I can't. I won't. She's all yours, Illes. Alet bless your union, and may your mistresses give you comfort, because that fae witch won't."

Illes laughed as if it was the funniest joke he'd ever heard, hard enough that Rodric joined in. Dorin did not. In fact, he froze in place, and only moved when his brother barreled by, shoving him out of the way. Not in fear, but in a rage so deep if he gave into it there would be two dead bodies before dinner.

Dorin inhaled through his nose and exhaled slowly through his mouth. Now wasn't the time. The time would be when they least expected it. He'd ruin them slowly, poison their food, chase away their women, and dull their fighting blades. He'd drug them and nearly suffocate them. And when they were desperate to die, he would feed them their own organs.

It was a nice fantasy. That's all it could be, truly. Instead, he would deny them the princess they so desperately desired. He renewed his vow to Alet and Zovog. He would protect Betony with his last breath.

He was desperate to see her, but she didn't show up to dinner. This upset his stepmother, but his father and brothers barely seemed to notice. Probably to Betony's benefit. They would have given her grief after her performance in the arena today. This way, they could all pretend it hadn't happened.

Dorin lingered in the shadows of the Great Hall, ensuring no one went to the guest house. His fingers and toes grew numb until he couldn't stand it anymore. His father's longhouse was dark and quiet. Loud laughter came from his brothers' house, but given the cold temperatures of midwinter, not a single person lingered outside. Except him. He crept to Betony's longhouse and slipped in once more.

She sat at the table under a feeble lantern with the brown dress in her hands.

"You missed dinner," he said.

She jumped, stabbing her finger with a needle. She stuck it in her mouth, and he watched hungrily.

"I didn't want to deal with your brothers tonight. I pleaded illness. Don't tell."

He slid onto the bench next to her. "I won't. What are you working on so intently you failed to hear me coming?"

Betony held out the sleeve she'd been embroidering. Light purple flowers dotted the fabric. When it was done, it would look like an entirely different dress.

"You're very talented."

"I know."

"And humble, too."

She laughed, and he basked in the musical sound. Betony took the dress back and folded it nicely on the table.

"You didn't come to see my embroidery," she said.

He stroked her cheek with a finger, and she leaned into his touch. "No, I did not. I came to make sure my brothers left you alone. What if I'd been them? You weren't ready."

She slid her blue knife out of her pocket and placed it on the table.

"I was ready. They make a lot more noise than you do."

He lifted it, and it vibrated in his hand, in his head, and in his heart.

"What is it?" she asked when he put it down.

"Is there something special about your knife? Whenever I pick it up, it's…"

"Singing?"

"Yes." That was the word for it, a harmony from a long-forgotten song.

"Of course it is." She laughed and nudged it toward him. "My grandmother gave it to me on my last birthday, but my staff already sings for me. Fairy-wrought steel always knows its true owner."

"Keep it."

"I—"

"For now. For protection. I'll collect it from you one day."

"One day."

She slid it back into her pocket. The firelight made her hair glow, limned her in golden radiance. He was wrong. He wouldn't be able to let her go when this was over. He never wanted to let her go.

"Betony, may I ask you something?"

"Yes."

His heart thudded wildly in his chest. Her answer to this question could break it or send it soaring. No matter her answer, he would protect her. It was vowed twice over.

"What will happen to us when this is all over?"

She cocked her head to the side and considered him for a moment. The pause wasn't helping his heart, and his mind started playing out all the possible answers.

"I don't know."

A tiny crack formed. It hurt worse than he expected, as though someone had pierced it with a barbed arrow and twisted.

"But," she continued, threading her fingers through his, "I also don't want us to end."

Foolish, foolish hope soared. He had to rein it in before his heart took over from his head.

"It may not be possible."

Betony lifted a shoulder, and a sly grin flashed in the dim light. "Never tell a Lorean royal they can't have what they want. We always find a way, Dorin. Always."

She leaned over and brushed her lips against his. The herbal scent of the tea she'd drunk was there, as well as the sweet taste that was all her. He ran his fingers into her hair, the silkiness of it thrilling him. She groaned into his mouth as he deepened the kiss.

Dorin loosed the laces of her dress and freed a breast, her skin as silky as her hair. How did she do it? Betony shuddered under his touch, and an instinctual possessiveness rose from deep within him.

She's mine, if I'm brave enough.

He sent a silent prayer to Alet, the god of life and all the possibilities that entailed.

He had no plan to get her home, no plan to nix his father's grand ambitions, no plan to deal with his brothers. Once the threat they posed was eliminated, he could claim what was his. Three words and she'd be his forever. But there was time to claim his forever.

Dorin pulled his tunic over his head, and Betony's fingers drifted over his chest and along his sides, avoiding the new bruises. He lifted the hem of her dress, bunching the fabric around her hips. He trailed a path up her inner thigh as Betony gasped and clutched at his arms. But he stopped before he touched the warm juncture calling to him, begging him for his caress.

Instead, he finished unlacing her dress, and she helped him pull it off. The garment dropped to the floor in a satisfying rustle, and she leaned on her arms. Her small, perfect breasts thrust toward him, demanding to be licked and sucked, and her legs were spread out before him, like an erotic banquet.

He stood and held out a hand.

"Come here, Princess. I need to show you something."

Confusion and frustration warred across her lovely features, and he pressed his lips together to keep from laughing. She quirked an eyebrow but took his hand. Dorin helped her to her feet and led her to the far end of the longhouse.

They stood in front of the mirror of silvered glass, the one his father had gifted his mother in the early days of their relationship. Spoils from a raid long before his birth, and the only thing he had left of hers. And it wasn't even his.

"Look at you...look at us."

He locked one arm around her waist and stroked up her side until he cupped her breast. As he brushed his thumb across her nipple, she arched back, but her eyes never left their reflection in the gray-clouded glass.

"I won't give you up. I won't give us up. I will fight for this, for us. You're worth it."

Betony's gaze met his in the mirror, and her brilliant green eyes shone with desire, want, and some deeper emotion. His heart skipped a beat when the word "love" came to mind.

"You're worth it, too," she whispered, grasping his arm. "But..."

He nuzzled her neck and licked the spot where it joined her shoulder. "But what?"

"You have too many clothes on."

Dorin nipped her gently and chuckled. He let her go as he toed off his shoes and removed his breeches. She watched his every move, her tongue darting out to lick her lips. Soon enough, his arm was back around her waist, his erection pressed into her ass. She tried to wiggle, and he pinched her nipple.

Betony hissed in a breath and bit her lip but stilled.

He returned to kissing her neck and strumming her nipple. She relaxed against him. He dropped the arm from her waist, allowing his hand to dip lower until he brushed two fingers against her slit.

"So wet, my love," he murmured.

She moaned in response and bucked her hips. He answered the unvoiced demand by slipping a finger into her warm depths. Her back arched, drawing his finger deeper, but she never took her eyes off the image reflected in front of them.

"Please, Dorin."

He slipped another finger into her and tweaked her nipple. She leaned into him, allowing him to support her weight, and her quiet cries filled the air. His thumb found the sensitive nub at her apex and rubbed.

She broke, her muscles clenching his fingers tightly in rhythmic waves, wild and beautiful as she fell apart.

As they subsided, he released her nipple and locked eyes on her reflection.

"Eyes on me, Princess."

Betony's passion-glazed gaze found his face in the mirror. Dorin removed his fingers and sucked them clean. Fire shone in her gaze, and her tongue once again traced the edges of her lips.

He tilted her chin up and back and kissed her. Her tongue found the seam of his lips and he opened, sucking on it, tasting her in an entirely different way. No matter how he did, it was exquisite, it was erotic. It was home.

Dorin guided himself to her entrance, her slickness coating him as he slid in deep. Betony gasped as he filled her, and she trembled around him.

One arm encircled her hips, steadying her, while his fingers found and circled the nub once more. He thrust into her in a slow rhythm. Their groans mingled in the cool air, and Betony rocked back, meeting him thrust for thrust. She panted, and her gaze found his once more. He could've sworn her eyes glowed, swallowing him up as he finally came, spilling himself into her. She bucked wildly an instant later as she found her own release.

Betony leaned forward and braced herself on the washstand, and he slipped from her, breathing heavily. As heavily as she was.

He gathered his princess in his arms and carried her to bed. He crawled in next to her and pulled up the furs. She snuggled into his embrace, and Dorin knew he'd found where he belonged for the first time since his mother died. He would do anything to keep her safe and by his side, gods-bound or not. Dorin, son of Piroska, bastard of Kalman, midnight man, and beloved of no one, loved Princess Betony of Lorea.

May Alet and Zovog have mercy upon his soul.

Chapter 29

*C*old air and hard hands dragged Betony from her sleep and her bed. Harsh voices spoke over her, and her sleep-addled mind could make neither heads nor tails of them. All she sensed in those first few moments was Dorin was gone, ripped from her as she slept. And she was naked.

Someone held her close, one arm around her waist and pinning her arms to her sides. Someone who was not Dorin. Because Dorin was on his knees five paces away, also naked, and Chief Kalman held a blade to his son's neck. Dorin's hands were tied behind his back, and a half dozen guards surrounded them, swords and axes pointed at her lover.

But the likely reason why Dorin didn't fight was the dagger held above Betony's heart. Whatever fight left in her disappeared. She went limp against the large body behind her, and Kalman smiled at her capitulation.

"I knew you were an intelligent woman the first time I saw you," he said.

He didn't leer, didn't seem to notice or care about her state of undress. But everything she'd learned about the chief of Clan Fher told her he would use her vulnerability against her. She'd try not to give him the opportunity.

"What do you want, Kalman?" She made a concerted effort to keep her voice calm. As long as they held a blade to Dorin's throat, she would do exactly as she was told.

"I believe you know."

"I've been roused from my bed and restrained. Let's pretend I don't."

The grin morphed into a sneer, but Kalman's blade never wavered. It hovered a hairsbreadth from Dorin's skin. Her lover held his tongue, but his eyes pleaded with her. It did not matter what he hoped she would do. With his life on the line, she had no choice.

"Fine, let me make it simple for you. Since you seem intent on fucking the least of my sons, I think you should upgrade. Marry my heir. With the support of Lorea, I'll be able to consolidate my power in Fuartir and become king in my own right. Your children will eventually inherit the throne, which is more than your father can offer."

The idea sickened her, but she needed time. Time to send for help, time to escape, time to save Dorin.

"Why should I?"

He pressed the blade to Dorin's throat. A line of blood appeared and drops dripped down his neck and splashed onto the rushes below.

"Did my bastard not tell you what he is?"

Bet kept her mouth shut, but panic flitted over Dorin's features.

"He's a midnight man, an assassin trained by the clerics of Zovog to kill using dishonorable methods—poison, 'accidents,' knives in the back. And you've been fucking him."

Her heart stopped for an instant. That explained…everything. Betony laughed, and surprise flickered over Kalman's face. The grip around her tightened, but the blade above her chest did not waver.

"He'll fit right in," she said. "Remind me to tell you stories about what it takes to marry into the Lorean royal family."

Kalman growled and yanked Dorin's head back, adding another line of blood. She stopped laughing, and a shiver threatened to give away her dread.

"Now, he's violated an honored guest. Twice dishonored my clan, and the price for breaking the laws of hospitality is death. I have the power to commute his sentence to banishment as an act of mercy for my heir's wedding."

As chief, he could spin the situation however he wanted. The truth was what he said it was, no matter the facts. He was leaving her with little choice.

"What about my oath? If you have me break it, the dishonor falls on the entire clan," Dorin said.

Kalman slapped him hard enough to split his lip. More of Dorin's blood dribbled down his chin and fell to the floor.

"You have caused me more than enough trouble. I offer you your life, if your lover values you for something other than your cock. The best thing you could have done was bring me her as a hostage. For that, you have my gratitude. Once she is married to one of my *true* sons, she will be with family. You, on the other hand, have become a liability. It is time for you to go."

Kalman threw Dorin to the ground and kicked him in the gut. Dorin curled into a protective ball as his father drew back his foot, aiming for the head.

"Stop." Betony strained against her captor. Her squirming had the guard…excited. She stilled. "I'll do it."

"Ah, she cares. At least you know someone in this world does." Kalman dropped his foot and dragged Dorin up by his hair.

"But I won't marry Rodric."

"Fine. I'll name Illes my heir. I don't like Rodric much, anyway." He took the handle of his dagger and crashed it against Dorin's head. Her lover crumpled, unconscious, to the floor. "Take him to the jail in town. He'll be put on a boat for anywhere but here immediately after the wedding. Tell him if he sets foot in Clan Fher land again, I'll personally cut his throat. And once I am king, he best stay out of Fuartir entirely."

The guards lowered their weapons, and two stepped next to Dorin and grabbed his arms. Tears streamed down Betony's face as they dragged her lover away. The man she truly wanted to marry. Someday. She needed to survive until she found him again. Then Idoya help Kalman. She would end whatever hope he had for a legacy.

Kalman gestured to the guard holding her. He sheathed his blade and let her go, but her legs wouldn't support her. She collapsed to the floor.

"I'll break the news to Illes. He'll be thrilled."

The chief turned to go. Betony pulled herself together, reminding herself what she needed most—time.

"I have conditions." She stood and refused to either cower or cover her nakedness.

"You are in no position—"

"I will wear a smile on my wedding day and make no mention of what happened here today to your people if you agree to my conditions."

He tilted his head and motioned for her to go on.

"One, I get to say goodbye to Dorin." Kalman opened his mouth to object, but Betony beat him to it. "With an escort approved by you."

"Very well."

She still needed time. It was unlikely help would arrive in the next few days, but a new dawn always brought hope. She had a good excuse. What bride didn't want a beautiful wedding gown?

"Two, five days to prepare my gown."

"Three days—sunset the day after tomorrow."

As expected, but she could live with it. "Fine, three days. And lastly, I want your most sacred oath, by Alet and by Zovog in front of witnesses, that immediately after the wedding, Dorin will be put on a boat and exiled, with no more threats to his life."

Again, a sly smile spread over Kalman's face. "I will enjoy having you as a daughter. Much more useful than Gizi has been. Her own marriage may finally bring me something of value. Done."

What she demanded was not unreasonable given the circumstances. He was barely giving up anything to achieve exactly what he wanted. Betony did not bother to explain he was getting more than he ever would want, and she would make their lives miserable until she found a way out of this mess.

"I expect the seamstress this morning. I can't get married in any of the gowns I currently have."

Kalman nodded and pointed at the guard behind her. "Stand guard outside. The only people allowed in are my wife, my daughter, and the seamstress. I'll feed your cock to the fish if you allow anyone else in. The rest of you, leave."

All the guards exited, the one who had held her looking particularly pale. Kalman followed without another word.

Betony collapsed on a bench, folding her arms and resting her head on them. She couldn't cry. Crying would solve nothing. She had done what she needed to do to save Dorin and buy her the time to devise a better plan. But without her magic, what could she do?

Nothing but go through with the wedding until she could escape. It might take months, maybe years, but at the first opportunity, she was gone. She would find Dorin again, and she would claim her happily ever after.

But first, tea.

She dashed away the tears that had leaked out despite her determination to not cry and pulled on her discarded chemise. After stoking the fire and placing the kettle on the hook, she busied herself with making tea. The seamstress arrived shortly with two gowns, only the hems unfinished. Kalman had planned well.

The woman laid out Betony's choices. One was a dark pink, almost the same color as her hair, with blue embroidery in abstract designs around the neckline. The other was a green the same color as her eyes, with golden leaves started on the sleeves.

"This one." Betony pointed at the green dress. If she was to be married, she would be a Lorean princess in all her glory. "You hem it and finish the edge. I'll decorate it."

"But Your Highness—"

"Are you going to argue with a princess, or are you going to do as you're told?"

Betony hated pulling rank or discounting a servant's expertise, but she needed to make a statement with her dress, one Clan Fher and Chief Kalman would never forget. She kept her expression as cold as Freylin, the Faerie Queen of Winter.

The color left the woman's face, and she curtsied low, keeping her eyes to the floor. "Of course. My apologies, Princess Betony."

She waved away the apologies. The woman helped her into the dress, pinned the hem and the seams for a perfect fit, and turned to leave.

"Return it as soon as possible so I may finish the embroidery by my wedding day. I will need as much golden or bronze thread as possible," Betony said to her back. "And I'm sorry for earlier. There's a lot to do in very little time."

More even than you know.

The woman dipped a quick curtsy before vanishing through the door.

The finished dress and the embroidery thread arrived with her midday meal. Ignoring the food, Betony stabbed at the fabric until her fingers were numb. She crawled into bed and fell asleep.

The next morning, she nibbled at some bread before going back to her embroidery. Unfortunately, it wasn't going to finish itself. The seamstress joined her after breakfast and worked on the embroidery near the hemline until she was called away to work on Rahel's dress. Despite the assistance, Betony's fingers were numb and bleeding by midday.

Gizi showed up with a bowl of stew for luncheon and a scowl. She dropped the bowl on the table with a clatter and sat with a dramatic sigh.

"Why don't you let the servants do that?" she asked.

Betony ignored her. Gizi kicked at her under the table.

"Hey, I'm talking to you."

Lifting her gaze from her nearly finished work, Betony focused her undivided attention on the brat. Gizi gulped at whatever showed on her face.

"I'll soon be your sister, Gizi, but I will always be a princess. You will give me the respect I deserve or face the consequences."

Her fingers continued to push and pull the needle through the fabric as she spoke. Gizi watched as if she'd been mesmerized by the simple motions.

"You could make yourself useful and put on the kettle," Betony said after a moment.

Gizi blinked, opened her mouth to protest, thought better of it, and did as Betony asked. As soon as the cup of tea was on the table, Betony put aside the embroidery and grabbed a spoon to eat. This time she was hungry, and she had to keep up her strength to get through the next few days. She shoveled in the stew without tasting it, sipping her tea in between bites. Gizi kept watching.

"Is there anything else?" Betony snapped.

She had no patience for this woman. And she did not appreciate being reminded of the fact she would soon be married to a man she despised, while the one she loved rotted in jail.

"Oh, yes. Father said after you ate, I was to bring you to town to shop for accessories. He said he would meet us at the mayor's house first to conduct some final business before the wedding."

Excellent, Kalman would keep his word.

"Why didn't you say so?" Betony finished her tea in a last gulp and left the remains of her stew with a clatter of spoon against bowl. "Let's go."

She grabbed Gizi by the hand and dragged her out of the house.

Chapter 30

orin huddled under his scratchy wool blanket. They'd dressed him in a ragged, stained tunic and some too-large trousers with thin knees while he was unconscious. No one had bothered to give him socks, shoes, or a coat, and thick metal chains bound his wrists and ankles together, allowing little movement. The blanket was the only warmth he had besides the straw pallet in the basement of the mayor's house. His head and ribs still ached from the blows his father gave him, but at least the lump from where his father had hit him had disappeared.

The small room served as the jail for Cseobar. Few people needed to stay more than a night after a fight or until they could be sent to the manor for the chief's judgment. It was a disgraceful end to his career as an assassin.

Betony was his safe place, and he slept too soundly in her presence. Caught naked and unaware, he had been subdued before he could put up any sort of fight. And the look on the guard holding Betony killed any other passing thought. The stinking whale turd of a man would have hurt her in deplorable ways if Dorin had offered even the least bit of resistance, of that he had no doubt.

Dorin assumed his father was waiting for Betony to marry Illes before he killed him, all the better to ensure her cooperation. Illes at least, and not Rodric. His father was cunning—Illes showed a modicum of restraint when necessary and would make a much better clan chief than Rodric. Kalman's promise to send him out into the wide world, never to step foot in his homeland again, had been merely a ruse to control her. He would never again see the woman he loved.

He wished he had one last chance to say it, but the likelihood was next to zero.

A guard had slid a plate of bread and a skin of water into his room this morning through the narrow gap at the bottom of the wood door. A small square had been cut out of the door and barred with thick iron. Through it, he got a peek out the glass window high in the wall across the way, the gray sky offering little cheer this dreary morning. Dorin's stomach gurgled with hunger, but the small repast was long gone. He expected nothing else until dinner.

Several pairs of feet tromped on the floor above. Murmured words seeped down the stairs, and the footfalls quickly followed. He'd recognize his father's steps anywhere, but there were at least two more people with him. A key jangled in the lock and the door flew open.

His father stood there, with a guard nearly as large. Behind them, a flash of lingonberry hair appeared.

No.

He took back his earlier wish. He didn't want her to see him like this. Beaten, bloodied, fucking shoeless, chained in the corner of his prison.

"Give us a few moments," Betony said imperiously, as regal as her mother.

The guard shifted unconsciously, responding to the command in her voice, but his father clapped a hand to the man's shoulder.

"Why?" Kalman asked.

"Would you prefer me to go willingly to the marriage bed, or do you want to drag me kicking and screaming?"

Dorin shuddered, not only from the picture of Betony going willingly to someone else's bed, but from her wintry tone. No matter how angry she'd been at him, not even when she'd first awoken after he'd kidnapped her, he'd never heard her so cold, so distant. *His* Betony was filled with flame, and passion, and kindness. This version was none of those things. And it was all his fault.

His father let go of the guard and signaled for him to leave. He turned to Betony and ran his hands over her sides and dipped them into her pockets. Then he grabbed her upper arms and pulled her close in a grip Dorin had experienced many times as a child. Despite the heavy fabric of her dress, she would wear bruises for a few days.

"Help him escape, and I will kill him myself, slowly, painfully, and bloody, and make you watch. Do you understand?"

Unexpectedly, Betony cowed before his father, her shoulders slumping and her eyes focusing on the floor. "Of course, my lord."

He shoved her roughly toward Dorin and strode out, locking the door behind him.

Betony crouched next to him, stretching out a dainty hand. Dorin flinched away. He'd done this to her, broken her spirit, doomed her to an involuntary marriage, took away her agency.

She dropped her hand. "Dorin, I'm sorry. I didn't mean—"

"Sorry? Why are you sorry? This is my fault. I knew better, but I slept with you anyway. I..."

He couldn't get the words out. He wanted, needed, to tell her how he felt, but the words stuck in his throat.

"Is it true? Are you an assassin?"

Yes, of course that's why she came. To shame him for his betrayal.

"Yes. The temple of Zovog trained me after my mother died. Jani's idea, though my father wholeheartedly approved. All the better to serve the clan. Serve the chief. Use the bastard so his legitimate sons could focus on fucking and fighting. Brought me in to pretend to be a manservant when I was eighteen. I thought...it doesn't matter what I thought. You were right—I should have run that night at the Fiddle and Drum. I should have left you alone. You'd be home with your family."

"Maybe, and maybe Lorant would have killed me. We cannot change the choices of our past, only make better ones going forward. But we don't have time for this." She dipped her fingers into her cleavage and pulled out a wooden disk. "Here, keep this close. The crew of *Zovog's Revenge* owes me a favor, and I'm giving it to you. Find them and tell them what happened. I trust they'll land you someplace safe and tell me where."

"You're assuming my father will do as he says." He refused to look at her.

"It's part of our agreement. Your life and an oath to guarantee it if he wants me to willingly marry Illes."

"You don't know my father. He'll renege."

"And that's why I'm giving you this." She grabbed his hand and placed the disk in it, closing his fingers around it. Her touch still filled him with warmth and desire, no matter the dire circumstances. Gods, he wanted so much more time with her. "I do not trust your father further than I can throw him, but I trust *them*. Please, Dorin, take it, let me do what is in my power to help you survive."

He regarded her for a moment, tears welling in her eyes, skin pale, and a tremble in her fingers.

"Why, Betony?"

"So I can find you, silly man. So I can get my happy ending the same way my sister and my brother did. Because I love you."

"You shouldn't."

"But I do."

He was the one shaking now. "Illes is possessive. He won't let you escape. And my father, he's ruthless. He'll see you dead before he sees you with me."

"I won't let them win."

Dorin pressed the token back into her hand. His next words were the hardest thing he'd ever said, but her life was the most precious thing in the world. "Use it for yourself. Run to the *Revenge*, and the crew will see you to safety."

"Fuck safety, Dorin, son of Piroska. My entire life, people have tried to keep me safe. My sister, my brother, my parents, the Queens of Faerie. Yet here I am. Safety never brought me anything worth having. I'd rather run for the rest of my life and have you by my side than live one more day in the safety of Avora."

She grabbed him by the tunic and pulled him to her, sealing her lips to his. Desperation, hope, and love flowed from her, and he breathed it in, swallowed it whole, and returned the kiss with passion and courage. He cupped her face in his chained hands and reveled in the feel of her for the moment they had left. Why not? If her plan failed, he at least had this last memory of her. And if it succeeded…well, then he had her, and they both got a happy ending.

His father's footsteps echoed down the stairs again. They broke apart, chains clinking softly, and Betony shoved the coin in his palm. But before she backed away, he clasped her wrist.

"I love you, too," he whispered, bringing her fingers to his lips.

The key jingled in the lock and she stood quickly. He tucked the disk in his pocket and assumed the same forlorn expression he'd worn when she'd arrived. She mirrored him, but the tears in her eyes were of joy not despair.

His father threw the door open, glaring between the two of them.

"Are you done?"

Betony dropped her gaze to the floor, once more the picture of a demure, browbeaten woman. "Yes, my lord. You have proven you keep your word. My thanks."

She slipped out, and her soft footfalls headed up the stairs.

Kalman's gaze burned with a fury Dorin was unfortunate enough to know well.

"You have been a boil on my ass since your mother birthed you, despite my order to end the pregnancy. I wish to Zovog you had never been born, but at least you have brought me the one thing that will win me a crown. For that, and for my word to the princess, your life is spared. I hope Zovog takes you sooner rather than later, but I thank Alet I'll never have to set eyes upon you again."

His father turned his back. It stung, but it didn't hurt nearly as much as he once feared. After all, he had the love of a fierce, intelligent, and beautiful woman. He'd be just fine without his so-called family.

"My mother had more courage in an eyelash than you have in your entire longhouse. And Betony is stronger and smarter than all your children put together."

Kalman said nothing and walked out.

Dorin brushed the pocket holding the disk. *And that's what I'm counting on.*

Chapter 31

*B*etony's heart soared. *He loves me.*

Then it sunk. *I'm marrying someone else.*

The only thing keeping her from screaming out her pain was the hope she would soon escape, find him, and get her happy ending. She barely paid attention as she and Gizi walked along the street, a guard trailing behind them. With each step, her stomach roiled and her heart ached more. Blessed Mother, how was she going to escape this mess? She had no magic, no way of contacting her family, and no option other than this farce of a wedding.

Gizi led her first to a cobbler. Betony smiled wanly and let Gizi do all the talking. She sat and the cobbler measured her feet for new shoes for the wedding. He had some soft brown suede that would complement her gown and little glass beads that perfectly matched the thread she used for embroidering it. This wasn't the wedding she cared about, but the cobbler wasn't at fault and her purposes were best served if she made the ordinary people think this marriage was a good thing.

They went to the market next. It was the middle of winter, the harvest long past and spring yet a dream around the corner, but there were preserves, and soaps, and dried herbs. Meat, both game and livestock, leather goods, and some woolens. Betony paused at a stall and fingered a fine pair of golden wool stockings, softer and more tightly knit than she'd ever seen in Avora. The Fuartirans had some exceptional goods and would do well in trading with Lorea, Teruelle, and even Faerie. As much as she appreciated Kalman's desire to move his people away from raiding and toward trade, his methods were ruthless.

"Do you like them, miss?" asked the middle-aged woman running the stall.

"It's 'Your Highness,'" Gizi said imperiously.

"Oh." Her face flamed, and she bowed the way Betony had seen the ordinary people of Cseobar do. "Your Highness."

Bet ground her teeth. If she had any chance, she would show these people this wasn't needed. Their aristocracy should be serving them. But today wasn't the day.

"How much for the stockings?" she asked instead.

They quickly came to an appropriate bargain, and Gizi paid the woman before dragging Betony to a final stall filled with sparkling trinkets. Her eye was drawn to a lovely pair of bronze hair pins with a spray of green, gold, and silver glass beads. She might not have a circlet to wear, but these would do nicely.

As Gizi counted out some silver pieces, a flash of black and white wings drew Betony's attention. A magpie launched from the top of the next stall and soared overhead, squawking as it passed. She hadn't seen many birds at all this far north in the winter, and if memory served from Ebon's research two springs ago, magpies were most commonly found in Lorea.

She bit her cheek to keep from smiling. It could be wishful thinking, her imagination finding salvation in an ordinary bird, but it was entirely possible help had finally arrived. She tried to convince her heart not to get ahead of itself, but it wouldn't listen, not one bit, and plans and possibilities whirled through her mind.

The bird made itself scarce, and she saw not a feather more of the creature on their walk back to the chief's manor. As soon as they entered the gate, Gizi shoved the small packages at Betony and took off, her longer legs making it impossible for Betony to keep pace. Not that she wanted to. She turned to the guest house. As she approached, the bird reappeared, swooping at the guard still following her.

She bit her lip to keep from laughing as the man swatted at the bird. It deftly dodged his attempts to bat it out of the sky. There was little doubt now help had arrived. Betony hurried into the house, leaving the door open. The bird flew in, and the guard chased after it.

"You're not supposed to be in here," Betony said with a royal stare that would have made her mother proud.

"But—"

"I'll take care of the bird. You stand guard or your chief will be informed of your transgression."

"Yes, milady."

He ducked out, shamefaced.

Betony slammed the door behind him, threw her packages on the table, and located the bird in the rafters. They studied each other for a moment, and she wished her magic was back. It would be the easiest thing in the world to tell the truth about this bird if it was. As if reading her mind, the magpie cocked its head at her and flew to the ground. Before it landed, a purple mist swirled and twisted around it, like thread on a spinning wheel, and a tall woman with black and white hair stood in its place. She rushed forward and hugged Betony.

"Oh, blessed Veitha, it's good to see you!"

Betony breathed a sigh of relief. Her family had come to her aid, and she might dodge this disaster without having to marry anyone she didn't want to.

"Hello, Sarsa."

"I fly hundreds of miles and all I get is 'Hello, Sarsa'?" But she didn't let go of Betony.

"It's so wonderful to see you all other words fled my mind," Betony amended, a waver of laughter in her voice.

"That's better."

"I understand congratulations are in order, sister. Mother was—"

Sarsa grimaced. "I can imagine. It was an impulse. We'll throw a ball when this is all over."

She gestured at the empty house. Bet noticed someone was missing.

"Where's Brumbull?" The little dragon was rarely far from Sarsa.

"A dragon is far less inconspicuous than a bird, even if he is a baby. He's waiting with Jadran and the others in the forest."

"Jadran is here?" She had to fight tears once more. The captain had been like an uncle her entire life, always looking out for her and her siblings. Even Rane, though she drove him to distraction.

"As soon as Vedel informed your father of your status as a hostage, Captain Jadran volunteered to come fetch you. He landed three days ago with a dozen other guards about twenty miles down the coast. They snuck to the forest and have been waiting for confirmation of where you were since last night. Hyssop contacted me, and I left Ebon on the other side of Fuartir to come find you. I've been searching the city and watching the manor for a few days. Now we need a plan to get you out of here."

"I have one."

"No you don't. *I* have a plan." She pulled a pendant out of her pocket, Bet's invisibility charm. "Put this on and we'll waltz out of here when it gets dark."

"You're not listening. It's not only me you're rescuing—the man I love is being held hostage to guarantee my cooperation. We're going to need serious fire power to rescue him. And that charm is just the start."

Sarsa grinned wickedly as she tucked the pendant back into her pocket. "I like the way you think."

"I'd prefer not to ruin any chance we have at peace with Fuartir in my lifetime. Can you contact Hyssop?"

"Yes, I have a scrying bowl at camp."

"Tell her I'm collecting my boon."

The grin vanished, and Sarsa shook her head. "Are you sure? I can get you both out."

Sarsa could. She was the Lady of Errozar, Faerie's spymaster and commander of its elite guard. She could also shapeshift into any number of useful creatures. But Betony didn't merely want to escape. She wanted to live her life on her own terms. For that, she needed to subvert Kalman's grab for power. He could never be king of Fuartir. She and Dorin would know no peace as long as Kalman held any hope for a throne.

"I'm sure."

Her sister-in-law took her arm and shoved up the sleeve. "What about this monstrosity?"

She poked and prodded at the iron-studded bracelet that cut off Betony's magic, shaking her hand out as the iron burned her flesh.

"They'll know something's wrong if I'm not wearing it. Are you or Hyssop powerful enough to take it off once the plan is in motion?"

Sarsa dropped her arm with a shiver. "Certainly. Hyssop is the most powerful fairy I know, including the Queens, and I'm not far behind, now that my curse is broken. Anything else you need?"

Betony smiled. "A mask and a witness."

Sarsa quirked a quizzical eyebrow but nodded. A smile grew into a laugh as she listened to Betony's instructions and witnessed her vow.

"So be it, Princess Betony of Lorea. Your vow is witnessed, and you will be held to the law of Faerie." Sarsa pulled her into another hug. "You Loreans have a strange way of picking a mate. And I should know, since Ebon picked me."

"What can I say? We're a bit selective when it comes to who we're going to spend the rest of our lives with."

"As you should be." Sarsa let go.

Betony walked over to her bed and pulled the small fairy-wrought knife from under the mattress.

"Make sure Dorin gets this."

"How long do we have?" Sarsa took the blade and made it disappear…somewhere.

"The wedding is tomorrow at sunset."

Sarsa hissed in a breath. "It's going to be close."

"Well, my godmother always enjoys making an entrance."

A wicked smile returned to Sarsa's face before another cloud of purple smoke rose around her. Betony opened the door and the magpie flew out. The guard on the other side flinched as it winged its way over the manor wall. Bet smiled sweetly and shut the door.

She picked up her embroidery and began work again. If she was getting married tomorrow, she'd better look her best.

Chapter 32

*W*hy did it take so long for the sun to set in the middle of winter?

Dorin had kept watch on the sun's progress all day. When it set, his life would change forever. When it set, he'd be put on a boat to gods knew where, never to return. When it set, the love of his life would be married to his asshole brother. At least it was the lesser of the two assholes.

But it seemed to inch across the clear blue sky, prolonging his torment to an intolerable degree.

Betony loved him. She would find him someday. It was his job to survive long enough to make her foolhardy plan a reality. Alet help him, but he believed if anyone could do it, Betony would.

A clap of thunder pulled him from his musings. He glanced out the sliver of a window again. The sun sat a hand's breadth above the clear horizon. Where had the thunder come from?

A thud above him, sounding exactly like a body hitting the floor, had him jumping to his feet, backing away from the door to his cell. Dorin had only the blanket to defend himself. He whipped it off and twisted it into a rope as best he could with his fettered hands.

Delicate footfalls on the steps filled him with hope for an instant. Could it be Betony? No, of course not. His father would be watching her as closely as a dog guarding a bone. There was no way he'd give her any chance to escape until she was safely married to Illes.

The lock turned, then the door burst open. A tall, thin woman with yellow hair—true yellow, like a buttercup in the summer meadow—and violet eyes stalked in, her face bearing a sneer of annoyance. A fairy, and not just any fairy. He'd never met her in person, but there was a portrait of this fairy in the halls of Avora. But she was not just any fairy. She was Lady Hyssop, godmother to all three royal Lorean children. Perhaps Betony had pulled off a miracle.

"Are you Dorin?" she demanded.

"Yes, my lady." He bowed, lowering his twisted blanket. It would be no use against her if it came to a fight.

"Excellent." She tossed the keys at him, and he snatched them out of the air. "Come along."

Hyssop walked out of the room without waiting for him. Dorin quickly unlocked his manacles, leaving them on the cold floor. Hyssop mounted the stairs and Dorin followed, his bare feet slapping against the cold stone floor.

"Where are we going?"

"To save my goddaughter, of course. The silly child was very insistent I rescue you first."

They walked up the stairs, the wood slightly warmer though rougher against his feet. The door was destroyed, splinters lying everywhere. Despite his caution, Dorin stepped on one and hissed in pain.

"My lady, a moment, please." He sat on a step.

"We do not have a moment—well, this is inconvenient."

Hyssop sat next to him on the step and examined his wound. Only a few drops of blood leaked from around the large splinter.

"Where are your shoes?" she asked irritably.

"Um, I was pulled out of bed. No one gave me shoes," he mumbled.

Heat flooded his cheeks, and a sly smile crossed the fairy's lips.

"Certainly, but it is also difficult to escape in bare feet."

Hyssop's fingers were unexpectedly gentle on his foot. She delicately removed the splinter, murmured some words, and with a golden glow, his skin was whole once more.

"Thank you, my lady."

She waved away his words. No—she was saying something in a language he'd never heard before. More green and gold light flowed from her fingers, and a moment later, a pair of black boots formed on his feet. The overlapping scales gleamed with an oily sheen.

"Dragon scale boots. As durable as fairy-wrought steel and sustainably harvested. Those scales came from a molting. Oh, and this is yours."

She pulled a small knife from a sheath at her waist, one among many. But the blade she handed him he recognized. It was Betony's, though she insisted it was truly his. When he took it, it sang, a deep resonance he felt in his bones and in his heart. He tucked it into his pocket alongside the debt token from the *Revenge*.

"It sings for you, doesn't it?" Hyssop shook her head with an amused squint.

"That's what Betony said. Why?"

"Some say fairy-wrought steel reacts to innate magic. Some say it stays in families. Some say it can predict love matches. I am over three hundred years old, and I don't know if any or all of these are true. All I know for certain is fairy-wrought steel knows to whom it belongs. If it sings for you, it belongs to you."

It would have to be good enough, but some ember of acceptance warmed his chest. For once, something chose him. Well, for twice. Hyssop's presence said Betony had, too.

The fairy clapped her hands together. "Now, if we stay much longer, someone is going to inquire about the outside door. Here, put this on."

She pulled a stone pendant off her neck. Also Betony's, her charm to turn invisible. He slid it over his head, gratified to have something of hers so close to his heart.

"How—"

Hyssop grabbed his arm and hauled him to his feet. "Less talking, more walking, please. Time runs short."

He followed her meekly, keeping his mouth shut for the moment. They passed one of his father's guards, sprawled on the floor, but his chest rose. He wasn't dead, disappointingly.

Dorin snagged a ratty coat hanging by the entrance and slipped it on as they exited the building through yet another shattered door. The cold hit him like a runaway carriage. He shoved his hands into his pockets and glanced once more at the sun. Time was running out.

"Can't we do whatever you did to pop into the mayor's house to get to Betony?"

"Yes, that is possible, but I thought you wished to survive long enough to kiss my goddaughter once more."

Oh... "We'll walk, then."

"Yes, that would be best. Keep up, northerner."

He did, but barely, fighting the pain of his earlier beating. Following Hyssop to his father's manor was an exercise in itself. He hadn't the breath to ask any more about the pendant, or the plan, or anything. The streets were oddly silent, as though they sensed danger walked their town. Or perhaps because most of the people were gathering for the celebration in the Great Hall.

When they reached the gate to the compound, the barest sliver of the sun sat on the hilltops.

"Halt!" a guard ordered.

Hyssop ignored him. Instead, blue light flickered into existence, and two tendrils wove through the air. The guards stared at them, frozen with fear, until the tendrils had wrapped tightly around their arms. Their weapons dropped to the ground, and the guards struggled against the magical bonds. The tendrils slammed them against the wall, and both men lapsed into unconsciousness.

Only a small part of him was sorry they weren't dead. Hyssop once again grabbed his arm and dragged him along.

"Everyone will be looking at me," she said. "I need you to use the charm and find a corner to hide in until you see the signal."

"Use the charm?"

She glared at him as if it were the most obvious thing in the world. "Say the magic word, of course. Have you never worked with a magical object before?"

He thought it best not to mention the zelizka he'd fastened to Betony. Besides, the bracelet required no magic word.

"No, my lady, I haven't." His heart raced at the idea of actively using magic. Part of him wanted to rip the stone from his neck and throw it as far from him as he could. The other part appreciated this small piece of enchanted rock was his best chance of rescuing Betony.

Her eyes widened. "Oh, well, I suppose you don't know the word. It's *assombrir*."

The rune on the stone glowed, and a shadowy veil dropped over him. Everything was a smidge darker, a tiny bit more blurry. He shivered—he was using magic, forbidden magic. And yet, he didn't care. There was no one left to dishonor—his mother was dead, the rest of his family had been tied to him only by blood. The one person he would truly miss was Delia, but without a doubt she would wish him well. He could do this. He could use magic, save his love, and flee.

"Say the word again, and the spell lifts," Hyssop said with a smile wide enough to reveal her sharp canines.

"And what's the signal?"

"You'll know," she replied enigmatically as she shoved him toward the Great Hall. "Now go."

He knew the exact right spot and moved quickly, all doubt left in the courtyard. The fairy followed him to the doors, treating the guards there to the same tender mercies she'd shown outside the gates.

Dorin slipped around back and snuck in through the entrance near the kitchen. He waited in the small prep area and peeked out of the curtain.

Betony stood on the dais in front of his father, wearing a gown that perfectly matched her emerald eyes. Golden branches and leaves were embroidered upon it, the embodiment of the Lorean coat of arms. Next to her stood his half brother, Illes, wearing a proud sneer, a fine linen tunic, and a fur jerkin. Gizi stood next to their father, and Rodric, with a scowl that should have scared Illes, stood next to their mother.

His father looked as glorious as a king, with a rich velvet doublet lined with fur, a fine sword strapped to his waist, and a half dozen gold arm rings. All he was missing was a crown.

"Welcome, one and all, to this momentous occasion. I have the honor of joining Clan Fher to the royal line of Lorea tonight. As a token of my joy and with the grace of Zovog and the blessing of Alet, I offer commutation of the death sentence of Dorin, son of Piroska. Instead, he will be banished for his blatant disregard of our laws of hospitality."

A weak cheer arose from those gathered. Half the town must be here, along with anyone of importance within a two-day ride. He recognized Chief Henrik from Clan Oles, and the leader of the heorthwerod of Clan Vadas. At least Betony had secured a promise for his life, and his father had commuted his sentence in front of all these witnesses. He couldn't easily renege and keep his position. But there were always accidents waiting to happen, and many a midnight man would be willing to take on an assignment as difficult as killing one of their own.

The doors to the Great Hall flew open, and a glacial breeze rushed through the crowd, followed by Lady Hyssop. The wind sent her hair flying in a halo, blowing her dress in front of her. She looked like a goddess bent on retribution.

Betony grinned as she turned to her godmother.

"Hello, child," Hyssop said nonchalantly. "It seems my invitation got lost."

At a subtle gesture from Chief Kalman, the guards rushed forward. Hyssop held out her hands, palms facing the guards, and muttered something lost in the chaos and shouts of the crowd. Green fog twisted out and wrapped around the guards, freezing them in place.

The rest of the assembly fidgeted in their seats, and a few tried to escape through the doors. Another wave, some blue light, and the doors slammed shut and the bar dropped into place, sealing them in. Dorin turned and locked the passage to the kitchens.

"Ah, better," Hyssop said. "Now, I understand my goddaughter is getting married today."

Kalman cleared his throat and stepped forward. "Yes, to my son Illes."

"Oh, no, I doubt that. You see, what you do not know is Betony is bound by a vow."

"Ridiculous." His father turned his glare from the fairy to Betony.

The princess lifted a shoulder in an elegant shrug. "You never asked if I was free to marry."

"It was implied," Kalman growled with enough menace Dorin had to stop himself from rushing to her defense.

"In front of a witness, Betony vowed to marry the man this belongs to," Hyssop said.

She twirled her hand in midair, sparks of red and gold swirling around her. She held her hand flat, and an object bearing an uncanny resemblance to the bark of a tree appeared. Hyssop held up her prize. A mask sculpted to imitate a maple tree in full autumn regalia with a dangling brown satin ribbon.

His mask.

Dorin's vision swam and his heart soared. By the gods, he loved his clever fae princess.

Chapter 33

The smile hadn't left Betony's lips since Hyssop had stormed in. Thank Idoya, she wouldn't have to go through with this farce of a wedding.

Rodric pushed past Illes and snatched the mask from her godmother. Apparently, after his father had so readily agreed to disinherit him to please her, Rodric had changed his mind about being married to her.

"Ha!" He placed the mask on his face. "Thought you could steal my inheritance, Illes, *my* bride?"

In theory, it should have fit. It wasn't sculpted to a particular person, but her instructions to Sarsa included an alteration. Spell the mask so only the man it belonged to could wear it.

Small sparks exploded from the mask, and Rodric ripped it off, dropping it to the floor.

"Zovog take you, fairy bitch." He reddened with anger as he charged at Hyssop.

Her godmother raised a hand, called the green fog again, and Rodric stood frozen midstep.

"Free my son," Kalman demanded.

"The spell will wear off soon. By that time, I assume my safety and that of my goddaughter will be assured."

Betony enjoyed this little bit of theater. What better way to prove to Kalman he couldn't control a princess of Lorea. What better way to show all of Fuartir that they messed with Lorea at their own peril. What better way to show Dorin she loved him, she chose *him*.

Illes picked up the mask and fitted it to his face. The same sparks greeted his attempt. But Illes had learned from Rodric's mistake. He took off the mask and handed it to Hyssop with a cool grin.

He turned to Betony and bowed with all the elegance of a court-raised lord, but his voice was as icy as the ground outside. "My lady, it appears I am not the man you are looking for."

Betony curtsied, a fake smile on her lips and a lump of dread settling in her stomach. Illes took a seat down with the rest of the crowd. Hyssop held the mask out to Kalman. He shook his head, a false smile hinting at a good nature that didn't exist and hooked his arm around Lady Rahel.

"I'm already married. Perhaps someone else is willing to try on the mask."

Hyssop turned to the gathering. "Are there any who wish to try? If it fits, the hand of Princess Betony is yours."

A few young men, many of them friends of Rodric and Illes, lined up in front of the fairy. They couldn't possibly believe the mask was theirs but dangle a beautiful woman and power in front of them, and common sense took a flying leap off a cliff.

Man after man tried. Man after man failed.

But the one man she wished to see wasn't here. Betony kept her smile glued to her face, but with each attempt, it became harder to do so. Where was Dorin?

Had her godmother failed to rescue him? She tried to catch Hyssop's eye, but the fairy refused to look at her.

When the last man in line sheepishly handed the mask back to Hyssop, Betony's heart sunk. Surely, if Dorin was here, he would have come forward. Perhaps he'd decided to take the chance and run. Any sane, smart man would. She didn't blame him, but her heart ached.

"Is there no one else?" Hyssop's voice rang off the rafters.

There was an awkward pause as her godmother stood silently, scanning the crowd.

A shimmer of light gray smoke appeared before her godmother. When it cleared, Dorin knelt on one knee in front of the fairy, still clad in rags, but all the more heroic because of it. Apparently, her godmother wasn't the only one who liked to make a memorable entrance.

Betony dug her fingernails into her palms to keep herself from doing anything to jeopardize this moment. Like throw herself at Dorin and kiss him senseless.

"Dorin," Kalman growled from behind her.

He tried to push past her to get to his son, but as he walked by, she drew his sword from his scabbard and pressed the point to his spine. The chief needed to learn he underestimated a princess of Lorea at his own peril.

"If I give it any more pressure," she hissed, "you'll be lucky to be paralyzed. Hold, let this play out."

Gizi and Rahel gasped behind her but did nothing. Should they move, she could injure him before they could stop her.

Hyssop glared at them. They were ruining her show.

"Apologies, godmother," Betony said. "Please continue."

Hyssop turned to Dorin. He was watching the whole thing with the tiniest grin. Goddess, she loved him.

"Do you wish to try, my lord?" Hyssop said in her most dramatic voice.

"I am no lord, but yes, I believe the mask is mine. I left it in the care of the most beautiful woman in Lorea somewhere around the winter solstice."

Flames grazed her cheeks at the compliment, and Betony couldn't tear her eyes away as Dorin took the mask from Hyssop's hands and rose. He locked his gaze to Betony, but his expression remained carefully neutral as he placed the mask on and tied the silken strings.

Instead of sparks, a golden glow flickered to life.

A wicked smile formed once more on her godmother's lips as she turned to Kalman.

"I am terribly sorry, my lord. But it seems this is my goddaughter's true match. Next time, perhaps you should ask before you make a mess of things."

In retrospect, not everything could have happened at once, but that's how it seemed to Betony. Kalman whipped around and knocked his sword from her hand. Betony ducked under the next blow and tumbled down the steps to the dais. She landed on her feet and pulled out her staff hidden in her expertly redone pocket. The blue metal caught the light from the torches and candles as she extended it, glowing almost as bright as the mask Dorin still wore.

Illes rushed his half brother and grabbed him by the neck. He snatched the mask and tossed it to the side. The glow vanished, and Illes stood with a blade to Dorin's throat. Dorin drew the small blade she'd given Sarsa and stabbed it into Illes's thigh. He roared in pain, but his grip loosened and Dorin dropped before his brother could slit his throat. The blade left a thin line to join the still healing wounds from Kalman's tender ministrations a few days ago. Illes's blade skittered off with an expert hit from Dorin.

Hyssop seemed oblivious. She grasped Betony's hand and pulled her close. Dorin and Illes continued to grapple without weapons.

"Veitha's balls, what is this?" Hyssop tapped the awful bracelet on Betony's wrist.

"What does it matter, fairy?" Kalman stalked closer, rage contorting his face. "Her lover will be dead, and she'll marry one of my true-born sons, or neither of you are getting out of here alive."

"It's a barrier, godmother," Betony replied, ignoring Kalman. "I'm cut off from my magic."

"What a wicked thing to do. No wonder you sent for me rather than solve this disaster yourself."

Hyssop wiggled her fingers and red sparks lit up the strip of leather. It turned to dust as power rushed into Betony. Goddess, how she'd missed it. She gathered the threads and stitched some into her staff.

Betony aimed her weapon at Illes, and a gust of wind blew through the Great Hall. The man flew across the room, landing limply in front of the door. Her lover swayed a little on his feet, but remained standing as he saluted her.

Kalman roared and charged toward Dorin. A black and white bird dropped from the rafters in a flare of purple, blue, red, and green magic. A black dragon with white scales dotted randomly across its hide appeared. It grew until it was the size of a horse and stood between Dorin and his father. Sarsa opened her jaws and roared. Kalman tried to stop, but she swiped her clawed foot at the chief and hit him in the jaw. He went down like a breaching whale, groaning briefly before falling quiet. He still breathed, unfortunately.

Hyssop was throwing around spells to freeze the guards in place while the townspeople and lesser lords cowered out of the way.

In another flare of rainbow magic, Sarsa emerged, shaking out the hand that had punched Kalman.

"Stop staring, Betony, and go get your betrothed," she said with a wink.

Betony ran to Dorin, heedless of the roiling crowd of people rushing for the doors. It was pointless, it turned out. As the first person reached the great, carved doors, they burst open and at least a dozen Lorean guards, led by Captain Jadran, poured in.

"To the princess!" Jadran called over the chaos. Brumbull flew over his head, screaming and looking fiercer than she'd ever seen the little rose gold dragon.

Betony grabbed Dorin's hand and examined him for wounds. He hadn't moved since she'd sent Illes flying. Besides a small trickle of blood on his neck and a glassy-eyed stare, nothing appeared wrong.

Soon, they were surrounded by the Lorean guards. The panicked guests streamed out of the Great Hall and into the night, some sobbing, some pale-faced, and some glowering.

"Not that one," Dorin said in a hoarse voice, pointing at a man dressed in similar regalia as Kalman. "Chief Henrik of Clan Oles. Witness."

Sarsa stopped him and led him to where Gizi sobbed by her father. Lady Rahel sat in her chair, pale and drawn. Hyssop stood glaring with arms crossed between them and the exit.

"Dorin, are you hurt?" Betony asked.

He swayed more on his feet, and his face had gone pale. He turned his gold-flecked eyes to her, and a smile crept across his lips.

"I'm fine."

Then he collapsed at her feet. Hands tried to pry her away, but she only held on tighter.

"Give the princess some room," Jadran ordered.

His voice was the only sound she heard. Her heart thudded so hard in her chest it drowned out everything else as she dropped to her knees beside her love. The staff clattered to the floor, and she pulled his head onto her lap.

No, this can't be happening. We won. We're supposed to have our happy ending.

Illes laughed coldly from the far side of the room as he stood on shaky legs.

"Did you think I was going to let him live?"

"But your father—"

"Spoke for himself, not for me. You would never accept your fate if he were alive, so I thought I'd…remove the temptation, visit the mayor's house before Father released him."

Betony's fingers found the trivial cut on Dorin's neck, his pulse fading under her touch. Betony sent a tendril of magic into him, all silver and gold. *Poison.*

She glared at Illes, but he only laughed harder. Hyssop muttered a few words and a pulse of gray magic twisted through the air and wrapped around his neck, cutting off the laughter. He clawed at it.

"Remain quiet, or the noose will tighten," her godmother said in a voice that brooked no more argument.

Illes nodded, his face red, and with a twitch, the tendril loosened enough for him to suck in air. He collapsed against the wall but said nothing further.

Betony poured everything she had into Dorin. Her magic sought the poison and dragged it out of his blood, depositing it as a thick, milky globule on the floor. She repaired the tiny wound, brushing her fingers against his skin.

Betony waited. And waited. Tears streamed down her face.

What seemed a lifetime later, he opened his eyes.

"Hello, love." He lifted a trembling hand to her cheek.

"Hello, my midnight man." She grabbed his hand and placed a gentle kiss on his palm. "You almost died."

"I knew you'd save me."

"Smart man."

"Oh, that was a lesson hard learned."

"Are you going to kiss me or are we——"

He pulled her down and kissed her. Sweeter than honey, hotter than a summer day, his lips demanded her, worshipped her, loved her.

"Ahem."

Betony looked up, finding Hyssop tapping her foot.

"Do you two need some privacy?" Sarsa asked from her seat next to Chief Henrik with Brumbull curled over her shoulders, keeping a sharp eye on the Fuartiran.

Dorin's face flamed, and Bet felt heat on her cheeks, too.

"What do you want us to do with these...I guess they're still people, even though they're shittier than dragon turds?" Her godmother gestured broadly at Chief Kalman and his family.

Guards with drawn swords surrounded them. Rodric and Illes were bound with Hyssop's magic, and Kalman looked worse for wear, a large bruise forming on his jaw. Gizi sat, tears and snot dripping down her face, while her mother was still as a statue.

"Chief Henrik of Clan Oles, will you carry a message to the Witan for me?" Betony asked.

The man nodded soberly.

"Tell them what happened today. Tell them any further incursions into Lorea and Faerie will be met with force, and I will personally convince the King of Teruelle to agree to a pact of mutual aid. If Fuartir is serious about peace, Chief Kalman and his family must be removed immediately from positions of power."

"That's prepos—"

Hyssop flicked her fingers and a gray gag wrapped around Kalman's mouth.

Henrik eyed the fairy, then addressed Betony. "You are a princess, not the ruler, not an ambassador, not even the heir."

"Chief Henrik, as I have often been reminded, the Fuartiran way is not the Lorean way." Dorin grasped Betony's hand. "Her father and sister will see her demands as merciful. Should you wish to continue to receive the mercy of Lorea instead of its wrath, I suggest you take Princess Betony's words to the Witan and send your decision to Avora as quickly as you can. Or else you'll add a very pissed off midnight man to your list of problems."

Henrik swallowed. "Yes, of course."

Sarsa let him go, and he scurried out of the hall. Hyssop pulled Betony to her feet, then grabbed Dorin under the arms and hauled him up. She shoved him toward Betony, and he stumbled into her arms.

Bet cupped his face and kissed him again. She would never tire of kissing him.

"No time for that." Hyssop shoved them toward the great doors. "Your ship awaits. You have until the mountains crumble to love each other and certainly enough privacy on the way home."

Home. Home would be nice, but as long as she was with Dorin, no matter where that was, she'd be fine.

Hyssop muttered some words, and the green spell wove around Kalman and his family.

"It will wear off before midnight, once we're well away. Don't follow us, or you will regret my goddaughter's mercy."

Rahel blinked her agreement while Kalman and his sons glared. Didn't matter. All that mattered was she had Dorin and they were going home.

"What happens now?" Dorin asked in a shaky voice.

Bet wrapped her arm around his waist. He was still a little unsteady on his feet. Dorin draped his arm across her shoulders and let her help him. They followed the fairies outside into the cold winter night, trailed by the guards. The stars sparkled brightly in the sky, and the moon lit their way.

"We get our happy ending," Betony said.

"Those exist?"

"Are you happy, Dorin?"

"Yes, very. Are you?"

Betony allowed her love for this brave, complicated man to shine through her eyes. "I am."

Dorin kissed her once more, gently, sealing the unspoken promise.

Epilogue

A year and a half later

Betony's happy ending began with a bang. Her door crashed open, and Dorin darted through the sitting room and ran to her bedchamber. She calmly shut the door and followed him.

Dorin was face down on her bed, shaking. He rolled over and his laughter filled the room. Bet couldn't keep a smile from her lips at the sound of it. He laughed often these days, and once her family had accepted she loved him, they embraced him. It had, however, taken several arguments and a stay in the pixie cottage for her parents to realize her threats of leaving with him were serious.

"Your nephew has sticky hands."

"What did Jonquil do?"

She sat next to Dorin on the bed. Her ice-blue gown billowed around them, encasing him in layers of tulle. He propped himself up on his elbows.

"He got into the honey pot and chased me into the castle. On our wedding day! You need to teach him some manners."

"Or you need to wait to dress for the wedding until after his afternoon tea."

He yanked on her arm, sending her falling into his embrace.

"Ah, you have seen through my nefarious scheme," he said before capturing her mouth with his own.

Every protest died on her lips as he explored her mouth fully, their tongues tangling. He tasted of honey, and she knew exactly how Jonquil got into his sticky situation. Dorin broke away, framing her face in his calloused hands.

"How did I get to be so lucky?" he murmured reverently.

"I'm still trying to figure that out. You kidnapped me and hauled me across Lorea with no one the wiser. Then we nearly died from hypothermia and a storm. And somehow your father failed to marry me to one of your brothers, despite his best attempts. And you survived an attempt on your life. You're either the luckiest man in the world, or some god somewhere truly loves you."

The winds of greater politics had all been blowing their way of late, too. The Witan had enough of Kalman's grabs for power and accepted the ultimatum delivered by Chief Henrik. One of Dorin's distant cousins was now Chief of Clan Fher, and he had been an instrumental voice on the Witan for obtaining peace with Lorea. Kalman and his family were exiled to a small farm far from the halls of power.

Dorin had helped, sneaking into the various clan strongholds to gather intelligence. The biggest point of contention was who deserved to be king. And her midnight man, in his sneaky brilliance, had suggested a rotating High Lordship to distribute power equitably. The Witan readily agreed.

Sarsa and Ebon were part of the negotiating delegation, and they had returned a few days ago with a new treaty to sign over the cold months. There would be a celebration in the spring once the storm season passed.

Dorin kissed Betony's nose and held her tight. "I don't care if the gods love me, as long as you do."

"I do, you know."

"I know. And I will love you until my last breath. Your fate is mine, Princess."

She pulled him back down and kissed him again. Sparks rose between them, the heat of their desire demanding more. A low moan escaped her lips, and Dorin swallowed it whole. Gasping, she pulled at the laces of his doublet as he snaked a hand under her skirt.

"We don't have a lot of time," she said when he finally allowed her some air.

"We have all the time in the world. It's not like they can start without us."

"Then shut up and kiss me."

He did, nibbling at her lower lip and slowly inching his fingers up her thigh. She dropped the laces of the doublet and fumbled with the buttons of his breeches.

Knock, knock, knock.

"Are you two done yet?" Rane's playfully annoyed voice seeped into the room.

"Give them a few moments to dress." Ebon's words were tinged with laughter.

Betony groaned, but Dorin chuckled again.

"We'll be out shortly," he called, before pecking her cheek and whispering in her ear. "Hold that thought until tonight."

Faster than she could anticipate, he rolled them and left her on the bed. Betony rose and straightened her dress. Dorin fastened his breeches and re-laced his doublet.

"Are you happy, Betony?" He twitched a loose curl behind her ear.

She pulled on his doublet and brushed off an imaginary speck of dust. "Yes, very. Are you?"

"Beyond what I ever believed possible. Ready?"

He held out his arm, and she took it like the princess she was.

"Ready."

They strode into the hall.

Ebon and Rane stood across from Betony's door, wearing matching knowing smiles. Rane had a hand on her belly, which was barely beginning to round. The babe should come this winter. Ebon leaned against the wall, his ankles crossed, the picture of a lazy lordling. His darkling eyes, however, missed nothing.

"Well, well, well. You two think you're getting away with something," Ebon said in a teasing tone, then stage-whispered. "You missed a button, Dorin."

Her soon-to-be prince flushed and fastened the last button.

"Do they know what happens on the wedding night?" Rane covered a faux shocked mouth, all innocence.

"I don't know, sister dear. Perhaps I should have a little chat with my almost brother-in-law."

"Shut up, Eb." Betony's smile belied her words, and her heart filled with the warmth of joy. She never wanted this to go away.

"You deserve only the best, Bet. I need—"

An elbow to the stomach cut him off.

Dorin shook his head. "You three…I can only imagine what it is to have a family you actually like."

"Oh, my love," Bet said. "You won't have to imagine much longer."

Dorin groaned in good humor when Ebon slung an arm around his shoulders.

"Welcome to the family. Don't worry, Nevar and Sarsa will fill you in. Make sure my baby sister is happy and you should be fine."

Dorin's shoulders shook with laughter, and Betony couldn't even come to his defense without spewing out a laugh of her own.

"There's no need to threaten the newest member of our family. I'm sure Bet can handle him herself." Rane shoved Ebon away and took Dorin's other arm in hers. "After all, from what I heard, she already has."

Betony and Dorin walked to their wedding surrounded by love and laughter.

And they lived happily ever after.

The End

Acknowledgments

Some books are just meant to be. They flow easily in the drafting phase, and the revision and editing process seems far too simple. *Midnight and Silvered Glass* was one of these (with the exception of Dorin's name—boy howdy, was he hard to name). After my frustrations with Ebon and Sarsa's story, this book was a nice way to conclude—for now—the Lorean Tales.

I owe a huge debt to *The British History Podcast.* Jamie, the host, has spent most of his time on the podcast so far on the Anglo-Saxon period between the Roman and Norman conquests. I loosely based some of the Fuartiran culture, politics, and warrior society on the information I gleaned from his in-depth and compelling storytelling. If you want a close look at British History and a smack in the face on how history does, in fact, repeat itself, please listen to this podcast. Plus, he's funny and his music choices are chef's kiss.

Peg and JA were excellent beta readers, as usual. My eternal gratitude for their input and kindness. Gail Delaney, editor extraordinaire, helped me put the final polish on this Cinderella retelling. Her advice is always clear, concise, and gentle. I couldn't ask for a better editor.

My initial plan for this book was to release it close to Dragons, Briars and Blades, so I was editing both DBB and MSG at the same time. Though I later changed my mind, it was too late—I had deadlines to meet. My adult daughter still lives at home and took over some of the cooking and errand running while I worked on these books. She also helped me out with some of the social media graphics to promote both books. She is totally awesome, and I tell her so all the time.

As you're reading this, my youngest is halfway through his senior year of high school. I can't believe I will soon be the parent to two grown-ass adults. Though he was busy with school, the high school musical, and doing all the other things a 16-17-year-old should (and shouldn't) be doing, he's a supportive dude, and I love him dearly.

And as always, I thank my husband. Getting two books done at once meant I had little time for anything else. God, he's patient. I lucked out.

Lastly, and most importantly, thank you, dear reader, for sticking with me. This is my tenth book. I wouldn't be here if it weren't for you all. I wish you always find good books and tasty beverages close to hand.

Other Books

by Emily Michel

Magic & Monsters Series

A widowed witch doesn't need anyone to save her from the monsters, but one hardened hunter can't let her face them alone.

Witch Hazel & Wolfsbane
Devil's Claw & Moonstone
Brimstone & Silver

The Memory Duology

How far will Hell's top assassin go to save the angel he was sent to kill?

A Memory of Wings
A Redemption of Wings

The Lorean Tales

A series of gender-flipped fairy tale retellings for adults.

Blood Magic and Brandy
(Snow White)

Dragons, Briars and Blades
(Sleeping Beauty)

Midnight and Silvered Glass
(Cinderella)

Standalones

Magic and Mint Martinis
Contemporary fantasy holiday romcom

Kissed by an Alien
Small-town, secret identity alien romance novella

About the Author

Emily Michel read her first fairy tale before kindergarten and has been fascinated with speculative fiction of all kinds ever since. She's traveled the world as a military family member, calling many places in the US and Europe home. She settled back in her home state of Arizona several years ago with her husband and kids. When not writing, Emily reads, walks, crochets, and pets her feline overlords. Her husband occasionally drags her out of the house for her own damn good.

Socially awkward and extremely introverted, she nevertheless participates in social media. Check out @EmiMiWriter on Facebook, Instagram, YouTube, and even, dear God, TikTok. If you want to be the first to know release dates, cover reveals, and sales, sign up for her newsletter at EmilyMichelAuthor.com. There are several short stories available for free when you sign up, including more of the Seven Sisters of the Silver Forest.

www.ingramcontent.com/pod-product-compliance
Lightning Source LLC
Chambersburg PA
CBHW031953240626
47153CB00003B/965